BLUE VENGEANCE

BLUE VENGEANCE

Alison Preston

Cover design by Doowah Design.
Photo of Alison Preston by Ruth Bonneville.

Acknowledgments
Lyrics from "For No One," written by John Lennon & Paul McCartney, ©1963 Sony/ATV Music Publishing LLC. All right administered by Sony/ATV Music Publishing LLC, 8 Music Square West, Nashville, TN 37203. All rights reserved. Used by permission.

Author's note: Although Norwood Flats is a real neighbourhood in Winnipeg, the locations of Nordale and Nelson McIntyre schools have been reversed for plot purposes.

This book was printed on Ancient Forest Friendly paper.
Printed and bound in Canada by Hignell Printing Inc.
We acknowledge the support of the Canada Council for the Arts and the Manitoba Arts Council for our publishing program.

Library and Archives Canada Cataloguing in Publication

Preston, Alison, author
Blue vengeance / Alison Preston.

Issued in print and electronic formats.
ISBN 978-1-927426-45-6 (pbk.).
--ISBN 978-1-927426-46-3 (epub)

I. Title.

PS8581.R44B49 2014 C813'.54 C2014-905381-9
C2014-905382-7

Signature Editions
P.O. Box 206, RPO Corydon, Winnipeg, Manitoba, R3M 3S7
www.signature-editions.com

for John,
best brother ever

Your day breaks, your mind aches
There will be times when all the things she said
will fill your head
You won't forget her

—from "For No One"
John Lennon & Paul McCartney

1

Spring, 1964

Danny stood bareheaded in the rain, watching his sister's coffin being lowered into the ground. A puddle was forming at the bottom of the grave. If they didn't hurry, it would turn into a pool. Cookie wasn't fond of getting wet. At Rock Lake she wouldn't even poke her toes in the water. She didn't understand going in the lake, not even as a young girl.

He wondered if he should mention it to someone, the minister maybe: *Hurry the heck up so Cookie isn't buried in a lake.* Grownups could be so stupid.

There was no point in asking for his mother's help. She had been weeping on and off for days, with tears Danny didn't entirely trust. He decided to speak out in a general way to the group at large.

"Cookie doesn't like the rain."

Aunt Dot, his mother's sister, turned and encircled him with her arms.

"No, Danny, dear. She didn't like the rain."

She held him close, pressed his face into her flat hard chest. At thirteen Danny was slight of build and not tall — not yet.

He pulled away, not wanting to hurt her feelings, but unable to stay smashed against her strange-smelling dress. Mothballs. Her funeral garb had been stored in mothballs. Danny decided he would rather wear clothes full of moth holes than go around smelling like that. Also, he was fairly sure the holes wouldn't happen. He couldn't remember ever seeing a moth flutter out of his closet or chest of drawers.

"Hurry up," he said. "We can't be dropping her down into a lake."

One of the men in charge of lowering the casket started up an electrical device that hummed. Reverend Badger paused in his droning. The casket, on its canvas bands, was lowered into the earth.

The reverend went back to where he had left off. "The days of our age are three score and ten."

"Fool," Danny said, quietly now. Only a certified idiot would include that line under the circumstances. The guy was certifiable. However long three score and ten was, it didn't apply to Cookie. She was fifteen years old. And would be forever.

Dot squeezed his arm.

The rain kept on, snaking down the sides of the shining wooden container that housed his sister. When they had picked it out at the funeral parlour Danny had thought it looked like a miniature palace furnished in satin and sparkles, but now he could see that it was just wood after all, and it wouldn't be shiny once it was in the ground. It would be dull and wet and soon rotten.

"For Christ's sake," he said now. "Fill in the hole around her."

There were no shovels in sight. A small yellow machine stood a ways off, partially hidden behind a tree. It looked as though it may have been responsible for digging the hole; perhaps it also had the job of filling it in. Danny got down on his knees and began to push the piled earth into the space around the casket.

"Danny, please." It was his mother's voice.

He didn't care.

Uncle Edwin, under orders from Dot, pulled him to his feet and led him away to one of the waiting cars. He didn't struggle. He knew by now that his efforts were useless.

Edwin sat with him as the rain pounded down on the black car that smelled of leather and cigars. It smelled like cigars because Edwin had lit one up.

Danny was glad that his uncle was the one chosen to be his minder.

They sat there, both of them dripping wet, Danny covered in mud, for what seemed a very long time.

A powder-blue '57 Cadillac pulled into the parking lot and sat. Just sat.

"That's the kind of car I'm going to have," said Danny.

"Well, in that case, you better plan on getting a darn good job," said Edwin. "Caddies don't come cheap."

The rain let up, turned to a drizzle. Edwin rolled down his window.

"Let out some of the smoke so the womenfolk don't get after me."

The crowd around the grave vanished inside the fog. Then figures walked out of it two by two, one by one, and in small clusters. Danny recognized his best friend, Paul, with his mum and dad; a few other kids from school with their parents; neighbours. He wondered who all the other people were: kids from Cookie's school, he supposed, and people who knew his mother—or knew of her anyway—people he'd never noticed, in the way that kids don't pay much attention to grownups. Was it possible that one of these strangers was his dad, and Dot and his mum thought it best not to tell him? He wouldn't put it past them. He didn't bother to ask Uncle Edwin. He'd be going along with whatever Dot had told him to do or risk her wrath.

Frank Foote was there. He was the one who'd found her, who'd tried to save her.

Then Danny saw another familiar shape emerge. She wouldn't know that she'd been walking inside a cloud. You never know it from the inside, when fog swallows you whole. Or almost never. He and Paul had tested it out until they thought they knew for sure. Then someone told him about paddling through a cumulus cloud on a mountain lake, and he knew he had further testing to do. Whoever had told him that said that the cloud had crisp perimeters. He'd believe that when he saw it.

The shape was Miss Hartley, the girls' phys ed teacher from Nelson Mac. She lit up a cigarette.

"What's she doing here?" Danny said.

"Who?"

"Miss Hartley. Cookie's gym teacher. Everybody hates her."

"I don't know, Daniel. I guess she wants to pay her respects."

"She should have paid Cookie some respects when she was alive." Danny reached for the door handle. "I've got a good mind to…"

"Leave it, Daniel." Edwin put a hand on his arm. "This is a hard day for everyone. Let it be for now."

Danny knew that what he was really saying was: you've already caused your mother enough upset for today.

He did as he was told and let it be, as he watched his mother bounce in her wheelchair across the soaked grass of the cemetery. She winced as she rode, at the mercy of the man who steered her, the driver of the funeral car. Danny took a measure of satisfaction from those winces.

The guests gathered in the church hall. Ladies served coffee and tea to the adults and a nasty orange concoction to the kids. To Danny the orange drink tasted like death — what death would taste like if it were in liquid form. Why couldn't they have had Orange Crush, say, or Hires Root Beer?

His friends kept their distance. He supposed they didn't know how to act around him, the way he didn't know how to act around his mum. He hoped it wouldn't last forever.

There were dainties, but they just made Danny think of Cookie, and how she would have hidden herself away somewhere and wolfed down scads of them. And then she would have thrown them up — in secret too — always in secret.

At the church there was no booze, except on the breath of some of the men. Church and liquor didn't go together. Not this church anyway. Norwood United. Danny supposed some of the men had flasks in the inside pockets of their suits. He knew that Uncle Edwin did.

Miss Hartley, the gym teacher, didn't come to the church hall. That disappointed Danny, as he was looking forward to having a word with her.

Back at the house the liquor came out.

"Rye whiskey and beer for the men; gin and sherry for the ladies," Aunt Dot said, as she bustled to get things in order.

Gin for the ladies. Danny wondered why it was divided like that, and if any of the ladies would have preferred beer, or any of the men gin. If there was a rule about it, none of them seemed to be breaking it, as far as he could see.

He tried the rye and the gin and couldn't believe that people drank the stuff. They both tasted like poison. Then he opened a beer and tried it. It tasted like piss, or what he imagined piss would taste like. He and Paul had been meaning to try it, but they hadn't gotten around to it yet. He finally sided with the older ladies and settled on sherry. It was thick and sweet with just a hint of poison thrown in. When he was throwing up later in the backyard, he thought again about Cookie, and how she had chosen to put herself through this disgusting act, to make it happen. He decided to give alcohol a wide berth for a while and then maybe just try one type at a time.

His dog Russell stood with him while he vomited, but looked off in another direction till he was done.

2

THE DAY AFTER THE FUNERAL THE SUN SHONE. THE ONLY clouds were across the river, sinking into the trees on the streets of Riverview. It was a drying day, but too late for Cookie's watery grave.

Danny went downstairs. He felt sick in his stomach and in his head. His mother sat at the kitchen table staring at nothing that he could see. Her hands gripped a cup of coffee that looked cold and oily, like the water beside the boats at the dock across the river. The water, though, was a swirl of colours from the gasoline that leaked from the boats' motors. He had often wondered why something as practical as gas was so pretty to look at. So far he had forgotten to ask anyone and he was certain that now wasn't the time. His mum probably wouldn't know the answer anyway. Dot might; she was a farm wife and knew lots of stuff city wives didn't.

She was at the sink washing glasses and small plates from the day before.

"I could have sworn I had them all yesterday," she said. "People leave them in the dangdest places. I found some of these way out by the back lane."

She wrung out her rag and hung it on a hook over the sink.

"Men," she said. "Oh. Morning, Danny. Have you seen any sign of the can opener? I swear I've looked everywhere. Edwin can open cans with a knife but I'll be darned if I go that route."

He wondered if she left the *good* out of *good morning* on purpose.

"Why couldn't they have waited one more day to dig Cookie's grave?" he said. "We knew it was going to clear today. Maurice Burchell said so."

Maurice Burchell was the weatherman on CBWT. He had taken over from Ed Russenholt a couple of years ago. At the end of

Ed Russenholt's weather reports, he had drawn a big heart around southern Manitoba with his chalk, and then, always with a smile, he'd said, *Ah, yes, for the Red River Valley, heart of the continent, it's going to be...* and told the local forecast. He'd acted as if the Red River Valley was the place to be. Danny missed him — missed his broadcasts.

"Say good morning to your aunt," his mother said and then went back to staring at nothing. It was located somewhere between her eyes and the back landing.

"Morning," he said and decided that he would leave *good* out of the greeting forever.

Dot dried her hands on a tea towel and scooted over to where he stood in the doorway. She may as well have been on wheels — casters, like on the table Paul's mum used to transfer items from the kitchen to the dining room and back.

She put a hand on his shoulder. "The funeral was scheduled for yesterday, Danny dear. It would have been too difficult to rearrange everything."

He didn't like the way she pronounced *scheduled*. She said it like *shed* and it sounded sloppy and dirty, like cow udders.

"We could've," he said.

Dot's eyes darted towards her sister and back to him.

"Would you like some breakfast, honey?"

"No, thanks."

"Just a piece of toast?"

"No, thanks."

"You've got to eat," said his mum, like she knew all about it.

But he was on his way back upstairs. He sat in his bedroom chair, looked out at the blue, blue sky and wondered how on earth he was going to get through the rest of his life.

3

ON SATURDAY, TWO DAYS AFTER COOKIE'S FUNERAL, PAUL came over to see if Danny could come out to hang around with him. Danny didn't know if he would be allowed to go; he wanted to, but he didn't know the rules for a week after your sister's death.

Dot encouraged him. "Go out, Danny. Have some fun."

They boarded a bus at the corner of Pinedale and Highfield. The plan was to go downtown on their usual rounds.

Aunt Dot had told him to have fun; maybe there still was such a thing.

A girl got on the bus at the corner of Taché and Coniston. Danny saw her reading a book while she stood at the bus stop, and she continued to read it once she got settled. She didn't seem to see him. He knew her; she was the girl who had helped him.

The title of the book was *Far from the Madding Crowd*. He could see it from where he sat. He didn't like the word *madding* and wondered if that was a solid enough reason to talk to her. But Paul was chatting away about going further afield when they got downtown, and the girl looked content. He decided to leave her to it.

When they stopped at Coronation Park, Paul stopped talking, and the inside of the bus was quiet for a moment or two. The girl looked over at Danny and smiled. Just a trace. He smiled too; at least he hoped he did.

It was impossible that the girl would not have been on the bus. Her presence across the aisle was a piece of the jigsaw puzzle that made up the section of Danny's life that took place following Cookie's death. It fell neatly into its spot and clicked.

The boys got off at The Bay. They climbed the wide stairs to the mezzanine floor, where they found two comfortable chairs side by side. There they sat and watched the people come and go, mostly women, often with their daughters. The ladies smoked; the daughters waited—impatient—hung around the fountain, dragged their fingers through the water, threw pennies.

Paul and Danny made up stories about the people they saw:

"That one has loads of man friends that her husband doesn't know about."

"That girl lets the boys in her class see her tits."

"Squeeze them too."

"That kid still shits his pants regularly."

Rarely did they make up anything kind.

Sometimes, if they stayed too long, a man who worked for the store would tell them to move along, especially if it was busy, and all the chairs were taken. They weren't doing anything bad, but they were boys. That in itself could be considered bad enough.

It didn't happen that day, but they tired before long and took the escalators up to the Paddlewheel Restaurant on the sixth floor.

Paul ordered a strawberry milkshake, and Danny struggled. Normally he would have ordered a root beer float, but he didn't want one now; he didn't want anything. Maybe water, but he couldn't order water. He didn't want to make Paul nervous. Finally he settled on a Coke.

Next they went to the sporting goods department on the second floor and admired the hunting knives, which were under glass. Danny tried to listen as Paul talked about what he would do with his, if his mum would only let him have one.

"All she lets me have is a measly old jackknife."

Danny fingered the one in his pocket as he followed his friend across Portage Avenue to Sydney I. Robinson on Vaughan Street.

"Let's look at the knives first and save the guns for last," said Paul, as they trundled down the stairs.

Sydney I. had a much bigger selection of knives.

"I wish they weren't under glass," said Danny. "Why do they always have to be under glass?"

"Why do you think?" Paul said. "Because a guy might go berserk and grab one and kill somebody before anyone has a chance to stop him."

He picked up a compass from the selection on top of the counter.

"This is nice," he said.

"You already have a compass."

"Yeah, but this one has a leather case."

"So what?"

"I like leather cases."

"May I help you boys with something?"

It was an older gentleman asking, dapper in his manner. Danny wondered if he might be Sydney I. Robinson himself.

"No thanks, sir. We're just browsing," Paul said.

Danny had heard his mum say a version of those words, except for the *sir* part. He supposed Paul's mum said them too.

"Are any of these knives rare?" he asked the man.

If he ever bought a hunting knife he wanted it to be rare.

"No. Not as such."

The man looked over Danny's head when he spoke and then moved on. Danny turned to watch a large hand come down on Paul's shoulder.

"I think you'd better put that back, son," said the man with the hand.

He was a burly man.

Paul took the compass out of his pocket and placed it on the counter.

With a hand on each of their backs, the man guided them to the rear of the store, where aromatic animal pelts hung on racks. He knocked on a closed door, and when no one answered he ushered them into a cramped office. There was a desk with a phone on it, two folding metal chairs, and merchandise. The merchandise took up every square inch where the desk and chairs weren't. The man asked the boys for their names and phone numbers and then made three calls: one to the police and one to each of their homes.

Danny thought later that maybe the call to the police was pretend, because no cop ever came. The one to his mum may as well have been pretend, because she didn't come either.

The burly man went back into the main part of the store to nab more criminals. Danny and Paul were left with a lady who didn't say one single word, just sat on a chair and looked at her fingernails from time to time. Paul sat in the remaining chair, and Danny sat on part of a cardboard box that poked out from the boxes piled on top of it. The woman crossed and uncrossed her legs more than once, and when she did that her nylon stockings rubbed against each other and made a sound that Danny liked. He pictured putting his hand there, where the stockings touched.

Paul's mum arrived, and the dapper man followed her into the room and introduced himself to her as Mr. Blandings.

"I'm so sorry, Mr. Blandings," Mrs. Carter said. "I assure you, nothing like this will ever happen again."

She clutched Paul's arm and yanked him out of his chair.

Danny thought Paul would speak up and say that it was him, not Danny who had stolen, but he didn't. They were both being painted with the same brush of juvenile delinquency. At that point he still expected a cop to burst in and he thought Mrs. Carter was just there to accompany them to the Vaughan Street jail and post bail. Or not. The Carters weren't rich, and bail could be in the thousands.

Paul's mum was usually very nice-looking. She didn't look so great right now because she was upset. Her nose was red and she trembled, but Danny hoped that Mr. Blandings saw past those things and got how attractive she was. Maybe he would think that her husband was dead or had run off, and that he had a chance with her.

"I'll hold you to that, Mrs. Carter," he said.

Danny saw the suggestion of a smile.

She herded the boys out to their family station wagon, and Paul still didn't say anything about how it was all his fault. She drove to the Blue house on Lyndale Drive and got out to see Danny to the door.

"I wouldn't trouble your mother with this, Danny," she said. "But they phoned her too. She already knows."

It wasn't me, he wanted to shout. *It was that asshole son of yours.*

But ratting out a friend was close to the worst thing you could do. He looked back at the car and saw Paul grinning from the back seat.

Dirty rotten asshole of a friend.

Aunt Dot greeted them. Barbara Blue was behind her, supporting herself on two canes. She only used them both when she was extra tired. That's what she said. Since Cookie died she had been extra tired all the time. She probably would have used her wheelchair but it was too big for the house.

She waited till Mrs. Carter left to say, "Go to your room, Danny. I don't want to look at you."

He fought back tears as he trudged upstairs. He sat in his chair, stared out the window, and thought about how they didn't even get a chance to look at the guns.

A little later Dot brought him a snack of fancy sandwiches left over from the funeral. He didn't eat them. They were cold from the freezer and they made him think about Cookie, which was worse than thinking about his so-called friend.

When he went to the bathroom he heard them talking. His mum said something nasty about Mrs. Carter's high heels and then, "My dear lost boy." She had tears in her voice when she said it.

Dear lost boy. That sounded promising. Maybe it wasn't going to be as bad as he thought. They were talking so quietly he couldn't grasp any more words. She sure hadn't spoken to him as though he was her *dear lost boy*, but there it was. Hard to fathom, but there it was.

4

DANNY COULDN'T GET OUT OF HIS BEDROOM CHAIR. COULD not.

From where he sat he had a view of the Red River and beyond it the pale green suburb of Riverview. But he didn't see it. Sometimes he caught a movement, a car or a passing bird, but if someone were to ask him to describe what was in front of him, he wouldn't be able to say. Cookie was his only thought.

He was eating a melted Jersey Milk chocolate bar, taking no pleasure from it. There was a fine line for Danny between a soft Jersey Milk and one that was too far gone. This one was past its best because he hadn't been alert to the rays of the sun on the table by his side.

A muted rage took a turn through his system and left as quickly as it came. It reminded him that he needed to do something, something connected to Cookie, but he didn't yet know what it was. There were only inklings.

His fingers were sticky from the chocolate. He licked them absently and wiped them on the front of his T-shirt. His thin body was lost inside of it. It had belonged to Cookie, who had been taller than him and plumper once, though not in recent months. According to their mum, she took after their dad's branch of the family. Danny couldn't know this for sure as he didn't remember his dad, and his mother said there were no photographs. She had often bemoaned the fact that it was Danny with his lean build that took after her side.

"It's more important for girls to be slim," she had said.

"Why?" Cookie and Danny both asked at the same time.

"It just is," said their mother in the unsatisfactory way she had of answering their questions. "Honestly, when I was young, people compared my shape to that of a wasp."

When they both looked blank she added, "You know…I went in in the middle; I had a waist."

She also had a sting.

It was Cookie who had taught him about the pleasure of soft chocolate. He hadn't known it since she died and he wondered if it would ever come back, and if it did, if it would be lesser somehow. A lesser pleasure.

Two weeks had passed since her death. The time had gone by in a blur—fog all through it, like at the graveside service.

Uncle Edwin went home after a week. He and Aunt Dot farmed a half section near Baldur, a couple of hours southwest of Winnipeg. Aunt Dot stayed on. She brought Danny his meals and encouraged him to have baths, even tried to jolly him out to the yard once for a game of catch, but mostly she left him alone. No one mentioned school.

Paul had dropped over a few times, but Danny refused to see him.

His dog Russell sat with him most of the time. She got up now to investigate voices in the kitchen. Paul and Dot. Then in the living room. Just Paul. Danny heard no response. Now there were footsteps on the stairs.

"Hi." Paul entered his room.

"Hi." Danny continued to look out the window.

"Your Aunt Dot said I could come up."

"So what."

"I talked to your mum. I told her it was all my fault that day at Sydney I. Robinson's."

"What did she say?"

"Nothing."

Danny had seen little of his mother. From time to time, he heard murmurs from the living room which was directly below his bedroom, so he figured she must be spending most of her time in there. She hadn't been up to see him, but she rarely made the effort to climb the stairs even under normal circumstances. Her bedroom and the only bathroom were on the main floor.

And he hadn't ventured down to see her. They had passed each other in the downstairs hall at night when both of them needed the bathroom at the same time, she using a cane even for the few steps it took her to get there. All he felt when that happened was irritation that the timing was so unlucky. They hadn't spoken; they could have been sleepwalking. He didn't feel at all like her *dear lost boy*. Lost maybe, but for sure not dear.

"Did your mum make you?" Danny said to Paul.

"What?"

"Did your mum make you come over and tell my mum that I had nothing to do with it?"

Paul didn't answer at first.

"She did, didn't she?"

"I don't know."

"Get lost."

Paul stood in the doorway for a minute, then shrugged and took off down the stairs.

Danny was glad Paul had owned up to his mother. But his anger didn't go anywhere; it seethed inside of him. It had been this way since Cookie's death, which he saw as murder, plain and simple. Somebody had to pay.

He needed to kill someone. That was the thing he needed to do. If he took a life, a bad one, it could help to even out with what had happened to Cookie. It was worth a try.

Dot came up to try and coax him to come down, now that Paul had come clean.

"Does Mum believe him?" said Danny. "Is she sorry?"

"Of course she believes him, honey."

"She's not sorry though, is she?" he said, staring out the window.

"We can't expect too much of her these days, pet."

5

When Danny thought about killing someone, the first person who came to mind was his mother, but he pushed that thought aside. You couldn't kill your mother. Somebody somewhere must have done it, but all the same. It seemed beyond his purpose of evening things out. He didn't want to go overboard.

He even thought of killing himself. When he went over in his head the last words Cookie had ever heard him speak he wanted to gouge out his own eyes and grind them into the dirt.

The idea of killing Paul wasn't unappealing, but that was for reasons totally unconnected to Cookie. And he didn't want to hate him—he missed the day-to-day fooling around—but he didn't know if it could ever go back to the way it was.

Really, there was only one person. He let his mind circle her for a while, circle and then land.

And he knew how he would do it.

He rose from his chair.

When he went downstairs, his mother was slouching against a counter in the kitchen, holding a mug of coffee. When she saw him, she dropped it on the floor. The mug didn't break, but the dark liquid splashed up onto the white cupboards and onto her greying robe and it spread like river water over the faded green linoleum.

Dot came running, and Danny kept walking.

"Where are you going?" she said, throwing a dishrag and a tea towel at the spill.

He stopped on the landing. "To visit Cookie's grave."

"Would you like something to eat first?"

She rummaged under the sink and found more rags.

"No, thanks."

"You're sure?"

He'd never been surer of anything in his life.

"For goodness' sakes, Barbara, get out of the way," said Dot.

Coffee surrounded his mother's bare feet, seeped under her long ugly toes.

"I can drive you." Dot had been using their old DeSoto for errands.

"No, thanks."

His bike was dusty, and one of the tires needed air, but other than that it was fine. He filled the tire and headed out. If it didn't hold the air he could stop at a gas station and top it up.

He weaved in and out of the cars on St. Mary's Road. Drivers honked at him and shouted comments: *stick to the sidewalk, buddy; hey, Mr. Magoo, watch where you're going.*

In his mind he saw himself being cut down, but not lucky enough to die. His injuries would worsen his life further. He would lie in a hospital bed with tubes and casts, and disgusting fluids would leak out all over him. People would hover, expecting him to try to get better.

He moved to the sidewalk, and things quietened down.

Cookie was lucky in a way. Death had been fairly fast, though Danny could imagine few worse ways to go. He changed his mind; she wasn't lucky, and it wasn't fast. It was a drawn-out affair, just like the sickness of cancer victims who waste away to nothing in their hospital beds. It took her years to die.

She was dying when she asked not to be cremated, but he hadn't known. They were playing Chinese checkers at the dining room table, and she was trouncing him as usual.

"Don't let them burn me," she whispered.

It surprised him, coming out of nowhere like that, with no preamble, but he knew right away what she meant because they had talked about it before: what they wanted to happen to them after they died. They had heard about cremation, it was becoming common in Canada, and it scared Cookie, made her think of Joan of Arc. What if she woke up from the dead during the fire? She also feared being buried alive, so made Danny promise that he would see to it that she was embalmed, that all the blood was drained out of her so she wouldn't wake up under the ground. She had read up on embalming.

Cremation wasn't even mentioned after her death, but neither was embalming, so Danny took it upon himself, with Edwin at his side, to speak to the undertaker and convey Cookie's wishes.

The undertaker was kind and unsurprised by these words from a young boy.

"Please promise me," Danny said, "that there is no chance in the world that my sister will wake up after her coffin has been closed."

"I promise," said the undertaker, and put his hand on Danny's shoulder as he looked into his eyes.

Danny believed him.

His tire was losing air. He stopped at a Texaco station to fill it up and then he gave the road another try. The cars had thinned. The streets had a wee-hours-of-the-morning look to them. What if one day all the adults decided not to go to work? And all the kids pretended they were sick and stayed home from school, and the old folks cancelled their doctors' appointments and bowling dates? What if everybody stayed home one day, all in the same city? For that one day the streets would be empty. He supposed the odds of it happening were very low.

The cemetery parking lot was empty. Danny imagined that he was the only person left alive in the world, living amongst the dead. He didn't know if he liked the feeling or not.

He found the grave. It had a small granite headstone that read: *Cordelia Ruby Blue 1948–1964. Beloved daughter and sister.*

Rage tore through him, like when he left the chocolate bar too long in the sun. But not muted this time and not soon gone.

Cordelia was Cookie's actual name, but no one had called her that in her entire life, as far as Danny knew. Except maybe teachers, at first, till they knew her.

He looked around at nearby graves. Some of them had flowers in various stages of death. He couldn't bear the thought of flowers wilting and dying on top of Cookie.

She was inside the coffin in the ground, right beneath his feet. He wondered if it was possible that some of her flesh was already gone.

As he stared at her patch of lawn he remembered a conversation he had overheard between his mum and Aunt Dot. It wasn't very long ago. They were talking about Cookie and how she had fainted in maths class and been sent home.

His mum had said, "It might just be the hole in her heart. I haven't heard of fainting as a symptom, but I suppose it's possible."

"Just the hole in her heart?" Danny had burst into the kitchen. It sounded disastrous to him—life-threatening. "What are you talking about—a hole in her heart? Who's going to fix it?"

Even when his mother explained it to him, he was certain that it would kill Cookie sooner or later, probably sooner.

"But can her heart handle having a hole in it? I mean with..." He looked over his shoulder to make sure Cookie wasn't listening. "You know...with the way she is, with what she does to herself."

"What does she do to herself?" said Dot.

"Nothing," said his mum. "It's gradually closing on its own, Danny. Dr. Briggs said there's no need for reparative surgery, at least not at present. He's keeping an eye on it."

"What does that mean?"

"It means we get it checked regularly."

"How regularly?"

"I don't know. Once every while."

"How often is that?"

"Danny, for goodness' sake. Twice a year. How's that?"

"Is that often enough?"

"Yes."

"Does Cookie know?"

"Of course she knows."

"Why didn't I know?"

"I guess no one thought to tell you. I'll be sure to tell you every little thing from here on in."

The hole in Cookie's heart seemed far from being a little thing to Danny, but he was sick of his mother's way and her words so he stomped off. He heard Dot ask again what Cookie did to herself, and his mother say, more loudly this time, "Nothing, Dot."

And sure enough, it wasn't her heart that killed her.

He walked his bike out of the cemetery and began the long ride home. His tire held up.

When he approached the screen door Russell flung herself against it from the inside. She greeted him as if he'd been gone for her whole life. His mother and Aunt Dot were in the front room. Dot was flipping through a *Family Circle* magazine; his mum lay on the couch with droopy eyelids. They were neither open nor closed. A forgotten cigarette smouldered in an ashtray on the coffee table beside her along with four bottles of pills, two standing and two on their sides.

Dot smiled at him; his mother didn't.

"Why does the stone say Cordelia?" Danny said.

"What?" said his mum.

"Why does Cookie's gravestone say Cordelia?"

"That was her name."

"No one called her that."

"I did."

"No, you didn't."

"Yes, I did."

"It's a stupid name." Danny tried to summon up a conversation between his mother and his sister. He couldn't remember her calling her Cookie, let alone Cordelia. Maybe she tried it out for a while before he was born, but not since he entered the picture. He was sure of it.

"The stone should say Cookie."

His mum sighed and looked at her sister. Dot had stopped flipping, but she held her tongue.

Danny stared at his mother. There was nothing about her face that he liked. He wanted to press it into the carpet till her nose broke. He could like that about it: a broken nose.

"We need to change it," he said.

"No."

"I'm going to save up and buy a new headstone."

"We're not changing it. Anyway, what are you going to save up?"

She had a point. He didn't have a penny of his own. He was at her mercy.

"I'll get a job," he said. "I'll steal."

There was money in the kitchen drawer. Perhaps he'd rob it.

"Oh, Danny." Dot stood up, but he was gone—up the stairs, where he slammed his door behind him.

He heard his mum's voice.

"Dot. Leave him."

6

The next afternoon Danny walked over to Paul's house. It was time to forgive him. He had been fine as a friend till the Sydney I. Robinson business, and Danny didn't want to think about that anymore.

It had been strange not having a sidekick. Paul had been around off and on since grade one. They even lay on top of each other once. It had stirred them both but they never did it again.

Danny knew that he was actually the sidekick. Paul was the main guy—the Lone Ranger to his Tonto—but he could never let him know that, not even if someone threatened to pull out his teeth with pliers.

Paul was in his backyard messing around with liquids and powders and beakers. Mrs. Carter was turning the earth over in a flowerbed. She was on her knees.

"Hi," said Danny.

They both looked up from what they were doing.

"Danny, hello," said Mrs. Carter.

Her first name was Jean. Danny wished that his mum's first name was Jean or maybe Donna—something other than Barbara. Barbara reminded him of fences that hurt you when you tried to climb them.

"What's up?" he said.

"I'm tryin' to manufacture an explosive device," said Paul.

"He could probably use some help," his mother said.

Danny cringed at her effort to bring them together. This was hard enough without a grownup all over them.

"Wanna go down to the river?" he said.

"Sure." Paul looked at his mum.

She stood up, and Danny noticed that she had very smooth legs, way nicer than his mum's. Hers had veins that stuck out.

"Paul's still not entirely out of the doghouse, Danny. If I let him go, this will be the first time for him to leave the yard since that dreadful day at Sydney I. Robinson, except to call in on you a few times. Under strict supervision, I might add."

"Will you let me?" said Paul.

"I wish you had checked with me before you agreed to go," said Mrs. Carter. "I'm inclined to think you haven't learned your lesson."

"Please, Mum. We won't be long, will we, Danny?"

"No."

It annoyed him to be hauled into it. What if they were long? Then what, would it be his fault?

"Well, all right then," she said. "But don't swim in the river. And don't do anything bad."

They started out the back gate.

"For goodness' sake, Paul, clean up your explosive materials before you go."

Paul rolled his eyes but started back.

"And that's enough of that attitude, young man. You're awfully quick to forget the trouble you're in."

Paul gathered up his stuff and put it in the garage.

"'Bye," said Danny.

"'Bye, Danny. Come back for supper if you like."

"Thanks, Mrs. Carter."

"Check with your mum first."

"I will."

They walked the short distance to the river.

"My mum is drivin' me nuts," said Paul.

"Your mum's great," said Danny. "You should try havin' mine."

They came to a clearing off the monkey speedway and sat down on a log.

"I hate my mum," said Danny.

"You can't hate her."

"I do."

"Why?"

"She's gone really weird since Cookie…you know…"

"Died?"

"Yeah. I mean, she's always been sick and stuff, but it's gotten worse. She's not like other mums. Yours, for instance."

"She never yells at you," said Paul.

"I wish she would. Silence is way worse than yelling."

"No, it isn't."

"Yes, it is. And so is quiet talk. You don't know."

He suddenly remembered her saying *my dear lost boy* and tears stung his eyes. He forced them back.

"She doesn't hit us or anything," he said, trying to bring back the hate—he couldn't have Paul witness his tears. "But she's still mean."

He realized he'd have to get used to saying *me* instead of *us*, and all the variations on those words. There were a lot of extras added on to the matter of your sister dying.

"Plus, she never teaches us…me anything. Aren't parents supposed to teach you stuff?"

"Like what?"

"I don't know…how to be. How not to die."

Paul was whittling a Y-shaped stick with his pocketknife.

"Maybe if you had a dad, he'd teach you stuff."

Danny turned to look at his friend. "That's a tremendously stupid thing to say."

"Sorry."

"Where the hell am I gonna get a dad?"

"Nowhere, I guess."

"What are you makin'?"

"A new slingshot. My old one broke."

Danny longed to tell Paul about his plan. He was bursting with it, but he resisted the impulse. He didn't want to put it in the wrong hands.

"Maybe if my dad is teaching me something, I could phone you, and you could come over and learn it along with me," Paul said.

"That's not a bad idea. What types of things do you think he'll be teachin' you?"

"I don't know. How to change a tire?"

"That's a good one. It'd be worth knowin' for later, when we have cars."

"A red '58 Thunderbird convertible," said Paul. "That's what I'm gonna have."

"I'm gonna have a '57 Cadillac," said Danny. "Powder blue." He pictured the car he had seen through the rain at Cookie's funeral.

"Powder blue's a suckhole colour," said Paul.

"No, it's not."

"Yes, it is."

They walked back to Paul's house for supper. Danny didn't let his mum or aunt know what he was doing, and when Mrs. Carter asked him if he had, he said yes.

Supper was meat loaf, mashed potatoes, and green beans.

Mr. Carter was a slow eater. Danny knew this from having eaten there before. He decided to take a bite only when Mr. Carter took a bite and to choose the same thing as he did each time. Meat loaf, beans, potatoes. Beans, beans, potatoes, meat loaf. He hoped no one was paying attention to what he was doing. It was the most fun he'd had since before Cookie died. He might tell Paul about it later, but he might not. It was more the type of thing he told Cookie.

7

DURING THE NEXT FEW DAYS DANNY CRUISED THE neighbourhood for suitable stones, which he brought home and placed on a shelf in the shed.

Since he was up from his chair and out and around, Dot decided she could go home, at least for a few days. Mid-week, Danny heard whispers coming from the living room as he sat at the kitchen table eating fried eggs and sausages that Dot had prepared for him. The words *pills* and *pull yourself together* were uttered more than once. From his mother's side of the conversation came mostly sighs.

She suffered from something called fibrositis. It was the cause of her fatigue and her pain. Heaven help you if you touched her—it hurt too much. She couldn't bear to be touched. She needed pills for all kinds of things: stiffness, sleeplessness, what she called her *excruciating pain*. There were some yellow ones that she took *just to make me feel a little better*. The pills worried Dot. In her opinion there were far too many of them, and she objected on the grounds that they didn't seem to help anyway.

"Do you want me to suffer, Dot? Is that it?" said Barbara.

"Of course not, Barb, of course not. I just worry that you're overdoing the pills, that you lose track of them sometimes."

"I'm a big girl, Dot."

The eggs on Danny's plate looked a little too jiggly this morning. He liked them sunny side up, but with no jiggle to them. Dot's mind hadn't been on her cooking.

Edwin drove in to pick her up. They left the cupboards and fridge full of *eats*, as Edwin called them, and a brand new pile of money in the kitchen drawer. The money in the drawer was nothing new. It always arrived by way of Dot.

Barbara got off the couch to say goodbye to her sister. It was the first time in a couple of days that Danny had seen her upright, and he wondered if the whole time he had stayed in his room, she had stayed on the couch—if she had remained horizontal except for her ghostly appearances on her way to the bathroom in the night. She put a hand on his shoulder now, a feeble unwanted pressure, and he forced himself not to shrug her off.

"Take care of your mother, son," Edwin said as he started up his Olds. "She'll need your help now more than ever."

Those words hit Danny hard in the gut. It hadn't occurred to him that he would have to look after anybody but himself. It reminded him of one Hallowe'en, when he was much younger. His teacher had passed out cards with little slits in them that were supposed to be filled with dimes. The whole scheme was called *The March of Dimes,* and it was to help people all across Canada who had been crippled by polio. Danny had thought that it was up to him to take his dime card to them wherever they lived and he wondered why none of his classmates looked as alarmed as he felt, with his silent questions about train derailments and dog sled travel to the Northwest Territories where he imagined some of them lived, in particular the ones he was responsible for. He was afraid to ask anyone for details, so he hid the card in a shoe box at the back of his closet and did nothing more about it. After a week or so, when the subject hadn't come up again, he stopped worrying.

He had a similar feeling now, when Uncle Edwin mentioned taking care of his mother. At first he had been relieved that Dot was leaving, but now he understood that he hadn't given any real thought to the meals that had turned up three times a day, or the clean clothes that fluttered and snapped on the clothesline. He did not doubt that he could cook and do laundry for himself—he and Cookie had been doing that for years. Well, mostly Cookie; he had helped. But when he thought about looking after the human lump on the couch, it seemed way harder than taking dimes to the Arctic Circle.

Dot kissed her sister on the cheek and Danny on top of his head and gave Uncle Edwin a look that went along with the way

Danny felt. If she were to speak then, he was sure her words would be: *Edwin, don't scare the boy.*

When she was settled in the passenger seat she rolled down the window. "We'll come in to town and check on you from time to time."

"When?" Danny said.

He knew it would be hard for them to get away. Farmers couldn't just up and leave anytime they liked, or anytime their sister lay limp and pathetic on a chesterfield. He had spent a week with them a couple of summers ago and watched them rise with the sun and work all day long. He had helped, but not very much; mostly he had sought out modest adventures with two brothers from a neighbouring farm.

Dot took his hand and squeezed.

"Soon."

She looked at her sister as she spoke. The line of her lips went straight across, no up or down to it.

Danny watched them drive away. He was on his own.

When he turned around, his mother was gone. He glanced at the house and saw nothing in any of the windows. He went inside and found her on the couch.

"Can I have a shelf in the shed all my own?" A stupid question but he needed to say something to sort of kick off their new life together.

And his thoughts had returned to the gathering of stones.

"Sure," she said.

He figured if he asked her if he could take a piss on the rug she would agree to that too.

She lay with the back of her forearm covering her eyes. The living room was thick with her smoke.

He started to open a window.

"Don't," she said.

So she cared about something.

8

DANNY ENLISTED PAUL'S HELP. THEY WORKED IN BACK LANES mostly. He didn't want the sharp edges of gravel, but they found rounded stones, often in groups.

"Why are we doin' this?" Paul said on day two.

"For slingshot practice, what else?"

"We haven't shot our slingshots once. This is weird."

"I thought it would be a good idea to gather up a million stones first."

"I'm sick of it."

Paul quit that day, so Danny did too. He didn't want to be weird.

They deposited what stones they had in the shed and biked over to the Rowing Club, where they sat on the dock and watched the rowers.

"I don't like rowers," said Paul.

"Why?"

"I'm not sure. I just don't."

Russell came scrabbling down to the dock and leapt into the river, splashing both boys.

"Jesus, Russell," said Paul.

Two rowers manoeuvred their way around the dog and glared at the boys as they lifted their craft out of the water and headed up to the club.

"Is that your dog?" one of them called out.

"No." They answered in unison.

"See?" Paul said. "They're assholes."

Danny took off his sneakers and socks and dangled his feet in the river. It was still a little swollen from the spring melt.

"Christ, that's cold," he said. "Imagine your mum thinkin' we might go swimmin'."

"She's out of her head," said Paul.

"No, she's not."

Paul took off his socks and shoes and lowered his feet into the water alongside Danny's.

Russell swam over in a frenzy of excitement.

"Easy, Russ," Paul said. "We're not comin' in."

"Do you have conversations at your house?" said Danny.

"What do you mean?"

"You know, do you talk to each other?"

"Not much. I mean my mum and dad talk, my sisters never shut up, but I don't listen. If I'm involved it's just mainly to be yelled at or ordered around."

"I guess that's normal."

Danny thought about the way his house was, had been as long as he could remember. At Paul's there were his two older sisters who put rollers in their hair and talked too long on the phone—like girls on television did—like Gidget did. And there was a mum who made good suppers and was nice about it if one was interrupted.

One day, last winter, when he had knocked on their door Mrs. Carter had answered and said, "We're just sitting down to supper, Danny, but I'll tell Paul you dropped by."

"Oh, sorry, Mrs. Carter," he said.

"It's okay, dear. We're eating a little earlier than usual. Sherry has CGIT. I can easily set another place, if you'd like to join us."

"No, thanks," he said and walked away. He remembered that he hadn't wanted to go home that day. But it had been too cold to do anything else.

They put on their socks and shoes now and sauntered back down Lyndale Drive.

"See ya later, alligator," said Paul when he turned off at Cedar Place.

"In a while, crocodile," said Danny.

"Not too soon, ya big baboon."

If only his mum could be like Mrs. Carter. He couldn't imagine her inviting a friend of his in for supper at the last minute. She rarely even answered the door. They never had people for supper except Aunt Dot and Uncle Edwin, and when that happened Dot did the cooking.

And why hadn't Cookie done normal girl stuff, like Paul's sisters?

His house wasn't like other people's. The missing dad was the biggest part, he supposed, but everything felt different there—even before Cookie died—and none of it in a good way.

9

SCHOOL INTERFERED WITH DANNY'S SLINGSHOT PRACTICE, but going to school was one of the things Dot had made him promise to do.

He practised at the river—aiming at trees, then at individual branches, then at single leaves. He didn't graduate to branches till he aced the tree trunks and he didn't graduate to leaves till he aced the branches. It was hard work. His arms felt strong as he pulled back the sling and held fast to the Y-shaped instrument that he had carved himself. He felt like a he-man.

"Leaves are way too feeble of a thing to aim at," Paul said.

He was coming by less and less often.

"What then?" Danny didn't look up from the task at hand. "Any better ideas?"

"I don't know. Squirrels? Cars? Shooting at nothing would be better than leaves."

It was true. Leaves were boring, and hitting them was practically impossible because of their size and their thin way of resting sideways on the air. Even when he did hit one (oak leaves were the easiest) it provided little satisfaction. You needed a good solid hit for that—if possible with some wreckage. But Danny stuck with it because he needed to perfect his aim and he couldn't think of anything else that presented itself in such abundance. It was his job, like it was Paul's job to practise piano after school—no fun, but it had to be done. And no question—he was getting good. That was what provided the scrap of satisfaction.

Birchdale Betty's yard had good stones. She had them trucked in. Whenever he got low, he would take a pail over and scoop them up by the handful. She caught him once.

"I see you, Danny Blue," she said, scaring him witless. "I've got my eye on you."

It was after dark, and he had thought for sure she would be inside her house. He should have known better. With her putting-green lawn and prize-winning flowers, she often stood guard against the neighbourhood hooligans who couldn't resist the dwarves and flamingoes that dwelled so happily in amongst her shrubbery.

"Put them back," she said, looming over him with a broom and her famous crazed eyes.

He obeyed her and ran all the way home.

There was no way he could conquer leaves, but he moved on anyway, to shooting at those same three things: tree trunks, branches, and leaves, but from different angles—hard left, hard right, and everything in between. It was time to advance to moving objects. He tried to enlist Paul for that, to throw things for him.

"Don't be an idiot," Paul said. "You can't hit moving objects unless you're Superman or someone like that. Probably he can't even do it. You know what? I'm tired of this whole thing. At least when we looked for stones we covered some territory. This is just stupid."

Danny no longer wanted to do the old things: ride bikes all over town, swim in the pool, go to scary shows at the Lyceum, walk around doing not much of anything.

"Let's go downtown," Paul said.

"I can't."

"Why not?"

When he didn't answer, Paul threw his own slingshot as far out into the river as he could and walked away.

It didn't take Danny long to realize that Paul had been right about the moving objects thing. What had he been thinking? He hoped there weren't other things that he was clued out about in regard to his plan.

He cared about the loss of his friend's presence, but not very much. It had been handy having him help with the search for stones, but tiresome listening to him whine. It played havoc with his concentration.

Now that he was on his own, he was free to do whatever he liked. He solved the moving objects challenge by becoming one himself. From his bicycle he shot at everything he saw that wasn't alive. He was good at no-hands—he had perfected that the summer before. He liked to chew Double Bubble while he rode, and blow bubbles as he shot—the bigger the bubble the better. Three activities at once. The only person he could have bragged to about it was Cookie.

Neighbours had come by at first with casseroles and pot pies, detailed instructions attached to the foil wrappings. When Danny showed them to his mum she didn't seem interested so he warmed them up in the oven himself and dished some out for each of them. Sometimes she ate hers; sometimes she didn't.

The only hard part about it was explaining to the women repeatedly that his mum was lying down. They never pushed. He came to suspect they were relieved not to see her. It meant they didn't have to figure out what to say.

Sometimes two of them came at once, with a supper apiece. Danny figured they came together in case his mum surprised them and made an appearance. It would be less awkward for them if they weren't alone.

These ready-made suppers eventually dwindled and then stopped.

Danny had no problem feeding himself with the eats his aunt and uncle left and he wore the same clothes several days in a row. He was beginning to think that wearing clean clothes was overrated. At first he didn't know if his mum ate or not after the ready-made meals stopped coming. He leaned towards not. The only disturbances in the kitchen seemed to be those he caused himself. So he started taking her some of whatever he was having: cereal, peanut butter and jam sandwiches, TV dinners, butterscotch pudding.

His mum had always been big on Swanson's TV dinners. Danny remembered watching her elation the first time she brought some home from the grocery store years ago, heated them up, and placed them in front of him and Cookie.

"Ninety-eight cents a pop," she announced gaily.

It was as gay as she got.

Cookie's eyes had grown big. She sometimes ate TV dinners in secret, any time of day, and then biked over to the Dominion store to buy more, to replace them before her mother found out what she had done. She spent a good portion of her allowance on them. She hadn't known that Danny knew, and he was too embarrassed to mention it. He also knew that in the past couple of years she had thrown them up soon after she ate them. For sure he couldn't mention that.

His mum usually thanked him when he made her a meal, but as with the neighbours' casseroles, she didn't always eat what he set in front of her.

"What would you like to eat?" he said one lunchtime when she hadn't touched her brown sugar and butter sandwich.

"Nothing, thanks," she said. "I'm having a little trouble swallowing lately."

So he kept on the way he was, giving her some of whatever he made for himself. The meal making wasn't difficult, and it didn't get in the way of his practice. Not much anyway. At the end of every day he washed the dishes and cutlery that he had used. The sink looked out over the backyard with its swimming pool and clothesline and shed. His thoughts could roam wherever they chose. Chores were something he and Cookie had co-operated on daily, and he missed her most during those times.

He was late for school off and on. Part of his preparations involved the study of his quarry: her comings and goings, her habits. She taught at Nelson Mac, and Danny went to Nordale, the elementary school, so he had to move back and forth between the two. The school year was drawing to an end; time was closing in.

Aunt Dot phoned daily to see how they were getting along. If he hadn't answered the phone, it would have rung and rung. He called his mother so that Dot could hear him, and she dragged herself, inside of her sheet or blanket, to the telephone table in the hall.

"Yes, Dot. We're fine. Everything's fine. For Christ's sake, Dot, we're fine."

Danny didn't like hearing her swear. It was just one more thing that had changed, one more thing to get used to.

Uncle Edwin and Aunt Dot made a day trip into town once a week at first, and then they began to come for a couple of days every two weeks or so. During these times Danny's mum would force herself off the couch and pretend she was going about the business of living a miniature life. She slept in her bedroom instead of on the couch, had baths, and put on clothes.

Dot and Edwin replenished the eats and the money drawer, did load after load of laundry, and cleaned the place up. Dot cooked and nagged Barbara about her pills, and Edwin mowed the lawn, pulled weeds, washed windows, did whatever he felt needed doing around the place. He even saw to the filling of the pool and cleaned it whenever he came to town. Danny never used it, but he didn't say so.

When Dot insisted on hiring a cleaning woman, Barbara fought it with what little fight she had.

"No, Dot, for heaven's sake, I can manage."

"You're not managing, Barb. I can see that. And too much is being put on Danny."

Dot won, and a woman named Lena began to come in once a week. She came recommended by a friend of Dot's, and her wages were paid up front for a full year.

Danny worried at first that Lena would be in his way, but he worked around her nicely. She even cooked and did laundry on the day she came, so it eased up on his chores.

Every day he shot 250 stones. By the time he turned fourteen on June 24, 1964, he was a pro. He thought of himself as a modern-day Billy the Kid. His favourite gunfighter was Paladin, a gentleman killer who only performed the deed when he had run out of other options. But Billy the Kid was, well…a kid. And Danny's mind was not willing to let in any peaceful alternatives. He differed from Paladin in that way.

Cookie was gone from the world, and Miss Hartley would pay.

Danny's birthday fell on a Wednesday. He thought that would be a good day to go to the cemetery and tell Cookie about his plan. As he rode out after school he thought about the first time she had mentioned her phys ed teacher's name. It was January, he remembered, around the time that he first heard "All My Lovin'" on the radio.

"Miss Hartley called me a scrawny cockroach," she'd said.

"Who's Miss Hartley?" said Danny.

"My phys ed teacher."

"What's a cockroach?"

"I don't know, but I know it's ugly, and everybody hates it and doesn't want to go near it."

"What happened?"

"We were all in the locker room changing into our gym clothes. I always go into the bathroom because I don't want the other girls looking at me in my underwear. She's always in there with us and she started yelling at me to come out and change with the others. What was so special about me that I needed extra privacy—stuff like that.

"I hurried but not fast enough, and she banged on the door of the cubicle. 'Cordelia!' she said. Oh, Danny, I hate her so much. I got the door open and she yelled at me to step out. Some of the girls had gathered 'round by then, and she said, 'Look at you. You're a scrawny cockroach. It makes me sick to look at you.' And she said. 'No wonder you want to hide.' And she told the other girls to have a good look at what no boy is ever going to want to touch or marry. She went on and on. Some girls giggled. Most of them didn't."

Danny winced now as he remembered the tears streaming down her face and how he had been unable to come up with anything to make her feel better.

He'd said, "Most of the girls didn't giggle," and then asked her if she'd like to play checkers.

She hadn't wanted to.

The only car in the cemetery parking lot was a pale blue Cadillac. Danny wondered if it was the same one that was there the day of Cookie's funeral. It had to be. Maybe it belonged to the groundskeeper. Maybe the groundskeeper was independently wealthy but wanted his job because he liked to hang around dead people, and it gave him a good reason for doing so.

He parked his bike and walked the short distance to Cookie's grave. Nothing about it had changed. It still said *Cordelia*. He sat down and told her what he had in mind.

When he looked up he saw a man standing a ways off, across an expanse of graves. The man was looking at him, or seemed to be. Maybe he was just looking in his general direction. Danny stared at him, and the man looked away.

Then he turned back to telling Cookie more about what was going on: his falling out with Paul, his developing skill with a slingshot, the worsening of their mum's health.

When he looked again the man was gone. He glanced at the parking lot and saw the Cadillac pulling away.

10

DANNY HAD TO DELAY HIS PLAN UNTIL FALL. HE HAD BEEN watching for over a month, but he needed more time to fine-tune the details.

Miss Hartley drove a Volkswagen that she parked on the street in front of the school. Danny often forced himself out of bed in time to watch her arrive. Classes didn't begin till five to nine, but she was always there by seven-thirty because of her coaching duties. The sporty girls got there before eight, carrying their gym bags.

She left at four most afternoons, unless there was a game. The tournaments had wound down now that school was almost over.

On the last Monday of the school year, Danny decided to go through a trial run. For the execution of the actual deed, he'd decided the days needed to be shorter. He wanted a slight cover of dusk, only slight, not enough to affect his sight line: straight to the temple.

The trial run got away on him. In his place inside the shrubbery by the house next to the school, he lost control of his intention.

He watched Miss Hartley walk briskly from the front doors of the school to her dark blue Beetle. She opened the door and threw her purse inside. He took aim—a trial run aim. She surprised him by partially closing the door and reaching over her windshield to retrieve a flapping piece of paper. It gave him more time. The angle wasn't good, but that was okay. He was a master of difficult angles.

A dog barked from behind him somewhere, a high-pitched sound that pierced his ear at the moment that he took his shot. He missed.

He stunned himself with his inaccuracy. The only thing he accomplished was a thunk to her windshield, satisfying in itself—Paul would have liked the thunk—but it was off the mark. He was too far away to see, but he could tell from the sound that he hadn't even made a star on the glass. Maybe, though, a nick that could grow into one. That had happened to the DeSoto once, when they had driven up to Rock Lake a million years ago. He wished for a star now. It could be a reminder to Miss Hartley that there would be a next time.

The dog's bark had both caused the shot and wrecked his aim. Danny was grateful for the wrecking part. It was too soon. There wasn't supposed to be a shot this day. He didn't have a hold on himself.

Miss Hartley looked around her, unhinged. Sounds escaped her throat, but no words.

Danny enjoyed the look on her face. It seemed to be a mixture of terror and guilt. Under the unexpected circumstances he couldn't have hoped for more. She knew how close she had come and she may not have known exactly why, but she knew she deserved it.

Clutching the stone in her fist, she ran back inside the school. She wasn't wearing running shoes, as usual, but ladies' shoes with a small heel. She went over on one ankle.

"Shit." She shouted it.

Danny laughed. It was the sort of laugh kids use when they make fun of others, but quieter. He didn't like the sound of it coming from his own throat.

He figured *shit* was probably the type of word Miss Hartley used all the time after school hours. She probably even said *fuck* sometimes, and women weren't supposed to say either of those words. She was a foul-mouthed pig when she was away from her job, even worse of a person than when she was at school.

Danny wondered if she was running to protect herself from another shot or just to report the misdeed to anyone who would listen. He suspected a little of each.

Almost immediately she emerged from the school with the vice-principal, Mr. Calder, in tow. Danny knew him from an errand he had run for his teacher on the day he had first seen Miss Hartley in action.

He was pleased with himself for not taking off when she went inside for those few moments. He wouldn't have had time to make a clean getaway.

Mr. Calder was not wearing a suit jacket, and his pants were pulled up impossibly high. Danny wondered if they had a longer zipper than standard pants. He vowed to himself that if he lived to be a hundred he would never wear his pants pulled up to his shoulders.

Miss Hartley waved her arms over the windshield and then faced Mr. Calder with her hands on her hips. Danny could hear some of her words.

"...could have been killed," she said.

The vice-principal looked nothing but tired. He stepped back from her noise and put his hands over his ears.

Her screeching stopped. Even she seemed to know that if a fellow grownup had his hands over his ears at the sound of her voice, it was time to shut up. They looked around them vaguely, never in Danny's direction. He was home free. They must have assumed that the culprit wasn't the type of person who would stick around.

Miss Hartley got in her car and wormed away down Birchdale, hunched forward, hands squeezing the steering wheel.

Mr. Calder took a handkerchief from his pants pocket, wiped his forehead, and went back inside the school.

Danny sat still inside the bush till the only car remaining was an old Hudson. A stooped man dressed in workman's clothes came out of the school, locked the doors behind him, got in the car, and drove away. Mr. Potter, Danny supposed: the janitor. Cookie had told him that she'd heard Miss Hartley yell at him more than once about the state of the gymnasium floor, so he was sure the old guy would be one person, at least, who wouldn't object to a fast-moving projectile aimed at her nasty head.

A warning shot had been fired. Miss Hartley could sweat a little. He toyed with the idea of another warning shot on the last day of school, but decided against it. He didn't want to take stupid chances.

When he emerged from the honeysuckle bush he backtracked till he came to Highfield. Birchdale Betty was in her yard squirting dandelions with a rod-like instrument. She fixed her loony eyes on him, but he was convinced that her only thoughts in life were about her yard, and protecting it from marauders. He crossed over and sauntered home down the back lane between Birchdale and Lawndale.

He thought about adding surprise sounds to his practice, like those of a barking dog, but he couldn't do that without another person. Also, he had to consider Russell, who could easily mess things up just by being there. She would need to be secured at home.

For the first time, he worried that he might be famous for his slingshot skills. Maybe it had gotten around...or maybe he wasn't famous at all. He hadn't heard his name shouted out during Miss Hartley's rant. And lots of boys had slingshots.

He liked the idea of being admired for his sharpshooting, especially when he was riding no hands on his bike, but he made the decision now to tone it down, appear average, maybe stop altogether for a while till his fame, if there was any, died down. He would feel Paul out on the subject. That wouldn't be easy; they hadn't seen much of each other these past weeks.

When Dot was in town the last time she had accused him of becoming a lone wolf. She said that was dangerous, but didn't say why. He didn't like being a lone wolf, if that's what he was, but these days he didn't know any other way to be.

When he talked to Paul he'd need to word the fame business in such a way that he didn't sound like a moron.

11

It was a little early for supper when Danny got home, but he boiled up three wieners and made hotdogs. He wanted to get it over with. He ate two, with mustard and Cheez Whiz. His mother ate none.

"I couldn't possibly face a hotdog," she said from her nest on the couch.

So starve then. Out loud he said nothing, just removed her plate from the coffee table.

The phone rang. He answered it and called her. She made getting up look like a gargantuan effort, but he wouldn't take no for an answer. How could she not get that if Dot didn't think things were normal, she'd come back? He had gotten quite used to not having her around.

His mother at least tried to sound breezy today.

Sometimes she told a lie—said she had caught some sun by the pool, baked some muffins, spoken to someone on the phone. Danny couldn't look at her when she lied, but at the same time, he didn't mind.

Dot made Edwin call sometimes. There was no way he would have done it without being forced. Those calls were shorter. His mum didn't work as hard for him, but still, everything was fine, just fine.

Danny waited till he was sure Paul's supper would be over and then knocked on his door to see if he'd like to come out. Russell accompanied him.

Paul seemed happier to see the dog than to see Danny.

"I'm meeting Stu and Stubby later," he said, "but I guess I could, for a while."

A well of loneliness swelled up inside him. Paul didn't really want to come out; he was just being polite, in his way.

They walked along in the tall grass by the river.

"Let's go down to the monkey speedway," said Danny, "where the blueberries are."

"They're not ready yet."

In summers gone by they had eaten the ripened fruit till their tongues and lips turned blue, and the thought of just one more made them sick. But it was too early in the season now, of course. And Paul had made this discovery without him.

He and Paul might find nothing to do, in an uncomfortable way.

Russell romped along beside them; Danny threw a stick. She snatched it up and kept running.

Danny hoped Paul would suggest that he join him and Stubby and Stu for whatever it was they had planned, which was probably just hanging around, but in a good easy way. It was something he had never had to hope for before. He had always just drifted along inside his friendships without questioning whether he was wanted or liked, whether his company mattered in a good way or bad.

He thought about inviting all three of them over for a swim in his neglected pool, but he didn't want to feel the way he'd feel if they said no.

Well, first things first.

"If you wanted to be famous for something," he said, "what would it be?"

"What do you mean?"

"I mean, say you wanted to be known the world over for something, what would the something be?"

Paul kicked at a clump of dry dirt.

"I don't wanna be known the world over for anything."

Danny watched Russell disappear into the bushes.

"Say you were forced to pick something."

"Well...I guess I'd like to hit like Mickey Mantle."

"Good one."

"Or play drums like Ringo."

"Another good one."

"Or maybe be a ventriloquist."

"Uh-huh."

It was time for Paul to stop reeling off things he wanted to be famous for. He hadn't even liked the idea at first.

They walked in silence, kicking dirt, kicking stones. Paul hit a stone that was too big and said, "Ow."

Russell bounded back, wet from the river, expecting praise. None came.

"Guess what I'd like to be famous for?" said Danny.

"Why do I have to guess?"

"I don't know. Just guess."

Paul looked at him as though he were someone he didn't know—had never known—and wouldn't like if he did get to know him. His oldest friend didn't like him anymore.

Danny slowed down, and Paul slowed too.

"Your slingshot," said Paul. "You'd wanna be famous for your jeesly shithead slingshot."

A train went by on the other side of the river, chugging its way slowly towards the CN station.

"I have to go." Paul quickened his step. "You're seriously certifiable."

He headed up towards Lyndale Drive.

Danny didn't follow. "Later, alligator," he called.

The train drowned him out.

Paul reached the top of the dike and was soon out of sight.

It hadn't gone well on any front. Danny still didn't know if he was famous because he hadn't asked the right questions, and his best friend was no longer his friend at all.

All this was Miss Hartley's fault. If he didn't hate her so much, he wouldn't have come up with the slingshot idea and he wouldn't have pissed Paul off this much. That didn't seem quite true to him, but as he moped along, he couldn't figure out what the real truth was. His thoughts rattled inside his head.

Russell shook herself down and leapt up in the air with all four feet off the ground.

"Good girl, Russ," Danny said.

It sure didn't take much to lose a friend. Maybe it had to do with more than his slingshot and how mean he had been to Paul after the Sydney I. Robinson thing. He regretted that now, even though Paul had deserved it. He wondered if maybe Paul had finally seen that he came from a creepy place. A standard family didn't have a fifteen-year-old girl in it who threw up everything she ate. A girl who died. And no dad, and an old mum who lived on a chesterfield. As far as he knew, no one but him and Dot and Edwin knew about the chesterfield part, but it wasn't impossible. People got to know stuff.

This total disconnection from Paul's world was worse than anything except Cookie's death. It practically equalled it.

To an extent he had always felt an apartness from the people in his life, even from Cookie. His mother no longer counted, and he couldn't remember meeting his father. There was Aunt Dot and Uncle Edwin and, till recently, friends that he had horsed around with: Paul and, to a lesser extent, Stubby and Stu. Paul had been the hub, friend-wise.

But he had always felt there was a missing piece, as if his own shadow had gone astray. When he'd had that thought he checked for his shadow a few days in a row, and there it was: long in the morning, short at lunchtime, and long again in the late afternoon on his way home from school, following him or preceding him wherever he went.

He had never felt the apartness like now. He was adrift like a balloon that had slipped through the fingers of a kid at a birthday party. The kid would cry, and the balloon would be forgotten and replaced soon enough with another one. Danny didn't want to be a balloon.

When he got home he went up to his room to assess his gear. There was a useless piece of crap cap gun that made a half-hearted sound. Often the rolls of caps didn't even work. The smell it gave off was good; it hinted at fire and destruction. But it couldn't put a dent in Miss Hartley or even in her windshield. Danny and Paul had sometimes used rocks to bang the strips of caps on the pavement to set them off, but there was only marginally more satisfaction in that than in hitting the pavement with rocks independently of the caps.

He picked up some spurs from his old cowboy outfit. They looked sharp, and actually were, kind of, but a piece of one fell off in his hand, and then another. He hefted a broken piece, took its measure as a weapon, and found that it easily snapped in two. Piece of shit spurs. No wonder he had never worn them.

There was a pea shooter. You could bother people with that, but nothing more. A yo-yo and a kaleidoscope—two items that had amazed him in his younger years, especially the kaleidoscope. Uncle Edwin had tried to explain it to him, but Danny hadn't wanted to believe there was a practical explanation. It was sheer magic, still was, but he didn't care about it anymore.

He put the yo-yo in his pocket and took the spurs downstairs to the kitchen garbage. Maybe he could still master *'round-the-world* and *walking the dog*. Other kids could do tricks with their yo-yos—even Cookie had been able to make it sleep, but Danny couldn't get the hang of anything but the most basic move.

A kid at school had one of those knives that opened in an instant when you pressed a button. It was confiscated almost immediately, before Danny could get close to it. The kid couldn't keep himself from showing it off. Switchblade. That's what it was called. Danny wished he had a switchblade.

He took his jackknife out of his pocket and opened it. It was difficult to picture his small knife causing any real damage. And even if he had a dagger or a sword, like Zorro, it would be messy and loud. Miss Hartley would scream like a banshee when he got going on her.

There was no choice, nothing to weigh. It had to be his slingshot. If he got caught he could run, like Billy the Kid. He could flee to the furthest tip of South America. Patagonia! They had learned about it in geography class. No one would find him there—not the cops, not Uncle Edwin and Aunt Dot. His mum wouldn't even search.

He could get a job washing dishes in Patagonia. There would always be dishes to wash; he could make a career of it.

12

It was a late afternoon in early July, and Danny was in his backyard shooting at Campbell soup tins. He had placed the cans on the flat fence posts that ran alongside their empty lot next door. His mum had posted a NO TRESPASSING sign on it, back when she still did things.

Soup was one of the main things that Danny made for lunch and often again for supper. He prepared it in a small pot, sometimes with milk, sometimes with water, depending on the kind of soup. He had a favourite pot by now, one he had grown attached to. When the soup was hot he poured it into bowls, placed one on a tray along with a little pile of soda crackers, and took it in to his mother.

When she didn't eat hers, Danny threw it down the sink. He didn't want to eat anything that her spit might have touched. The soda crackers went back in the box.

He ate his soup in the kitchen with a piece of toast. He had started out making toast for his mum, but it usually went to waste, and that hadn't sat well with him. Wasted bread meant he had to go to the store more often.

She was most inclined to eat tomato soup. Danny could tell by her bowl that she even crumbled the soda crackers into it. That was something she used to do before Cookie died. So he made it regularly, even though it wasn't close to his favourite. It hurt his tongue. The ones he liked best were Scotch broth, which you made with water, and cheddar cheese, which you made with milk. He also made tomato soup with milk, so that was another thing he had to lay in regularly. But that was easy; the Spanish Court store had milk. It had bread too, but it wasn't as good as what he got at Dominion or the A&P.

He shot the cans off the fence posts one by one, then replaced them and did it again. Soon his mind began to wander, so he took a break and sat on the stoop. Wielders of slingshots shouldn't have wandering minds.

Russell sat with him.

A girl stood outside the gate. The girl he'd seen on the bus. He didn't know how long she had been there. She was a small girl, but older than Danny by two years. He knew that because she had been in Cookie's room at school. Her hands were pushed down into the front pockets of her jeans. She stared at him.

"Hi," said Danny.

She didn't answer, but she came closer, right up to the gate.

"I was thinking," she said.

"You were?"

"Yup."

"Come on in," he said. "I can hardly hear you."

She came inside the yard and closed the gate behind her. She wore no shoes. Russell walked over slowly with her tail wagging, also slowly. The girl put her hand down for Russell to sniff. The dog did so.

The girl came closer.

"I'm Janine," she said. "I was friends with Cookie. I was there the day you saw Hardass being mean to her."

"I know who you are," he said.

How could he forget? He sounded unfriendly to his own ears; he didn't mean to. Janine was the girl who had helped, and who he had seen on the bus reading the book that had *madding* in the title. And she said she was Cookie's friend. That was good news. He hadn't known Cookie to have any friends in the past couple of years. Since she started at Nelson Mac her old ones seemed to have drifted away.

Janine didn't mind his tone, not outwardly, anyway. She seemed the sort that didn't mind much, the sort that wouldn't let an incidental like an unfriendly tone get in the way.

"I was thinking you might want an assistant," she said.

Russell circled her and sat down. The girl crouched and scratched her behind her ears.

"What do you mean? An assistant for what?"

"You know. For your slingshot practice and that."

"Oh, jeez."

"Don't worry."

"I'm not worried," he said. It was a lie.

Had his fame reached as far as girls who were way older than him, who should be thinking about makeup and garter belts?

The day she referred to was just three months ago when Cookie was still alive. Danny's teacher had asked the grade eight class who would like to take a message for the principal over to the high school. The hands of most of the kids had shot up, of course—anything to get out and taste freedom, however briefly. She picked Danny; he couldn't believe his luck. The message contained a list of all the grade eight kids from Nordale that would be heading over to the high school in the fall.

A few of the other kids chanted *teacher's pet* after him as he snatched his jacket off a hook in the cloakroom and dashed out the door. It was good-natured chanting, and Danny smiled to himself as he walked down Highfield with a spring in his step. The April wind was cool, but the sun was high enough and close enough to warm his face when he raised it skywards.

He left the list with the vice-principal, Mr. Calder, and was deciding which roundabout route he would take back to Nordale as he walked past the gymnasium on his way out.

The double doors to the gym were open, and he saw a class of girls lined up in their white shorts and blouses. He didn't see Cookie at first; she was out of his line of vision. When she appeared she was panting hard and her face was blood red. She was the only one running and she was barely able to keep putting one foot in front of the other. To Danny she looked like a person about to have a heart attack. And she was so thin. He hadn't seen her in shorts for a long time. When had she gotten so thin?

The rest of the class watched: some snickering, some with worry on their faces, some slack-jawed, some turning away in embarrassment. He wanted to mow them all down.

"Come on, cockroach," Miss Hartley said. "If you can't run, crawl. Look at her, girls. Watch the stinky cockroach. Puke stink. I can smell it from here."

Cookie looked close to collapse.

Danny hesitated for a second or two. Did he want all these beautiful awful girls to know that the feeblest person in the class was related to him? He made a beeline for her at the exact moment that Janine stepped away from the others and moved forward, calling out words of protest.

She got there first, and put her hand on Cookie's arm to slow her down and then stop her. Her legs folded beneath her and she crumpled to the floor.

"I can't do it," she gasped, all bony and bruised.

Danny and Janine kneeled together, between Cookie and the teacher, who yelled at them to get out of her gymnasium and march right down to the office. They propped Cookie between them and walked her out of the gym and out the front door of the school. They sat on the grass, still brown and damp from winter, while Cookie caught her breath. No one followed, but Danny was ready for them if they did.

The three of them walked to the Blue house on Lyndale Drive. It was chilly despite the sun, and the girls in their gym wear weren't dressed for it. They stopped several times on the way; Cookie had trouble holding on to a breath once she caught it.

"You're gonna be in trouble on account of me," she said.

"Trouble, shmouble," said Danny.

"Do I stink?" she said.

"No, Cookie. You don't stink," he said.

Cookie turned to Janine and pleaded with her eyes.

"No," said Janine. "She stinks. She positively reeks."

She left them at their gate.

Their mother didn't want to know.

"The teacher called her a stinky cockroach," Danny said, after Cookie had gone upstairs. "She was the only one left running."

He hadn't gotten into trouble, and neither had Janine. But not getting into trouble meant nothing. Miss Hartley was still there.

Danny insisted that his mum write a note to the school saying that Cookie had a hole in her heart that made her weak and fragile, and could she please be excused from phys ed for the rest of the year. And he planned to insist that she write another one when school started again in September. They all knew that wasn't the reason for her weakness, but it could have been.

"You look different," Danny said to Janine now.

Her gaze was steady, steadier than Cookie's had been. Her eyes had often darted from side to side, as though looking for a way out. He wondered if Janine was sixteen yet. Cookie would have turned sixteen in August, if she weren't dead.

"I cut my hair off."

"It looks nice," he said. "It suits you."

"Thanks." She tugged at a strand next to her ear. "It could use a little evening up in spots."

He didn't know where to take it from there. He wanted to ask her to sit down beside him on the stoop, but it seemed beyond him, so he stood up instead and stepped down onto the grass.

"You've got a good setup here." Janine gestured towards the fence posts.

"Thanks. It works pretty well for me."

"Well, what do you think?" she said. "About me helping, I mean."

"I don't know."

"It'd be good. I promise I won't be in your way."

"Helpin' with what exactly?" He hadn't voiced his plan to anyone, not even Paul.

"With you becoming the best slingshot shooter in Canada."

Her look faltered; she wasn't telling the truth, not the whole of it. Danny admired everything about her, even her lie.

"That's it?" he said.

"I've seen you on your bike. No hands. Once even blowing a bubble at the same time."

He was so delighted she had seen it that he had to move, get his feet off the ground. Russell sensed the joy and behaved for a moment or two as though she was about to receive a snack.

"I'm not sure I need a helper." He looked at her, met those steady eyes.

"You missed, didn't you?" she said.

The words hung in the air between them. Danny couldn't snatch them back; they weren't his to snatch.

"Don't talk any more." He walked over to the shed where he fetched a y-shaped piece of dogwood from his shelf.

"If you're gonna help me, it would be good for you to have your own slingshot, so you understand the ins and outs of it."

She reached into the back pocket of her jeans and brought out as fine a specimen as he had ever seen. It made his look like something Fred Flintstone would carry around. Hers was uniformly solid, and the rubber and leather sling looked strong and full of purpose.

"Wow," he said. "Where'd you get your hands on that?"

"So I'm allowed to speak now?"

He smiled. "'Course."

"I made it." She handed it over.

"What kinda wood is it?"

She had left the bark on, except where the grooves were, and he liked that rough-hewn look. His weapon looked naked and tired next to it: the slingshot of a simpleton.

"Willow," she said. "We have a big old willow tree in our yard."

"The rubber," he said. "It's red."

"Yeah. It's from an inner tube."

She lifted her chin towards a black inner tube that floated on the surface of the pool along with the elm seeds and aspen fluff.

"Like that one, except red."

A picture of Cookie, cold and rubbery from the river, flashed behind Danny's eyes.

"The rubber of red inner tubes is more elastic. You can pull it back further."

He pulled and saw that she was right.

The grooves were perfect and the rubber was tied with strong twine. The leather pocket for the stone was expertly attached; there were uniform slits to slip over the tubing.

"There's a dead squirrel in your pool," Janine said.

He followed her gaze. He handed the slingshot back to her and went to the shed for the skimmer that Uncle Edwin used to clean the surface. Handling it with ease, he scooped the squirrel out of the water and tossed it over the back fence with one smooth action. It was done before Russell had a chance to get involved.

"Nice one," said Janine.

"Where'd you get the leather?" he said.

"It's the tongue from a pair of my dad's old shoes."

He whistled quietly. "It's a beaut." He laid the skimmer down.

"I have to go now." She put the slingshot back in her pocket. "I have to make supper for my dad, but I could come back later and start in on being your assistant—set up cans and stuff."

"Why do you want to help me?" Danny said.

"I just do."

"But why?"

"Cookie was my friend. I mean, not so much lately, with what she got up to and everything, but...well...she was kind to me, back before..."

"Back before what she got up to lately."

"Yeah."

Danny hadn't known that anyone else was aware of *what she got up to lately*. He wasn't even sure that his mum realized the extent of it.

"Plus, I hate Hardass and I'd like to do something to her."

Danny smiled. *Hardass*. So it wasn't just about him becoming the best slingshot shooter in Canada.

"What if we get in serious trouble?" he said.

"We won't."

"Where do you live?"

"On Lyndale. Same as you but at the far end."

"Maybe I could come there."

He wanted to get a look at the tree with the good wood, maybe find himself a decent branch. Maybe she would give him a strip of the red tubing.

"No," she said. "That wouldn't be good. I'll come here, or we could meet somewhere. At the river, say."

"Yeah, okay. Tomorrow? Two o'clock?"

He too had a supper to make and he had to digest this new development.

Russell saw her to the gate.

As she walked away, she said over her shoulder, "Your grass could use a mowing."

Danny looked around him. It hadn't been cut since the last time Uncle Edwin was here, and that was well before school let out for the summer. He tossed the piece of uncarved dogwood over the fence into the vacant lot. Then he got the push mower out of the shed. After one go-round the grass looked practically as long it did before he started, so he did it again.

"That oughta do it," he said to Russell.

When he went in the house, his mother was on the couch. He hated the couch almost as much as he hated Miss Hartley. He started opening windows.

"What are you doing?" his mother said.

He ignored her at first.

"What are you doing?"

"I'm opening windows. The house stinks. It smells like lazy bums live here."

He went into the kitchen, dumped a can of cream of mushroom soup into a pot with water, and heated it through. Usually he added milk to mushroom soup—it was better with milk—but not this time. He didn't want it to be better.

When he took the tray in to his mother, she didn't look at him.

"Thanks," she said.

He didn't say, *you're welcome.*

It was the first time he didn't say it, and the painting of Scottish cows did not crash down from the wall, and the breeze continued to drift through the freshly opened window. It felt as if there were worlds of things he could not say, or say, and get away with it.

After supper he retrieved the dogwood from the lot next door. What if he never saw Janine again? What if he never found a willow tree? What if he did, but couldn't find a suitable branch? He placed the rough wood back on its shelf in the shed.

Why had she said it wouldn't be good for him to go over to her house? Maybe she had a sick mother too. She was making supper for her dad.

He liked the way she talked, there was something about it.

It was a relief to have something to think about other than Miss Hartley. Janine had called her *Hardass*. He liked that too. He wondered if she had been there the day that Cookie was made to feel bad in the locker room. Probably.

Sometimes he thought it would be enough just to hurt Miss Hartley; that held its appeal. He could keep her captive, tie her up in the shed, naked on all fours. Feed her hard crusts of mouldy bread and dirty water between the hurting. That way she would know what was happening to her and why. He could buy a whip. But mostly he just wanted her gone.

From time to time, since Cookie's death, he had thought about dying, as it applied to himself. It was a faint, barely uplifting desire. Maybe he could talk to Janine about it, hear some of her thoughts.

He wanted to believe in heaven, but by now he knew that everything he'd learned at Sunday school was a steaming pile of crap. He'd liked some of the stories, but not the impossible ones. Even they might have been okay if the stupid teacher hadn't tried to convince them that they were true. Some of the kids had believed her. He'd known that from the looks of amazement on their faces.

Danny liked far-fetched stories, like *Gulliver's Travels*, because no one had spoiled them by telling him they were true. Still, *Robin Hood* and *Treasure Island* were the best, because they could have happened in real life. He'd only read *Gulliver's Travels* and *Treasure Island* in comic book form, but he intended to read the books as soon as he had some time, once this Miss Hartley situation was out of the way.

There was comfort in Janine knowing about his plan, if she really did know about it. It eased his load somehow. But he worried about having been unaware of her watching him the day of the botched trial run.

You missed, didn't you? That's what she'd said. She had seen him.

She couldn't know for sure how far he wanted to take it. Could she? No. It was as unlikely as the story about Jesus waking up after three days of being dead. She couldn't know, but she could have an inkling; she seemed pretty smart. She could probably make a yo-yo go 'round-the-world.

Maybe she could help him by making unexpected loud sounds as he took aim. Mimic a barking dog, say, or the blast of a train's whistle.

His real plans were starting now, with Janine. Her appearance in his life shifted things for the good.

He took his yo-yo out of his pocket and after a few tries made it sleep for the first time in his life.

13

At one o'clock the next day, Danny started walking towards the St. Mary's end of Lyndale, where Janine had said she lived. He couldn't wait for two o'clock, had no idea why he'd suggested two.

Lyndale Drive formed the arc of the D that framed the Norwood Flats. It had been built as a dike during the flood of 1950. One end of the arc was at the Norwood Bridge, the other at St. Mary's Road. Danny's house was in the middle.

It was hot. The air in the lane shimmered as he saw her moving towards him down the lane. She was carrying something that required both hands. When he got close, he saw that it was a flat of eggs.

"What the...?"

"Yeah," Janine said. "It's eggs. Don't worry. They're rotten. My dad's going to kill the egg man."

"There must be what...three dozen eggs here? This is great."

In Danny's house the eggs used to come in pristine one-dozen cartons from the A&P or Dominion store. It hit him that eggs were another thing he could make for his mum and him to eat. Dot must have already bought some; she'd served them to him lots of times. He'd have to learn how to cook them, but how hard could it be?

Janine's eggs were nothing like the ones from the A&P. Hers came from an egg man who her dad was going to kill, and there were feathers attached to some of them.

"I thought we could balance them on the fence posts with gravel," she said, "and you could shoot them. They seemed too good to throw away. My dad was glad to know they were going to be put to use."

It would be very satisfying to hit an egg. Danny thought of Paul. He would have liked to shoot at eggs, especially rotten ones. But it was too late for Paul.

He and Cookie used to eat milk chocolate eggs at Easter (when Jesus purportedly woke up after his three-day death). They got them at Wade's drugstore. It would never happen again.

Sometimes she hadn't been able to stop once she got started. He tried to step in a couple of times—not with the Easter eggs, but other times—when he saw that she was eating way too much for it to be okay. She had told him to go away in a voice that scared him, a low voice that wasn't hers.

It had turned into a secret thing, the eating too much, and Danny wondered if that could have been his fault, because of poking his nose in.

With Cookie being his older sister had come an assumption that she knew better than him. Still, she only made it to fifteen. How much could you really know after only fifteen years or so? During some of those years you could barely walk or talk. His mother was forty-nine, and she didn't even know she was supposed to get up off the couch.

Cookie had seemed pretty normal in her younger days, before the weird eating got a hold on her. She had gamely gone along to the toboggan run in the winter and taken a couple of slides down the riverbank. She hadn't liked it much. Danny hadn't either—it was scary—but they both felt as if they were supposed to like it because everyone else did. He wondered for the first time if in reality no one liked tobogganing. He hoped so. Cookie liked the post-tobogganing part the best: the indoor part with cocoa and baby marshmallows.

Skating was different. She took to the ice, sailed across it. Forwards like a speed skater, backwards with a grace she shared with no one else on the ice. There were three rinks at the Norwood Community Club: two for hockey and one for "pleasure." Cookie had owned the pleasure rink, a boy named Butch Goring, the hockey rinks; people stopped to watch both of them. But that was a long time ago, when she'd had a friend or two. He hadn't known one of them might have been Janine. Cookie had hung up her skates a few years ago.

"Too busy," she'd said when Danny asked her why.

He realized now that it was probably true. She had taken over most of their mother's responsibilities as her illness worsened, and Barbara Blue came to rely on her more and more.

"What are you thinking about?" Janine said now.

"Nothing."

"You look sad. Are you thinking about Cookie?"

"No."

They had walked the short distance back to his house.

Janine lined the eggs up on the fence posts, placing pointy bits of gravel from the lane around each one to hold it in place.

Danny admired her while she worked, pretended to be watching the placing of the eggs. The skin on her bare arms was golden. He wanted to taste it.

The moment of connection was satisfying, more than with soup tins. The eggs were almost alive. Russell and another dog from the neighbourhood snorfelled around them.

"Go on," Danny said. "Find something else to do." He drove them off and turned to Janine. "Would you like to have a go?" The eggs were about half done.

"No. I'm fine," she said.

She put up more eggs as he knocked them down, seeming to enjoy her role as sidekick.

"It's you who needs the practice," she said.

Again, he wondered if she knew the scope of his intention.

14

THE NEXT DAY JANINE ARRIVED WITH A SMALL PAPER BAG HALF full of ball bearings.

"These are perfect," Danny said. "Where did you get them?"

"My house. My dad had them."

Danny stuck his hand in the bag and let the smooth round projectiles run through his fingers.

"Won't he miss them?"

"Nope. He said I could have them."

"Does he know what you want them for?"

"He didn't ask."

She took out her slingshot and placed one of the silver orbs inside the leather pocket. She looked around her for a moment or two and then aimed.

There was an oak tree in the vacant lot next door. At its apex the glossy leaves stood out against the pastel sky. She took her shot and the topmost leaf disappeared.

"What were you aimin' at?" Danny said.

"What I hit."

He looked back at the treetop and wasn't sure now if the leaf was gone.

"Paul thinks leaves are too feeble of a thing to aim at," said Danny.

"Who's Paul?"

"My former friend."

They took the ball bearings with them to the icehouse on the corner of Lyndale and Gauvin Avenue. They bought two solid bricks of ice for twenty-five cents apiece and set them up in the scrubby lot behind the building. They shone in the sunlight.

Janine joined in this time. She was at least as good as he was. They shot till the bag was empty and then gathered up as many of the ball bearings as they could find. They were too precious to leave behind.

At the river they sat down in the long grass, Janine cross-legged, Danny with his legs sticking out in front of him, supporting himself with his two brown arms. Russell joined them there.

"Why is Paul your former friend?"

A fist formed in the centre of Danny's chest and settled there. It was a tiny fist, the size of a small sour crabapple, but too big for a spot that had no space for it.

"Because I just want to practise with my slingshot, and he wants to do other stuff, like we used to. It's kinda my fault."

"Maybe you can be friends with him again…after."

"Yeah, maybe."

"Don't you have any other friends?"

"I did. But they might not be my friends anymore either." He thought of Stu and Stubby and the way they all vied for Paul's attention. The fist inside his chest clenched.

"What kinds of suppers do you make for your dad?" he said.

He didn't want to think about things that hurt his insides.

"Nothing special. He has his favourites, but they're simple, and he's easy to please. Why do you ask?"

"I have to make stuff for my mum and I never know what to make."

"What does she like?"

"Nothing."

"Hmm, that makes it hard."

A dog barked from somewhere far away. Russell's ears twitched and then settled down. Danny stroked her stiff coat and wondered if a dog of the same size and breed as the one barking now had sounded the same a thousand years ago. He suspected so.

"She needs a bath," said Janine.

"Yeah, I guess."

"Why is she called Russell if she's a girl?"

"She's mostly Jack Russell terrier, so we figured on either Jack or Russell and finally chose Russell."

"Who, you and Cookie?"

"Yup."

She rubbed one of Russell's ears and the dog closed her eyes and tilted her head back. Janine wiped her hand on her shorts.

"She's kind of big for a terrier, isn't she?"

"There's other stuff in her too, Lab, we think, because of her size and her floppy ears."

Russell knew they were talking about her and shifted her gaze from one to the other and back again. She looked doltish, and Danny hoped Janine didn't think so.

"What are you makin' for supper tonight?" he said.

"Beans and toast probably. I make that at least once a week."

"Hey, I forgot about beans. I could make that. She used to like beans, I think."

"What's the matter with her? I mean, is there something more than Cookie dying?"

"Yeah, she's got fibrositis."

"What's that?"

"It's a disease that means everything hurts, and you don't sleep and you sometimes have trouble swallowing."

"Sheesh. That covers a lot of bad stuff."

"She can't stand it if you touch her because even the lightest touch hurts."

"Jeez, your poor mum."

"Yeah, I guess."

Danny stood up. There were beer bottles strewn around the area, and he took a few shots, this time with stones from his pockets. He missed two out of five.

When Janine said she better get going, he asked her which house on Lyndale was hers.

"It's on the other side of the street from Rock Sand's house," she said, "and not as far east."

"Who's Roxanne?"

Janine looked at him sideways.

"Rock Sand," she said and spelled it for him. "You're kidding, right?"

"No."

"He's a guy. I can't believe you don't know who he is."

"Well, I don't. Why would I?"

"Everyone knows who he is."

"I don't."

A vertical line appeared on the smooth skin of Janine's forehead between her brows.

"Hmm. Maybe he's more of an eastern Norwood phenomenon," she said.

Danny was sick of the conversation. He didn't want to think about which way was east and some guy whose house was probably full of sand that got under your fingernails even right after a bath and turned up inside your sandwiches.

"So who is he?" He didn't want to care, but he did.

"Well, he's kind of a rebel, for one thing. He doesn't take any guff from anybody."

"What's so great about that?"

"I didn't say it was great. Did I say it was great?"

"No. I guess not."

"He is great, though. For all kinds of reasons."

"Like what?"

"Well, let's see...he's cool and smart and he plays the guitar and is full of good ideas."

Danny didn't know anyone who was cool. Maybe Paul verged on it.

"Lots of people are smart," he said, though he was hard-pressed to think of any of those either. A couple of his teachers maybe. Uncle Edwin? Perry Mason was smart, but Janine would probably think he didn't count. Paul for sure wasn't smart; he was an imbecile. A coolish imbecile.

There was no arguing with playing the guitar. George Harrison played the guitar, and one-quarter of the girls in the universe wanted to marry him. All the ones who didn't want to marry John, Paul, or Ringo.

"Plus he's got weights in his basement," Janine said, "that he lifts to make his muscles stand out and so he can beat people up if he needs to."

"Why would he need to?"

"Well, say someone was giving him a hard time for something."

"Like what?"

"Well, I don't know, do I?"

"Is he a greaser?"

"Yeah, I guess people would call him a greaser."

"Greasers are idiots," Danny said, but he said it quietly, and Janine was so starry-eyed she didn't seem to hear him. He was glad. He was heating up inside, but he didn't want to have a fight with her.

"His biceps are hard as rocks. He let me touch one."

"What's a bicep?" Danny said, leery of the answer.

"It's an arm muscle. Arm muscles are called biceps."

She said this as though she knew everything in the world, and part of Danny wanted her to go away.

"Plus, he has a car," Janine said. "A really neat one. It's old, but it's in mint condition, and he does all the work on it himself. I think it's a model of car they don't even make anymore."

Danny understood what was great about having a car. You could take girls into the back seat and touch them all over.

"Why would anyone wanna be a greaser?" he said, not meaning to, wanting the talk to go back to what they made their parents for supper.

"In Rock's case," said Janine, "I think he was born one."

"I don't think that's the kind of thing you're born to be."

She reached in the bag for a ball bearing and stood up to shoot.

"He's got blond hair," she said.

Danny didn't like Rock Sand. He didn't like the way Janine's eyes went when she talked about him. She missed the shot.

"What were you shootin' at?" he said, needing her to admit it.

"It doesn't matter," she said. "I didn't hit it."

At least she came clean.

"Greasers don't usually have blond hair, do they?" Now Danny wanted to take issue with something.

She rolled her eyes. He preferred that to the faraway look she'd had a moment ago.

"Marlon Brando has blond hair," she said.

"No, he doesn't."

"Yes, he does."

"No, he doesn't. And anyway, he's an actor, not a greaser."

Janine rolled her eyes again, but Danny knew he had her on both counts. He'd read in one of his mum's old movie magazines that when Marlon Brando turned up with blond hair it was "from a bottle." That meant he dyed it, just like women did. That made him a sissy.

"You said this guy has good ideas," Danny said. "Like what?"

A moment or two passed before she came up with one. "He's going to get so good on the guitar that he'll play in a band."

"Yeah, and?"

"He drives like the wind down the highway with the windows open."

"How can he drive like the wind in a rickety old car that they don't even make anymore?"

"He just can, okay? It's not rickety."

It was Danny's turn to roll his eyes. He wanted to stick his finger down his throat and throw up on Janine's feet. *Cookie.*

She was setting herself up for another shot.

"Don't waste the ball bearings," Danny said. "We won't be able to find them, if you shoot them into the trees."

"I'll shoot them where I want to," she said. "They're mine."

She picked up the bag and took off. Danny stayed at the river for a while. He had thought the ball bearings had become both of theirs.

Russell had strayed off, but she came bounding back now.

"You're a good girl, Russ. I'm sorry if I've been ignorin' you. I've got a lot on my mind."

Back at the house he lifted her into the bathtub. It was something he couldn't have gotten away with before Cookie's death. Now he was certain his mum wouldn't care, in the unlikely event she even noticed. He decided he would pick up a new movie magazine for her—try to find one with Doris Day or Natalie Wood on the cover. She used to like both of those movie stars. He wished his mum were Doris Day, with her lively way and her freckly smile.

After he put Russell outside to dry off he went to the cellar pantry to look for beans and found none.

It worried him that he had angered Janine. He didn't want to lose the one person he could talk to these days. There was Russell, but she couldn't answer back when he asked her questions. Sometimes he liked to pretend that Russell could talk, and he imagined the kinds of answers she would give. They would be jolly kind-hearted answers no matter what. Even if he told her his plan for Miss Hartley, she would root for him, scamper along beside him all the way.

Danny and Janine still hadn't talked about it out loud. They had hinted at it, when they talked of targets and lookout positions and good cover, but they had yet to discuss the degree of damage they wished to cause, to call it by its name. Maybe she would vanish if she knew how far his intentions went. Maybe she thought he just wanted to hit Miss Hartley on her scrawny, no-account ass.

15

THE DAY AFTER THE ROCK SAND CONVERSATION IT WAS cloudy and cool. Danny rode his bike to Wade's, where he found a *Photoplay* with Elizabeth Taylor on the cover. There was an article about Natalie Wood inside; she was in a movie called *Love with the Proper Stranger*. He liked the sound of that.

The breeze he caused as he travelled through the streets felt fine against his face. At the A&P he picked up pork and beans and dog food, along with the usual stuff like milk and bread and, of course, Swanson TV dinners. On the way home, when he turned onto Lyndale Drive, he tried to pick out Janine's house. His bike wobbled with the load, so he decided to take the groceries home and come back on foot.

He had known her for only three days, but he couldn't imagine a day without her. If she moved away, or worse, stopped wanting to hang around with him, he wouldn't be able to stand it. He might become even less of a person than his mum. He'd lie down on the floor—the cellar floor—and accept neither food nor drink. All that would be left of the old him would be his plan, floating around in the atmosphere, with no one to pull it off.

It was a real worry, because the thing was, Janine was a girl. And not only that, she was probably two years older than he was. It made no sense for her to be his best friend.

When he got home he fed Russell and used the new can opener that Dot had bought to open a can of beans and put them on the stove to warm up.

Then he picked some wild flowers from the vacant lot next door and put them in a small vase. He didn't know what they were called; he hoped they weren't weeds.

A few minutes later he placed a tray containing beans, toast, flowers, and the *Photoplay* on the coffee table beside his mum. He caught a glimmer on her face. It came and went, just like that.

She started to cry. He left the room and ran out the back door, leaving his own beans on the kitchen table. A mother who wasn't much of anything was one thing, but a crying mother was something else entirely.

He began the walk down Lyndale towards St. Mary's Road. Janine had said she lived across the street from Rock Sand, but not as far east. If he couldn't find her he could ask someone where the greaser lived and proceed from there. If he was as famous as she let on, everyone in the area would know which house was his. Danny didn't know which way was east and he hadn't asked because he felt so stupid about not knowing who that asshole Rock Sand was.

He cut through the field behind the icehouse to see if their chunks of ice were still there and was amazed to find that they were. They didn't even look much smaller than they had the day before.

Past the icehouse there were eight small houses on one side of the drive and several more on the other. He walked down the front street with no luck, so tried the back lanes. Behind one of the scruffy little homes he spotted her in the yard, sitting on a nylon lawn chair beside a wiry man who Danny took for her dad.

He had a cigarette resting on his lower lip, as if he had sticky spit, or it was attached with Mucilage. It bobbed up and down while he talked. He held an accordion between his legs, but wasn't playing it. Danny had never known anyone who owned an accordion or any musical instrument other than a piano. Pianos were everywhere. Most girls seemed to take lessons, and even some boys (Paul, for instance).

Janine or her dad must have said something funny because they both laughed. The dad's turned into a cough, but Janine's was clean and hearty. It was the first time Danny had heard it. Her dad punched her shoulder gently and tousled her short uneven hair.

As she recovered from her laughter, Danny saw her see him and pretend that she didn't. It alarmed him. She must be pissed off about the way he acted when she talked about Rock Sand.

He went home, and wasn't in the house for five minutes before she knocked on the back door. Russell stood beside her wagging her tail. When Danny opened the door, they both moved to come in, but he stopped them.

"No. Let's sit on the stoop."

He didn't want her to know how dark and musty his house was compared to hers, which was probably full of laughter and music and board games.

The screen door clacked shut behind him, and they settled themselves in the backyard.

"Why did you pretend you didn't see me?" Danny said.

"Sorry."

"Why, though? Was it because I told you not to waste ball bearings?"

Janine looked puzzled for a second or two and then laughed. Not the hearty one, though.

"'Course not."

She cuffed his shoulder, like he had seen her dad do to her.

"Was it because we argued about the colour of Marlon Brando's hair?"

He stayed away from Rock Sand, even though he was sure he was the real reason—something to do with him.

"No, you crazy idiot," said Janine.

"Why then?"

She invited Russell to sit down beside her and concentrated on giving her ears a good scratch.

"She's clean," she said.

"Yup. I gave her a bath."

"I didn't want you to see where I lived," said Janine. "I mean, obviously you already had; I saw you see me. But for a second I thought I could still hide it."

Danny was so relieved that it wasn't about anything he had said that he almost started to laugh, but he noticed that Janine's eyes had filled up. He didn't want her tears to spill. They might be even harder to take than his mum's.

"Why?" he said.

"Because you're rich, and I'm poor."

"What?"

"You heard."

Danny looked down at Russell. She was staring straight ahead. He faced Janine again.

"What's that got to do with anything?"

"Everything."

"I'm not even a hundred per cent sure we're rich."

"Have you noticed what your house looks like compared to mine?"

Danny looked at his house.

"No."

"You've got a swimming pool, for Christ's sake."

Danny looked at the pool with its deflated inner tube and sprinkling of debris. A blanket of rotting elm seeds had turned black and scummy.

"I haven't swum in it yet this year." He knew that wasn't any kind of point.

"So? You could have."

"But you and your dad were laughin'," he said. "Sittin' side by side, laughin' at something one of you said."

"So? What's that got to do with anything?"

Everything.

They sat on the stoop for a while. The breeze picked up and rustled the treetops, wafted against their faces. Danny wondered what it would feel like to be a topmost leaf, at the mercy of the wind and the seasons and stones shot from slingshots.

"I don't expect you to understand," said Janine.

For a second he thought she was talking about leaves, what it would feel like to be one, and he was set to argue.

"I've never really thought about people's houses before," he said after that second had passed. "I mean, what they look like from the outside."

He could see from her face that this was of interest to her, and it pleased him that his words had done that.

"Do you and Russell want to come over and meet my dad?"

"Sure. He looked sorta neat, the way he could smoke without the cigarette leaving his mouth."

Danny figured since he was so good at riding his bike with no hands, smoking that way would be a cinch once he got started on it. Maybe afterwards, in the fall. If he was still friends with Janine, he could go over to her house and smoke no hands with her dad.

They took a winding route back to her house and entered the yard from the lane. There was no fence, just lots of greenery for Russell to root around in. Her dad was still outside but the accordion was nowhere in sight. He was squirting oil into parts of a lawn mower. Janine was already at his side. Danny approached slowly, as if he was entering a special place where he might not belong.

"Come on over, Danny," Janine said. "This is my dad. His name's Jake. Jake, this is Danny Blue, the kid I told you about."

Her dad held out a hand, and they shook. His eyes squinted against the smoke that floated in front of his face.

"Danny, is it? Short for Daniel?"

"Yes, sir."

"I had a brother named Daniel once, a long time ago."

Russell hadn't made it past the scrub at the far end of the yard.

"That's your dog?"

"Yes, sir. That's Russell."

Danny wondered what Janine had told her dad about him. Did he know about Cookie? About his slingshot skills?

"Is Daniel not your brother anymore?" he said, for want of something better to say.

"He died, I'm sad to say, when he was just a young whipper-snapper."

"Oh. I'm sorry, sir."

"Call me Jake, son. We're not in the army."

Danny had never heard of calling someone's dad by his first name, but somehow it made sense in this case.

"Sorry, Jake." By now he wasn't sure what he was apologizing for.

"Nothing for you to be sorry about. It wasn't you killed him."

Janine's dad seemed nice enough, yet Danny felt he wasn't able to say quite the right thing. Not so far, anyway.

He wanted to ask who or what killed his brother, but he figured that might be another wrong thing. Or not wrong so much, as not quite right.

"It was polio got him," said Jake. "Epidemic of '36."

Jake had the same thing going on with his words that Janine did. They had an interesting way of talking. Not the words they chose to say, but what they did with them.

"I'm sorry for your loss," Danny tried. It was the comment that he had heard the most at Cookie's funeral.

Jake smiled. The crevices in his face went all the way around it, from his chin to his eyes and across his forehead. He had a lot of crevices for a dad. Usually you had to be a grandfather before you had that many. Other than that he didn't look all that old. He was skinny, in his sleeveless undershirt, and gave the impression he'd had a hard time of it in one way or another.

"Thanks, son," he said.

"My dad was in the war," said Janine, as though she knew that Danny was wondering about the hardships her dad had been through.

"Oh?"

Most dads he'd met had been in the war, but he had never come across one that talked about it. He didn't know if his own dad had been in the war. If so, he'd probably deserted. They were probably still looking for him so they could put him to death by firing squad.

"Danny doesn't want to hear my war stories, honey." Jake's smile wasn't so big now, and that put an end to that.

So Janine said wrong stuff too.

"Jan tells me you're a dab hand with a slingshot."

For a moment Danny didn't know what he was talking about because he didn't know who Jan was and he'd never heard the expression *dab hand* before. But he soon put it together.

"Yes, sir. I mean, Jake."

"That's good, son."

Danny wanted to tell him not to call him son. It reminded him of the burly man at Sydney I. Robinson's and that whole terrible day. But he didn't figure kids were allowed to tell grownups what to call them. Then again, Jake had told him not to call him *sir*.

"I prefer not to be called *son*," he said.

Jake smiled. "Well, good for you, boy. It's good for you to speak up for what you don't like. I can't very well ask you not to call me *sir* and then turn around and call you *son* if you don't like it, can I?"

Exactly.

Danny didn't like being called *boy* either, but let it go. Maybe it was just a one-off. If it turned out not to be, he could deal with it another time. The effort of talking to Janine's dad was wearing him out.

"Do you wanna go down to the river?" he said to Janine.

"Sure. Let's go."

They left Jake to his lawn mower and walked away down the lane.

"Your dad calls you Jan."

"Yeah, sometimes."

Russell trotted along beside them.

Danny waited till they turned left onto the drive before he said, "I'm worried that I'm too famous for my slingshot skills."

Janine stopped walking.

"What are you talking about?"

"I'm talkin' about, if I do something with my slingshot that causes some sort of result, I'm worried that everyone will know it was me."

Tiptoeing around the plan wasn't easy, but Danny didn't want to be the first one to say the word that started with *k*.

This was as close as they had come, except for when she had mentioned that he missed. *You missed, didn't you*? He heard it in his head from time to time; he even saw it—letters forming words inside his eyes—like Jake's cigarette smoke, but more particular in shape.

"Let me do it for you," said Janine.

That took him by surprise.

"No. Jesus, no," he said.

"I'm as good as you."

"That's not the point."

She took her slingshot out of her back pocket, picked up a smooth round stone, aimed at something on the other side of Lyndale Drive, and shot in a clear straight line.

"What were you aimin' at?"

"What I hit."

She picked up another stone. "What is the point?"

Danny took a couple of shots himself, hitting his targets both times.

"It's not your fight," he said. "Are we even sure we know what we're talkin' about, that we're talkin' about the same thing?"

"Of course we are. I told you. I saw you that day."

"Did anyone else see me? Does everybody in the world know what I did?"

"Nope. Just me."

"How do you know that?"

"I just do. We would have heard about it if it was out there."

"And you didn't tell anyone?"

"'Course not."

"Your dad seems to know I'm a dab hand with a slingshot. What about him?"

"I didn't tell him what you did. What you didn't do. What we're going to do."

She started walking again, and Danny and Russell followed along.

"Honest," she said.

They sat down on a patch of grass near the river's edge.

"I bet you wouldn't have missed that day if it hadn't been for the barking dog."

"Yeah, that's what I think too. But I'm glad I missed."

"Why?"

"It was supposed to be just a trial run. I need to be readier."

"Maybe I could make sudden loud sounds sometimes when we're practising," said Janine.

"Yeah. I thought of that too, but I think it would completely destroy my concentration if I had to wonder when and what your next sound was gonna be. I'll just have to chance loud sounds."

"You need nerves of steel for something like this."

"Like Superman."

"My dad said that he had nerves of steel before the war."

"Maybe we could time travel back to before the war and get your dad to go into the future and do it. Then we could zoom back to the present, and he could go back to the past, and no one but us would know what had happened. Your dad of the past wouldn't exist in the present."

"He was shell-shocked in the war," said Janine.

"Shell what?"

"Shell-shocked."

"What's that?"

"Messed up inside his head in certain ways. He wasn't the same when he came back as he was before he left."

"How not the same?"

"I don't know exactly because I didn't know him before he went, but I guess for one thing, he no longer has nerves of steel."

"Maybe it's good that you didn't know him before," said Danny, "so you don't have to compare the two versions."

"Yeah, maybe. I like him fine the way he is now. He was an electrician before the war and now he works on an assembly line at Kub Bakery."

"I noticed he smells a bit like bread."

"Yeah." Janine smiled.

"Where were you when you saw me?" Danny said.

"In the lane behind Birchdale Betty's house. I was heading to the school grounds, to cut through, when I noticed a bush move—a honeysuckle—the type cats go berserk over. Bushes don't usually move, so I went closer to see whether it was rabbits or kids necking or what. Turned out it was you."

"You actually saw me."

"Yup. I peeked in the back of the bush, and there you were. And then you did what you did."

"Jesus. Imagine me not knowin' you were right there."

"I'm quiet."

"Did you see the afterwards part?"

"Just the part where Hardass went screaming into the school. I took off down Balsam. I had my slingshot with me and I didn't want them thinking I did it."

Danny told her about what had happened next, Mr. Calder's appearance on the scene, how that had gone.

"I feel sick," he said. "What if it had been someone else who saw me, like Birchdale Betty?"

"It wasn't, so quit worrying about it. She doesn't leave her yard unless it's in that boat of a car."

"Birchdale Betty hates me."

"She hates everybody. Who doesn't she hate?"

"I don't know, her husband?"

"No. I'm pretty sure she hates him too. I heard her yelling at him once, when he was vacuuming the trees. She shouted that he wasn't doing a good job, that he was missing spots. She even said, *what good are you anyway*. That's not a very nice thing to say to your husband."

"I wish you hadn't told your dad about my slingshot skills."

"Sorry. I shouldn't have. I'll try and get him to forget about it."

"How?"

"Maybe by talking about other things you're good at."

"I'm not good at anything else."

"You're smart in school, aren't you?"

"Well, I'm pretty good in maths, I guess."

He was exceptional in maths and good in everything else except phys ed but he didn't want her thinking he was some kind of suck who studied all the time.

"Your dad shouldn't know," he said.

The grass was damp. When they stood up, they had damp rear ends. They walked, following the curve of the river.

"Lots of other kids have slingshots," Danny said. "Nearly every guy in my class had a Wham-O hangin' out of his pocket last year. I think they were in style or something."

"What's a Wham-O?"

"It's the one you can order from the back of comic books. I sent away for one. I think it was one of my *Lone Ranger* comics that had the ad in the back pages. It was pretty good actually; I might still have it lyin' around somewhere."

"Jeez. I must have read the wrong comic books."

"What comic books do you read?"

"Well, none anymore, of course, but I used to read a lot of *Archie* and *Little Lulu*."

Of course she doesn't read comics anymore. Danny wished he could take back his little-kid words.

"Let me do it for you," Janine said again. "People probably do know how good you are."

"Maybe just you and Paul and your dad and me," Danny said.

"Likely more."

"Maybe."

"Nobody knows how good I am," said Janine. "My dad, but he doesn't count in terms of me."

"What do you mean?"

"Well, if I were to do something bad with my slingshot, my dad wouldn't let anything happen to me. He'd lie or kill to keep me safe."

Kill. She'd said the word that hadn't yet been spoken.

Danny envied her a dad that would kill to keep her safe.

"If I do it," she went on, "and they suspect you, they won't be able to prove it because you won't have done it."

"There'll be circumstantial evidence."

"What?"

"Circumstantial evidence," said Danny. "You hear about it all the time on *Perry Mason*. It's when there's no actual proof, like fingerprints or bein' caught red-handed, but there are so many things that point to the culprit that they capture him anyway and send him down. Like in my case, it would be my hatred of Miss Hardass and my skill with a slingshot."

"It won't go to trial like on *Perry Mason*," Janine said. "Kids don't go to trial."

"Where do they go?"

"Reform school. It's a home for juvenile delinquents. But neither of us will have to go there. We're going to plan this and pull it off so that won't happen. It'll be perfect, and I'm going to be the one to do it."

"What if you get caught red-handed?"

"I'll pretend it was an accident. Like I said, no one knows how good I am except you and my dad and me. I could be just learning, and the shot goes wildly astray. Stuff like that happens all the time."

"It does?"

"Yeah. I've got a second cousin with a glass eye because of a slingshot accident."

"Really?"

"Yup."

"Who shot him?"

"Me. I was just learning. See? I'm experienced in these things. I got in no trouble over it. Zero trouble."

"Was it really an accident?"

"Of course. I like my second cousin."

"What's his name?"

"Who cares? Plus, it's a her."

"And she didn't die."

"No. She didn't die."

Danny was mildly disappointed. He wondered if she was making up the story just to talk him into letting her do it. Then he realized it didn't matter one way or the other, like the cousin's name didn't matter. Janine wanted to help him. Period.

"Do you have lots of cousins and second cousins and stuff?" he said.

"No. As far as I know, just that one second cousin. Around here, anyway."

"How do you have second cousins without havin' first cousins?"

"I'm not sure. I don't know the legalities surrounding it."

"I don't have much in the way of cousins."

Danny figured they had a lot in common family-wise: her with no mum (that he had seen), him with no dad (that he had seen); both of them with no brothers or sisters (anymore, for him); no cousins to speak of except the one-eyed girl. As far as he was concerned, second cousins were too distant to even mention, unless they'd had eyes shot out. He had a dog.

"Do you have any pets?" he said.

"Yup. A cat named Pearl. You'll meet her."

Any time she said anything about the future, even if the future was just later that day, Danny's heart leapt up with the knowledge that he would see her again.

"Pearl loves honeysuckle bushes. She rubs up against them and goes cross-eyed."

"That's funny," said Danny.

"Yeah."

Neither of them laughed.

There was no doubt in his mind that she was as good as he was with her aim. In fact, they both knew she was better. But still.

"You can't do it," he said. "There'll be trouble, and it shouldn't be your trouble. It'll be way too suspicious that Miss Hardass gets targeted twice. Mr. Calder will figure it out."

"I want it to be my trouble," said Janine. "She's a vile human being. Plus, Mr. Calder probably hates her. Didn't you say he put his hands over his ears while she was screeching at him?"

She picked up a stone.

"It's true," said Danny.

"Like I said, if I do it, and they suspect you, they won't be able to prove it. Never mind circumstantial evidence. You can be somewhere else, somewhere definite where a trustworthy person sees you and can stick up for you."

"Who?" he said.

"I don't know. Another teacher, maybe. The janitor, Mr. Potter. We could plan it so you're inside the school in full view of people while I'm outside doing it."

"Mr. Calder," said Danny.

It was sounding more and more like a good idea.

"Sure. And it'll be an accident. You can't get punished for accidents."

"Can't you?"

"Nope."

Janine fit the stone neatly into the pocket of her slingshot and aimed for something low, far into the shrubbery.

"What were you aimin' for?" Danny said.

"What I hit."

Danny turned up towards his house.

"Where're you going?"

"I have to go home for a while, think things over."

"Okay. We'll talk some more soon."

Janine headed back the way they had come.

"You can swim in our pool if you want to," he called after her, in case he had been too abrupt.

She waved without turning around. Every single thing she did enchanted him more.

16

LATER THAT AFTERNOON, THE CLOUDS DISAPPEARED, AND Danny sat on a Muskoka chair by the pool popping peanuts into his mouth and flipping the shells onto the ground.

Russell lay across his legs. She was far too big for anybody's lap. She was covered with peanut dust, and broken shells had attached themselves to her fur. Her eyes were closed and the warm rays of the afternoon sun caught the rear half of her body.

The Blues were practically the only family in the neighbourhood with a swimming pool in their yard, and Danny thought, for the first time, how odd that was. His family would not be on anyone's list as one likely to have a pool.

In previous summers he and his friends had used it — Cookie, not so much in recent years. On extra-hot days other kids would knock on the door and ask politely if they could have a dip to cool off. Mrs. Blue had allowed it; she hadn't told them to go away. But Danny knew she didn't like it. She was on edge till they cleared out.

It was inevitable that teenagers would take liberties at night, with beer in their bellies and no fear to speak of. Then she would make a fuss. She would even phone their parents if she knew who they were. At night the kids were at least partially naked, so as soon as Danny heard them, he would rush to the bathroom window to see if he could catch anything interesting. Boys' dicks and asses mostly. The girls were slower to get out of the water once they were in and they weren't as flagrant as the boys; they usually left their underwear on. But on occasion, he had seen a breast or two and a hint of something dark down below. It was worth the wait.

No one came knocking this summer. Danny supposed it was because of Cookie's death. The pool was out of bounds now, for fun and frolic.

It must have been different once, before him, before Cookie. Maybe his mum and dad had had some good years, before their kids and her sickness came along to spoil everything. Maybe they had swum together in the pool. He liked to think the Blues were a welcoming family at one time. There was no reason for him to think that, other than that he liked to.

He didn't remember his dad, except as a word: *dad.* A notion of a person.

There was an arm—big and sturdy with lots of hair—soft against his face. That might have been his dad.

He remembered a time when he and Cookie were little, and they had peeked around a wall into the front room to see their mother sitting in a sunbeam, sewing a button on her taffeta dress.

"Daddy?" Cookie said.

Their mum looked their way but didn't speak.

"Daddy," Cookie said again.

She set aside her sewing and looked past them out the window.

The memory felt so hollow that Danny wanted to fill it up with a better one, even if he had to make it up.

When he was old enough to notice that other kids had two grownups in their houses instead of just one, he'd asked his mum about it.

"Your dad died," she said.

Aunt Dot and Uncle Edwin were there when she said it and they both got funny looks on their faces, so Danny didn't believe her. And then, later that day, Dot and his mother whispered in cat voices. It was the first time he heard them hiss.

He waited what he considered to be a substantial length of time and then he said it again.

"Where's my dad?"

"I told you. He died."

"No."

"Yes. Now leave it, Danny."

He was still young enough not to know that a couple of hours wasn't a substantial length of time under those sorts of circumstances.

When he had given up on asking his mother, he asked Cookie.

"Where's our dad?"

"I don't know," she said. "Somewhere."

That was enough for him. He had a dad out there and he would wait for him to come home. His dad would be nicer than his mum.

As time went by, Danny and Cookie made it their business to get to the bottom of the puzzle of their missing dad. Cookie became the asker, Danny along for moral support.

Their mother started out by denying again that he existed and then, when they wouldn't give it up, she ignored them, went about what she was doing, even if it wasn't much. She didn't bustle like other people's mothers. Danny wanted a mum who bustled.

They pegged her for a liar. They even made up a game surrounding it. Cookie would be the mum, Danny the kid.

"Where's our dad?" said the kid.

"He's dead," said Cookie in an irritated mother voice.

"*Liar, liar, pants on fire*!" the kid would shout.

Then they would both dance around, singing it," *Liar, liar, pants on fire, hang them up on a telephone wire*," till their real mother shouted up the stairs.

"Cut it out up there!"

They speculated on their father's absence. Was it their fault for being born? Had their dad wanted no children? Had they behaved so badly as babies that he couldn't stand them for one more day and escaped to a far-off land where no one knew his name or what he had run from?

Cookie had more memories than Danny of him. She knew enough to draw a picture of him. He was shaped like an elongated pear. One of the juicy ones that they took outside to slurp on in summer. The drawing looked more like a pear than a person, but Danny praised her anyway and said they could use it as a guide when they went searching.

He imagined their dad climbing up and down grassy knolls with a stick over his shoulder. The stick held a large handkerchief—father-sized—bulging with tasty foods that Danny and Cookie never got at home: fried chicken, crackers with more flavour than soda crackers, potato salad. Their mum cooked potatoes all the time, but she never made them into a salad like other mothers did. Mrs. Carter added mayonnaise and celery, and radishes in summer.

They wondered to death what became of their dad. One of Danny's speculations was that he was a magic man. He had kept his talents to himself over the years and behaved like any other dad, made a living like any other dad, but he could see into the future. And he saw that the future in the house on Lyndale Drive was bleak. It wasn't their fault, his and Cookie's. They hadn't been bleak kids, not yet, anyway. It was the fault of their mother.

Maybe their dad couldn't face a future with her and her illness, so he did the thing that made the most sense. He ran off and joined the circus, putting to use the powers that he had kept to himself for so long. He read people's fortunes, helped them with decisions in their lives, their futures. In short, he did good.

"Maybe that's it," Cookie said when Danny told her his latest theory.

"Yup, I think it is."

They found themselves being happy for him, cheering him on in his endeavours, and then they would remember that he left them, and a shadow would fall over the hillside rambler, who ended up in a travelling show of wonderment.

Finally they put it to rest. Out loud, anyway.

Danny shifted in his lawn chair now, and Russell dug in. He shifted some more, and she resigned herself to getting up.

There was a small whisk hanging from a hook inside the back door. Danny fetched it and a dustpan and cleaned up the scattered peanut shells around his chair.

17

RAIN FELL IN THE NIGHT, BUT IT STOPPED BEFORE DANNY rolled out of bed. Clouds still hung heavy in the sky. It was the kind of day when Cookie would have once said, "Let's play board games."

He wondered if Janine liked to play games. She probably had loads of girlfriends that she hung around with on days like this, experimenting with hairdos and talking about girl stuff, like bras and Kotex. She didn't have much hair to work with, and it always looked about the same, and her breasts were small under her T-shirts. She wouldn't have to think too much about what size of brassiere to choose—likely the smallest one. Maybe she and her friends just hung around, like he used to do with Paul: walking around the neighbourhood, poking at things, inventing wild scenarios that would never come to be. He missed Paul, but not as much as he did before Janine entered his life.

He'd never noticed her with girlfriends, but they must exist. The only time he'd seen her with other people was the day they'd rescued Cookie. It was hard to imagine her in a dangerous pack of girls that stood around whispering and giggling, but it must happen. Who wouldn't want to hang around with Janine? You'd have to be mental. She said she read a lot, that that was what she did when she was on her own, but she must have friends, mustn't she?

When he went downstairs, Aunt Dot was in the kitchen with his mother. A new carton of Buckinghams sat on the table between them. It had already been opened.

"Hello, Danny dear," Dot said.

He hadn't known she was coming and he didn't think his mum had either. She was at the table in her housecoat, trying to sit up straight, her hair flat against her scalp. They exchanged a glance, mother and son, united in their desire to get on with things in their own way.

"Hi, Auntie Dot," said Danny. "Is Uncle Edwin here too?"

"Yes. He's outside skimming the seeds and whatnot off the pool. Are you using it, Danny?"

"Well...I lounged beside it yesterday."

His mum lit a cigarette from the one she was ready to put out.

"How are you getting along?" said Dot. "Since no one ever answers the phone around here, I thought I better drive in and ask you in person."

"Sorry. I answer it if I'm here." Danny immediately regretted his words. He had ratted out his mother. He looked at her again, and this time it felt as though their shared bond was one of distrust.

"Morning, Daniel." It was Edwin at the door.

With no thought, Danny ran to his uncle and threw his arms around his waist. Edwin brought with him the smell of the farm—manure and prairie grasses. To Danny's horror, he felt hot tears spill down his cheeks when Edwin's strong hand pressed against his back. He let go and made a beeline for the front hall, where he sat down on the telephone chair out of sight. His face burned with his baby-girl behaviour.

A chair scraped against the kitchen floor.

"I'm going to lie down," his mum said.

"Oh no, you're not," said Dot. "Barbara, we need to talk. For God's sake, Edwin, sit down."

Danny had never heard her so upset. She wasn't one to take the Lord's name in vain. Another chair scraped, as Edwin sat.

Dot's voice eased up a little.

"You're not managing," she said. "I'm going to stay for a while. Edwin, you'll have to get along without me. You can hire someone from town for a few days to help with the house chores and the milking."

Danny heard his mum sigh, and when he poked his head around the corner, saw her head resting on the table from two feet out. Her back made a flat surface. You could have set teacups on it.

"You go, Edwin," Dot said. "I'll borrow some of Barbara's clothes."

Edwin's chair scraped again, and Danny returned to the kitchen in time to see him put his hat on.

"Can you two not get up without scraping your chairs along the floor and driving a person to distraction?" said Dot.

Edwin and Danny exchanged the tiniest of smiles. Neither of them wanted to get caught; it was no time for smiles.

Dot followed Edwin to their car. Danny went too, but stopped when he got to the shed. He had a few stones in his pocket to add to the ones on his shelf.

He could hear Dot's voice clearly. Her words were all about his mum snapping out of it and performing her duties as a mother to her remaining child.

Edwin spoke, but more quietly. Danny couldn't hear what he said. Probably not much—maybe *yes, no*, or *mm hmm*—whichever he thought fit in best.

"I've a mind to take that child home with us and leave Barbara to it. This is too much for Danny, Edwin. Surely you can see that."

Again, Danny couldn't hear his uncle's words. He hoped he was arguing against Dot's idea. It wasn't possible for him to go and live with them. He wished he could relive the last several minutes and act in a more manly fashion.

"I don't know, Edwin. I just don't know."

Even Dot's sighs were louder than Edwin's words.

It started to rain. Edwin got in the car and pulled away, and Dot marched back to the house. Danny waited a few minutes. He didn't want to go in, but the rain began to come down hard. He found Dot in the living room, straightening up the couch and surrounding area. His mother had disappeared into her bedroom.

"How are you really getting along, Danny?" Dot held a ratty-looking blanket in her arms.

"Fine, thanks."

"Honestly?"

"Yes, honestly." He smiled. He needed her to believe him.

"Are you hungry, dear?"

"A bit, I guess. I usually have cereal or toast about now."

"Are you doing all your own meals, honey?"

"Yeah, pretty much. But it's not hard. I'm okay with it."

"Are you making your mother's meals as well?"

"We had beans on toast yesterday."

"Who prepared it?"

"Me."

"Is your mother doing anything at all?"

He picked up an overflowing ashtray and started towards the kitchen.

"Oh my, oh my, oh my." She followed along behind him, her arms full of bedding. "I'm just going to run down and throw a load in the washer."

"Okay," said Danny. "I'll have some cereal."

"No, you won't. I'm going to make you a proper cooked breakfast."

Danny stirred some Jiffy into a glass of milk while he waited for Dot.

"I could make you some hot cocoa," she said when she came upstairs and saw what he had in front of him.

"I'm good with cold Jiffy, thanks."

"We need laundry detergent," Dot said. "I'll make a list."

She found everything she needed to make fried eggs and pancakes. There was no syrup in the cupboard, but she made some out of sugar and water.

"You're doing a good job, Danny."

"Thanks."

She went to get her sister and force her to sit back down at the table. The pancakes tasted good, and Danny took a small amount of pleasure in watching his mum try to impress Dot with her eating, as though she did it all the time.

"We're going to give your hair a good scrub after breakfast," Dot said.

"I..." Danny began, but when he looked up from his food, he realized she was talking to his mother.

He had a mum with dirty hair.

"What would you think about coming out to the farm for a while?" Dot said to Danny. "For the rest of the summer, say?"

"No, thanks."

He spoke around a mouthful of pancake. Everything on his plate was drenched in syrup.

"I love pancakes," he said.

Dot sat down. "We have them all the time out at the farm. The hired men are fond of them too."

"I can't leave," Danny said.

"Maybe we could talk your mum into coming too. That way you wouldn't have to worry about her."

His mum's fork lingered halfway between her mouth and her plate for what seemed a very long time. A small piece of pancake rested on top of it.

"I can't go," Danny said again. "I have swimming lessons, baseball, and summer fun club."

His mum turned to stare at him now, but he didn't care. She'd have to be retarded to object to his lies.

He could come up with more if he needed to. Lying had become a necessity. Dot's idea was unacceptable.

"Well, we'll see," said Dot.

"Thanks for breakfast, Auntie Dot. It was delicious. May I please be excused?"

"Certainly, dear." Dot busied herself with the cleanup.

Danny went upstairs, where he sat in his chair and stared out at the rain. It was really coming down. He used to like the rain, but ever since Cookie's funeral it had felt like an enemy. This morning it was conspiring with Aunt Dot to take him away from his house and Janine and his plan. Not Russell. He knew they would allow him to take Russell with him. He reached down to pat the smooth clean head of his dog. She was only five years old; she probably had a good five or ten years left before she died.

He heard his mum and aunt in the bathroom. His mum let out a couple of *ows*. His aunt was, indeed, giving her head a good scrub.

18

Dot made salmon sandwiches for a late lunch. The three of them ate in silence around the kitchen table. Afterwards, Danny put on his baseball cap and a pullover and stuck his slingshot in his back pocket. The lace broke on his left sneaker. He retied it, using what remained. When he got home he could look for a new one, in secret, so Dot wouldn't make a major production out of it. It was still raining, but he couldn't wear a raincoat or take an umbrella. He could imagine the sneer on Paul's face if he saw him scurrying along underneath his mother's umbrella.

The clouds were so heavy that it was darker than dusk. He ran over to Janine's house. The lights turned on in the houses lent them an air of warmth and comfort. His mum hadn't been letting him switch on lights at home.

"It's summer, Danny," she'd said from the couch, the back of her hand over her eyes. "We don't turn lights on in summer till night time."

He hadn't heard that rule before. He suspected it was a new one. Not for the first time, he wondered if Miss Hartley was the wrong target.

As he'd left the house today, he'd stared into his mum's lengthened face at the kitchen table and turned on the light in the back landing, just for fun. When he got to the lane he heard Dot's voice shouting after him, something about rain gear, but he pretended not to hear.

By the time he got to Janine's, he was soaked. He stood on the stoop and peered through the kitchen window. She and her dad were sitting at the table. They drank from steaming mugs and moved their hands as though they were playing a game. He knocked on the door.

"Danny," said Janine. "Come on in."

They were playing Monopoly. She gave him a towel and dry clothes—a green T-shirt that he'd seen her wear, and jeans that must have been hers as well—and sent him to the bathroom to dry off. He left his underwear on even though it was damp. He didn't think his ass, balls, and especially his dick should touch Janine's clothes directly. The T-shirt had an iron-on picture of the Rolling Stones on it, and the jeans had beads woven in somehow to cover one of the back pockets. He wouldn't be able to go out on the street in these clothes, and nothing fit, but they weren't too bad.

"We've just started, Danny," Jake said, "if you'd like to pick a man and jump in. Jan's running your clothes through the wringer to give them a head start."

Danny chose the milk bottle. He and Cookie had always fought over it. He was amazed that neither Janine nor her dad had chosen it. Janine had the thimble, Jake the shoe. He smiled at Jake, who winked back at him.

In a couple of hours the sun came out. The game could have gone all day, but they packed it in and declared Janine the winner. She had bought Boardwalk and Park Place on her first two swings around the board and never looked back.

Danny pegged his clothes to the line in the yard and set his sneakers out to dry. He and Janine sat on old cushions on the stoop with their legs stretched out in front of them. The eaves dripped and the leaves sparkled in the sunlight.

Janine's sandals were crisscrosses of red, yellow, and blue.

"Your toenails are red," Danny said.

"Yeah."

"I've never noticed your toes before."

"Probably because my toenails have never been a colour before." Janine tilted her head to the side as she studied her feet. "My dad said I could paint either my fingers or my toes, so I picked my toes."

"Why just one or the other?"

"I don't know. I guess he didn't want me overdoing it."

"That makes sense."

They admired the willow tree, its branches drooping with the wet, and discussed the slingshot Danny would carve some day soon.

"Do you kids want some Johnny cake?" Jake spoke through the screen.

By the time they had eaten their fill and helped to clean up the kitchen Danny's clothes were dry enough to put on.

"Let's go out," said Janine.

She went to get her slingshot, and Danny tied on his damp shoes. They started walking. A cool wind had come up, and already the gravel in the lane had dried under the sun.

"People have seen us together," Danny said. "If you're the one to do it, they'll suspect that you're doin' my dirty work for me."

"Danny, no one knows how much you hate Hardass. Or do they? Have you been announcing it to everyone?"

"Of course not."

"Well, stop worrying then. You only think that people will suspect you because you suspect you. No one else does."

Danny tried to step outside of himself to look at things from a different angle, but he couldn't manage it.

"We could ease up on hanging around together if that would make you feel better," said Janine.

Danny sat down on a curb on Lyndale Drive and looked off towards the river.

"I don't wanna ease up on it," he said.

She sat down beside him. "Let me think about it some more."

They watched the occasional car drive by. Danny recognized Mr. and Mrs. Carter in their beige Plymouth, with Paul in the back seat. Mr. Carter smiled and honked his horn, and Mrs. Carter waved gaily. Paul stared straight ahead.

"There's an example right there," Danny said, "of people seein' us."

"Yeah, but they're not seeing us in relation to Hardass."

She stood up. "Oh, man. I've got a great idea."

"What?"

"We can pretend you're teaching me. We can practise in the school grounds, not give a hoot who sees us."

"Yeah, and?"

"And I can get her by supposed accident, like we planned, and come clean right from the start."

Get her. He still wasn't sure Janine knew how far he needed it to go. She was winning him over, though, to the idea of her being the one to do it, and that wasn't all good. There were good parts to it, a letting go of sorts for one, but it might not be a good thing to let go of. A sick feeling, a familiar one, lay heavy in his gut. He couldn't remember when he'd felt it before. It might have had something to do with Cookie, or not. It was about him not being good enough. Not slingshot wisé, he was good enough that way. Person wise. If he let Janine do it for him, it meant he wasn't a good enough person—he wasn't doing his best. He wanted to lie down on the road and succumb to the leaden weight that dragged him down.

"You'll be looked down upon forever," he said.

"No I won't. It'll be an accident, like when I put my cousin's eye out."

"Second cousin."

"Whatever."

Did she not get that a real accident and a fake one differed from one another? That she might feel different after the fake one than she did after the real one? Did she not have those types of thoughts?

She was so cheerful that he started to think perhaps it was a good idea—never mind her lack of thoughts—and then no it wasn't, and then yes it was. He felt as if his head was full of butter that had melted and then turned hard again.

"Come on," Janine said. "I want you to meet someone."

19

THEY CUT THROUGH THE ICEHOUSE LOT TO SEE IF THEIR ICE WAS still there, and it was barely a puddle. Danny was astounded that from the first day to the second it had seemed practically the same size, and then from the second day to the third it almost vanished. Janine wasn't astounded, just suggested that once it got seriously started on melting it picked up speed. They walked down Lyndale to a tidy little house with yellow trim. Janine knocked on the door, and no one answered.

They sat down on the front steps.

"Who lives here?" said Danny, knowing the answer.

"Rock Sand." Janine's voice broke in two. "Now he's someone who really is famous. In these parts anyway," she added, perhaps remembering that Danny had never heard of him. "He's famous just for being who he is," she went on, answering the question he had no intention of asking.

Now he went from not wanting to be famous at all to wanting to be world-renowned. It didn't matter for what, as long as it beat out the legendary asshole whose front steps he was sitting on and whose name ground your teeth down to dust.

"Why don't we go?" he said.

"I think it's just an aura about him that makes him famous," said Janine.

It angered Danny that she answered questions that he didn't ask and ignored the ones he did. And her eyes went funny again, like the other time she talked about Rock Sand, as though they were seeing something that he couldn't. It made her look mental. It made her look like Russell in one of her denser moments.

"You know how some people just have an aura about them that makes them special?" she said.

"No."

Danny was unsure about his answer. It was possible that he liked Janine so much because she had an aura about her. Part of it, he knew, was that she seemed to like him, without him having to do much.

But another part of it might have to do with auras. He would look the word up in the dictionary when he got home.

"How do you spell aura?"

"A-u-r-a."

"I don't wanna meet this guy. Why do I have to meet him?"

"Well, jeez. You don't have to. I thought you might want to. You know, to broaden your horizons."

"I don't want my horizons broadened."

"Sure you do."

"No, I don't."

Danny looked at her to see if the dreamy look was still there. It wasn't. She was back on planet earth.

"That way is east, right?" Danny pointed towards St. Mary's Road.

"Yes. Jesus, Danny. Do you not know where the sun comes up?"

"I guess I haven't really thought about it before."

"It's not the kind of thing you think about," said Janine. "You just know it, like how many toes you have or what your middle name is."

"My middle name is Arthur." He took out his jackknife, opened it, closed it again, and put it back in his pocket.

"Does he live with his parents or is this his very own house?"

"Oh no, he's got parents. He's not an adult or anything, but he lives in the basement. His folks pretty much leave him alone."

"Let's get out of here." Danny stood up.

Janine stood too, and they walked to the front sidewalk and began a discussion about what to do next. Her cutoffs were too big for her, as if they had once been a pair of her dad's old jeans. They hung on her hips, and Danny could see her belly button, and slightly lower, to either side, the hint of an indentation.

An old black car came towards them and stopped near where they were standing.

He felt the change in her. Her body shifted into a different gear, one that lifted her clear out of their conversation and towards the car.

"Let's go down to the river," he said uselessly.

A boy got out of the car and reached into the back seat for an electric guitar that he slung over his shoulder. He was small in stature, but the muscles in his arms bulged, stretching the cloth of his T-shirt. It was stretched further by a pack of cigarettes. He took a deep drag from one as he approached. It had no filter.

"Hi, Rock," said Janine.

Danny didn't like the way she said his name. Plus, who the hell would name their kid Rock? His parents must be retarded.

"Hi, Jan."

So this muscle-bound freak was in the secret club that got to call her Jan. Him and Jake. How many other boys and men belonged to the club? He wanted to join it and he wanted to run as far away from it as he could get.

"This is the guy I was telling you about," said Janine. "Remember?"

"Hi, guy-that-Jan-told-me-about."

They'd been talking about him. Sweat began to trickle down his sides.

"I have to go now," he said, staring hard at her.

"No, you don't," said Janine.

"Yes, I do."

"A minute ago we were talking about what we were going to do next."

"So what."

Rock laughed and crushed his cigarette under his foot. He wore black boots that came up to his ankles. They had chains attached to them.

"I'll leave you kids to your bickering." He walked down the sidewalk and disappeared around the corner of his house.

"Thanks a lot," said Janine, again the person who had stood beside him before the car's arrival had changed the whole world.

"Thank you a lot," Danny said. "You told him about me too. Who haven't you told about me? I don't wanna be told about."

"I didn't give him any details."

"Yeah, just like you didn't blab to your dad, and then he goes ramblin' on about me bein' a dab hand. Don't you get that the fewer people that know about me the better?"

"I didn't tell Rock about your slingshot skills, and even if I had, we can trust him. He's cool."

"This is unbelievable. If you didn't talk about my slingshot skills, what could you possibly have talked about? There's nothing about me except my slingshot skills."

"Cookie."

"You told him about Cookie?"

"Yeah."

"What about her?"

"That she died."

"What else?"

"That she was my friend and your sister."

"What else?"

"Nothing."

"You're nuts."

"No, I'm not."

"Yes, you are. You're nuts about him, and that makes you nuts in all ways."

"No, it doesn't."

"Yes, it does. And you're stupid to think you can trust him. Why did you have to talk about Cookie with him?"

"Sorry."

Danny decided on the spot to carry out his plan alone. He couldn't trust her, not with thoughts of Rock Sand messing up her head.

"I'm not stupid," she said.

"Well, maybe not. But nuts for sure. And a blabbermouth."

"I'm not a blabbermouth. I didn't blab about Cookie. I just talked."

She walked away from him, up Lyndale and back to the path by the river. Danny followed and caught up. He wasn't done with her.

He chuckled. It was a mean chuckle, the kind that accompanies the word *amused*. He had noticed that people who said they were amused never really were. They were filled with something bad—hate maybe, or envy—and they pretended they were amused. His mum said it sometimes: *It amuses me that Jean Carter thinks she can get away with spike heels at her age*. He heard her say that to Dot on the day Paul's mum dropped him off after the Sydney I. Robinson incident. She only said it because her own legs were lumpy and white, and Mrs. Carter's were shapely and smooth and tanned. He knew it.

"What?" said Janine. "What could possibly be funny?"

"Your heart-throb. He's short."

Danny laughed out loud and bounced along beside her. He skipped ahead a step or two and walked backwards. He had imagined Rock to be six feet tall at least.

"He's not my heart-throb," said Janine. "Where'd you get that stupid word? And he's not short."

"Yes, he is. He's a pipsqueak."

"He's not as short as you."

"Yes, he is, and besides, I'm way younger than him. And his eyelashes and eyebrows are white."

"So what."

"He looks like a sissy. No wonder he lifts weights. He has to protect himself from all the people who make fun of him. And he has a ducktail. Nobody has a ducktail anymore, not even morons."

Janine turned towards him. Her face had hate on it, inside of it. He had gone too far, but he couldn't stand her starry-eyed carrying on. Who did she think she was, Sandra Dee?

She started to run back towards her house.

"Oh no. Wait."

"Go away, Danny."

"Sorry, wait up." He ran after her.

"Leave me alone, you little prick," she shouted. "If you follow me, I'll tell everyone in the universe what you're gonna do. I'll testify in court."

Danny stopped. He didn't see anyone, but that didn't mean anything. Somebody could have heard.

Janine stopped too and faced him.

"His eyelashes are beautiful, and he's a good kisser too. Best I ever had." She wasn't yelling anymore.

"Kids don't go to trial; they go to reform school." It was the best he could do.

He turned around and walked towards the river. The upper half of his body strained to leave the rest of him behind.

How many other people had she kissed? He knew very little about kissing as yet. Once last year three older girls had held him down in the school grounds and taken turns pressing their lips against his. Two of them pressed really hard. One of them didn't, and he didn't hate it. His body responded in an instant.

Frank Foote had driven the girls off that day. Just his appearance on the scene seemed to deflate the girls' intentions somehow. He had been walking by the school with his younger sister, pushing her in her wheelchair. She suffered from something horrible that she'd been born with and she couldn't walk or even talk. People said she probably wouldn't grow to be very old. Frank could often be seen pushing her up and down the streets of the neighbourhood, talking to her, pointing things out.

He was a good brother to her, Danny thought now. If only he could go back to Cookie's last day and change just a couple of the sentences he had spoken. The last words she heard from him should have been kind.

She had been the same age as Frank and Janine. He wondered if she'd had any ideas about what a good kiss was. If so, it would have been only in her imagination. He was almost certain there were no real kisses in her life. Not that kind, anyway—the kind Janine was talking about.

A picture came to him; he'd seen it before. It was what he thought of as his first memory, and he attached the age of three to it. That might be right.

His mother was sitting in a chair in the front room. It was around the time of Cookie saying *Daddy* to her as she sewed.

There was a sunbeam this day too. Maybe it was the same day, the same sunbeam.

Cookie crawled up onto her lap. Their mother's arms hung down on either side of her chair. They made no move to encircle her daughter, to touch her in any way. The lack of movement was out of whack. It puzzled Danny then, and he wondered about it again now. His mum had used her arms for practical reasons, to move Cookie and him from place to place: bath mat to tub, road to car seat, dewy grass to dry cement. Surely it was too early on in her illness for touching to have become such a problem for her. Or maybe that was one of the first symptoms. Yes, maybe that was it. A grimace was attached to every effort she made, then and now.

Had Cookie ever known their mother's arms in the way he knew was missing that day? He knew he hadn't.

By the time he got home the cool wind had calmed, along with his distress.

His mum and Dot were sitting down to supper.

"Danny, finally. We'd about given up on you," said Dot. "Do you realize it going on seven o'clock?"

"Sorry. I guess I lost track of time."

It was Sunday, so Dot had cooked a roast with all the trimmings.

After supper he helped with the dishes, and when Dot and his mum were settled in the living room, he hauled the dictionary off its shelf in the dining room and looked up *aura*. There were three meanings. One of them had to do with headaches and epilepsy, so he discounted that one. The other two were much alike, but one seemed to apply to the very air we breathe, and the other to something more particular. It said: *subtly pervasive quality or atmosphere seen as emanating from a person, place, or thing.*

Okay, emanating. Emanate: *to flow out from a source or origin.*

In this case, the aura emanated from Rock Sand, who was the source. Danny wished the dictionary went into more detail. Both words, *aura* and *emanate*, were vague. They offered nothing he could sink his teeth into. All he knew for sure was that the emanation from Rock surrounded Janine and pulled her in. Away from him.

He needed an emanation, a first-class one, so that he could gather Janine in to himself. It was hard to think about. He doubted he had it in him to be the source of an aura, not a good one, anyway. If he could muster one up at all, it would probably be prickly like a cactus and stinky like the garbage under the sink when he let it sit too long.

Anyway, he had for sure ruined things with her. There was no fixing what he'd said.

He went into the bathroom and locked the door. He forgot all about Rock Sand for a few minutes and thought about Janine's heart-shaped face, as it was before he had damaged it with his words, and then he fixed his mind on the smooth golden indentations hinted at above the line of her cutoffs where they hung down low and caught on her hips. If he could lick one of them, slowly, he would give up anything else he had hoped for in his whole life, including his plan for Miss Hartley.

For the rest of the evening he stayed in his bedroom. He wondered about the possibility of having a television installed in his room, so he could watch the shows he used to watch with Cookie before his mum took to the couch. *Cannonball* was his favourite. He supposed some rich kids had TVs in their rooms. And, according to Janine, he was rich. There was no way he was going to sit in the same room as his mum for even half an hour. Plus, Dot was there and she'd probably talk through the whole thing.

He sat in his chair and thought about having no friends. He was on his own again. But he knew which way was east; that was something, he supposed.

20

When Danny woke up the next morning, he thought for a couple of seconds that he had already done it, and his stomach turned.

He thought back to the time before he had hatched his plan. A lightness suffused him and he arose from his bed. He didn't have to do it. It surprised him to realize how good that made him feel. Then it worried him.

By the time he got dressed he knew he hadn't left his plan behind.

His jackknife lay on his desk along with a few stones and a nickel from yesterday. He put them in his pocket and started down the stairs. Then he remembered that Dot wanted to take him home with her, and his steps slowed.

"Morning, Danny." She looked him over. "There's a pile of clean clothes in the laundry basket." She forked sausages onto a plate for him. "I just haven't folded them yet."

"Thanks, Auntie Dot."

His mum looked up for a moment; her eyes were at half-mast.

As his aunt chattered, he thought about Janine. There was no way she could still like him after yesterday. Also, the trust he'd had in her had wavered when he saw the way her eyes went when she talked about Rock Sand. It vanished completely as he watched her transformation in his presence. She was crazy for that guy. She would tell him their secret when he kissed her. Danny knew that from Cookie's old love comics. That's what kisses did. They caused people to give up their secrets. And he knew she would let Rock kiss her again. That's what the look on her face meant, and that's what she meant when she said the word *aura*. And it went further than kisses. She wanted to do it with Rock Sand. She probably already had.

Danny groaned, and his aunt and dozy mum both looked at him.

After breakfast, he rummaged around in Cookie's closet till he found her old copies of *Young Love*. He spent a good part of the morning poring over them and by the time he was done he knew he couldn't use Janine as an accomplice, even if she forgave him. The beautiful women in the comic books looked exactly like Janine did when she talked about Rock. They ended up with the men of their dreams, but they got there at the expense of everything else in their lives. They left a trail of crap in their wakes. Danny did not wish to be part of that trail.

None of the dreamboats in Cookie's comics looked anything like Rock Sand. If there was an opposite of him, these comic book men were it. Some of them even wore ties.

What had Cookie seen in these stories? He had never thought about this sort of thing in terms of his sister. He had just taken her comic books for granted, as she must have done with his Superman and cowboy comics. Had she longed to be like these women with the stars in their eyes, and the tears spilling down their cheeks? He could not fathom it.

He wondered if Cookie would have turned out differently if they'd had a father. For sure she would have in some ways. Maybe the detail in her nearly sixteen years of life would have differed enough from what had been that she'd still be alive. It dizzied Danny to think about it.

There were some *Little Lulu*s and *Archie*s mixed in with the love comics. He had read his share of *Archie*s, but he put some *Little Lulu*s in his room for later so he could find out what the attraction had been for Janine.

When he went back downstairs, his mum was on the couch, and Aunt Dot was in the kitchen making potato salad. He sat at the table and watched. There was no point in avoiding his aunt. She was more likely to think he was getting along okay if he was present and forthcoming.

"I'm very fond of potato salad," he said.

"This is going to be a good big one, sweetie. It should do us for a few days."

Us. How long was she staying?

A few years ago on a hot day in summer, Danny had decided there was no good reason he and Cookie shouldn't have potato salad just because their mum never made it, and he went about giving it a try.

He chose a time when she had gone to lie down. It was something she did a lot, even back then. He went to the cellar and came back with three big potatoes. He was going to cook just two, but Cookie said he better do three because they should share it with their mum.

She scrubbed them clean, while Danny searched for the utensil that his mother used to peel them. It had been invented specifically for that purpose. He peeled carefully, cut each one into four pieces, and plopped them into a saucepan that Cookie had filled with water. Then he placed them on the stove to boil.

Both of them knew that this was the most important part, because it could go terribly wrong since it involved the stove. He put the lid on the pot, and turned on the burner. They both stared at it till Danny remembered that he had heard someone, maybe Aunt Dot, say, *a watched pot never boils.*

So they got out a deck of cards and began a game of War. Their mother came into the room a little later and took the lid off the pot to see what was inside. When the potatoes began to boil she turned down the heat. When they were done, she drained them.

"I'll take it from here," Danny said.

"What?"

"We're making potato salad."

"Oh. Okay." She rinsed them with cold water.

She left the room, and Cookie and Danny smiled at each other.

He got the Miracle Whip out of the fridge and looked in the vegetable crisper where he found celery and radishes. The celery was on the limp side, but he figured the limpness would be disguised inside the salad. He cut the potatoes into smaller chunks, as small as he could manage, put them in a bowl, and added the dressing. Cookie sliced the celery and radishes. They mixed it all together, added salt and pepper, covered it with Saran Wrap, and put it in the fridge. It looked a little soggy—Danny suspected he had added too much Miracle Whip—but not too bad. There were worse things than soggy.

They played a little more War, and then Danny went outside to cool off in the pool. He looked forward to presenting the salad at suppertime to round out whatever his mum was making. She still did most of the cooking back then.

"Danny. Supper," she called out the kitchen window.

It was five o'clock. They always ate at five, earlier than anyone else Danny knew. It was too early, in his opinion, and he didn't get why it had to be that way. He had asked his mum once.

"Well, it's good to get it out of the way, isn't it?" she'd said.

After supper she would get them to clean up so there wasn't a trace of anything left in sight. Not a crumb.

Danny and Cookie were often hungry again when it was time for bed. If their mum heard them messing about in the kitchen, she would say, *The kitchen is closed.* She said it in no uncertain terms.

On the day of the potato salad, when Danny entered the kitchen Cookie was already seated at her place. He saw that there was a hamburger in the centre of each of their plates. Potato salad went with hamburgers. People ate them together when they had barbeques in their yards or went on cookouts to City Park. This was good.

He went to the fridge to get it. He moved things around and around.

"Sit down, Danny," said his mum.

"But where's…where's…?"

"Your sister ate it."

Danny looked at Cookie, who stared down at the table, turning red to the roots of her hair. She wore it in a ponytail that day.

"But…"

"Sorry, Danny," she said.

"But…"

"Sit down," said his mum.

It would do no good to say anything else. He had walked into a silent period. He couldn't taste his burger, and no matter how many times he chewed each bite, it was never ready to go down.

As soon as supper was over he went outside again. He didn't see Cookie again that day, but when he went to bed there was a note on his pillow in her left-handed scrawl: *sorry danny.*

The events of that day, potato salad day, were etched deep in Danny's brain as the start of it all. There must have been inklings before that, but none that he had taken in.

She had scarfed down the entire potato salad by herself, after they had prepared it together, for the three of them.

The next day he asked her about it. "Why did you do that, Cookie?"

"I don't know."

"What were you thinking about when you did it?"

"I don't know."

"Did you forget that it was for all three of us?"

"No."

"I don't get it," Danny said.

"Me either," said Cookie.

He remembered asking his mother about it.

"Do you think Cookie eating all of the potato salad has to do with the hole in her heart?"

"What do you mean?" said his mum.

"Maybe she's trying to fill it."

Danny realized now, as he sat at the kitchen table, that he was alone in the room. He heard murmurs from the living room and slipped out the back door without explaining himself. A risky business with Dot there. That was one good thing about when it was just his mum and him: he never had to explain himself. Dot required explanations.

At the school grounds Danny found a good stick and threw it over and over and over and over again for Russell.

In recent years Cookie had asked him more than once, more than twice: *Danny, do you think I'm fat?*

No, he always said. But that was all. Maybe he should have said more. Picked some efficient words to say that would have worked to make her feel better.

He blamed their mum, always harping on about Cookie's shape, her unfortunate shape. He pictured how thin she had looked in her gym clothes last April.

Please come back, Cookie. I'll do better.

21

Danny didn't see Janine for the rest of the week. He made a point of staying away, and she made no effort to be in touch. More than anything he wished he could turn back the clock to before he made fun of Rock Sand. He tried to remember what the last straw had been, what had caused her to run. Was it when he called him a pipsqueak? Or maybe it was when he made a joke of his hair. If only he could go back and not make fun of him at all.

He tried to tell himself that she wasn't as wonderful as he thought. He sure didn't like the part of her that admired that greaser the way she did. It was distasteful—one of his mum's words. It was no good to examine it too closely though. He didn't want to turn it into not liking some part of himself that he hadn't known about before. That happened sometimes: dislike turned itself around and faced the other way.

Thoughts of Paul crept in from wherever they dwelled, and he pushed them back again. And thoughts of Cookie. She had loved him no matter what. She got mad at him for sure, but love was always there, like the river.

He'd heard of hermits who lived in shacks in the woods. He wondered if they were happy or sad. They couldn't be happy. But if they were too sad they wouldn't be able to do all the hard stuff they had to do to stay alive, like chop wood, kill food, and patch holes in their leaky roofs. Sadness took away your strength. He remembered the days of sitting in his chair, before his plan took shape, before Janine. He couldn't have played with Russell then, let alone patched a roof. Perhaps the hermits were medium: neither happy nor sad.

It seemed a miracle to him that in the days following Cookie's death he had managed a trip downtown with Paul. He supposed he did that during a sinking-in period, while the enormity of what had happened settled into its place, with him a permanent fixture in the middle of it.

He didn't know what to think about that wouldn't make him feel bad, so he took his slingshot to the river and concentrated on smooth round stones and topmost leaves in their shades of green.

Aunt Dot didn't question why he was around home so much, and he was grateful for that. He guessed she didn't want to make him feel worse about having no friends by talking about it. She gave him chores to do, and he was even grateful for that. He biked to the store for her, and to the library and the drugstore, and he helped with the dishes and the yard. He even dusted once when she asked him to, though that was a chore he could have done without.

When he woke up on Saturday morning his first thought was of Janine. And then he remembered that he had wrecked their friendship and that even if he hadn't, he had decided she couldn't be his accomplice.

He hadn't seen her for six days. His decision and the wreckage didn't seem so fixed now. The decision was his alone; he could reverse it or change it in any way he wanted. The wreckage was up to Janine.

After his last bite of toast with apricot jam, Danny headed out. He was wearing a long-sleeved shirt, and Dot commented on it.

"It's warm out, Danny. Seventy-five already, if that's to be believed." She nodded towards the thermometer attached to the outside of the window frame.

He wondered what she would do if he told her to go to hell.

"Go to hell, Aunt Dot," he said on his way down the lane. The words didn't seem so bad if you said them cheerfully. They were just groups of letters. They could fall apart.

He hoped Janine could forget the horrible things they had said to each other. He would be on his best behaviour and act as though everything was normal, as though he hadn't behaved like a moron the last time they were together.

Russell trotted along beside him. They approached the backyard from the lane. No one was there. He found her sitting on the front steps with a large cat—white, grey, and orange in colour.

Janine hadn't seen him yet. Everything in the world depended on how her face looked when she saw him standing there.

"Hi," he said.

She looked up. A quiet smile materialized on her face.

It was enough. *All's right with the world.* It was a line from a song he'd had to sing in stupid music class. But it made sense now.

"Hi," she said. "Long time no see. Hi, Russell."

The dog swished her tail from side to side, but kept her distance. Whimpers escaped her throat. Her trepidation due to the cat's presence clashed with her joy at seeing Janine.

"Hi," Danny said again. "Is your dad home?" He wished that on the way over he'd thought up a better topic to open with.

"Yeah. He's sleeping." She stood up. "Go sit on the stoop. I'll get us some Kool-Aid."

When they were settled in the backyard with their sweet cherry drinks, Danny said, "I'm sorry."

"Never mind."

"But…"

"I mean it. Never mind."

"Okay."

The cat leapt up and insinuated itself between them. Russell sat on the grass a short distance away and shifted from one haunch to the other.

"This is Pearl," said Janine.

"Hi, Pearl." Danny held out his hand to her.

She nosed it tentatively and gazed up at him.

"She's beautiful," he said.

They sat in silence for a while, and he knew he wouldn't tell her that she was no longer his accomplice.

"Don't tell Rock Sand about our plan," he said.

"I won't."

So she thought they still had a plan.

"Promise?"

"Promise."

"Have you already told him?"

"No."

"Honest?"

"Honest."

She crossed her heart.

"I'm gonna go home now." He stood up. He worried if he said anything more, he would destroy their wobbly truce. Why had he mentioned Rock's name first thing like that?

"Why?" said Janine.

"I have to…my Uncle Edwin's comin' by, and I wanna see him."

It was a lie, it came easily.

"Liar," said Janine.

He looked down at his shirt, his long sleeves.

"What is it, Danny?"

"Nothing."

"Let me tell you a secret," she said. "A big one that I'll trust you with, so you'll be able to trust me with yours."

"Are you sure?" He sat down again. "I probably wouldn't wanna tell me a secret if I were you."

"I want to. It's about my dad." She glanced over her shoulder. "Just let me check to make sure he's sound asleep."

When she was gone, Pearl turned over onto her back with all four legs stretched up. Danny rubbed her tummy. Russell growled low in her throat.

Janine returned. "He's down for the count."

A thin layer of white cloud covered the whole sky and turned it a misty blue. Two brown squirrels chased each other around the yard and up the trees and across the telephone lines.

"I wonder if squirrels ever relax," said Danny.

"You don't ever see them sitting around. I think it's either they're busy or they're asleep."

"I'm glad I'm not one."

"They're probably okay with it, not knowing any other way of being."

Pearl turned onto her side, a mound of fur in a hazy sunbeam.

"My dad's an off-and-on drunkard," said Janine. "He doesn't drink for long stretches of time and then he can't stop himself and he goes on a bender. He just got back from one a couple of days ago."

She took a long drink of her Kool-Aid.

"So he doesn't even come home at night?" Danny said.

"No."

"Where does he go for his benders?"

"Beer parlours. In hotels."

"How long does he go on them for?"

"It depends. The longest he's ever been away is five days."

"And you, stay here all by yourself?"

"Yup."

"Don't you worry about him?"

"Yeah. All the time. I'm afraid he'll get killed by a car or beaten to death by another drunk. He goes to those hotels on Main Street. I followed him once. Well…twice. He sleeps there, I guess.

"The thing is," she went on, "the reason it's important that it's a secret is the Children's Aid Society. They take me away from him if they find out that he's left me on my own. Somebody told on him once."

"Who?"

"I don't know. They wouldn't tell me. I'm guessing Old Lady Horndog across the street and down. She's always peeking out from behind her curtains. *Salope*!"

"Sal-opp?" said Danny.

"Bitch,"said Janine.

"And what's the Children's Aid Society?"

"It's the outfit that takes you away from your home if someone tells them that your dad leaves you alone sometimes even when you're totally able to look after yourself. They're a bunch of assholes who don't listen to you or answer your questions."

"Assholes," Danny said.

"Yeah. Next to my dad dying, the thing I'm most afraid of is them taking me again. If they try, I'm going to run."

"So they've taken you before?"

"Yup."

"What do they do with you when they take you?"

"They put you in a house with people who are in it for the dough. People are paid to take you in. I only had a nice person once."

"It's happened to you more than once?"

"Yup. Once you're in the system, they can pop up any time to spy on you and destroy your life if they don't like what they see."

"What about when you were little?" Danny said. "Did he leave you alone then?"

"He didn't do it when I was little. It just started happening after..."

"After what?"

"Nothing."

Danny didn't press.

"You could stay at my house when he goes on his next bender," he said. "That way they wouldn't find you. You could have Cookie's room. My mum probably wouldn't even notice."

He pictured sneaking into her room at night and slipping under the sheet next to her. They would both be naked and they'd press up against each other, the whole length of them, front to front.

"Does your mum's sickness mean that she doesn't notice things?" said Janine.

"Well...she takes a whole bunch of pills for pain and sleep and everything else, and they make her groggy. It's gotten worse since Cookie died; she barely stands up. I won't be surprised if one day she wakes up and her legs don't work anymore. She'll fall to the floor in a pile of skin and bones."

"She'll probably snap out of it."

"I doubt it," said Danny. "She's pretty old for snappin' out of things."

"How old is she?"

"Forty-nine, I think. Anyway, you could stay at my house. You could bring Pearl. Russell would adjust."

Russell wagged her tail.

"Hi, you two."

Jake stood inside the screen door with a cigarette attached to his lower lip.

"Hi, Dad." Janine leapt up, and Danny did too.

"How about some pancakes?"

"That'd be great. Will you stay for pancakes, Danny?"

"Sure. I love pancakes."

He was full of Aunt Dot's scrambled eggs and toast, but no way would he refuse.

"Okay. You two carry on, and I'll call you when they're ready. Hi, Russ."

Russell clambered up the steps, forgetting all about Pearl for a few seconds. The cat hissed and was gone. Russell peered inside the screen door, wagging the whole rear half of her body. Jake let her in, and her toenails scratched riotously on the kitchen floor.

"I don't like maple syrup," Danny confided to Janine.

"Me neither. We make our own syrup: one cup white sugar, one cup brown sugar, one cup water, boil for one minute."

"That's what we do too!"

Jake seemed like the kind of person who might feed Russell bits of bacon and pancake right from the table, so Danny put her outside before they sat down to eat. He didn't want her to develop bad habits.

The pancakes were at least as good as Dot's. Jake insisted on doing the cleanup as well as the cooking.

"He feels guilty because of his bender," Janine said when they were back outside.

"Why doesn't he get fired from his job?" Danny said. "Does he mainly do his benders on weekends?"

"Actually, yeah. He's very regimented about his drunkenness—does it on long weekends, holidays, those sorts of times. Now and then he screws up—like this time—and misses work, but only once or twice a year. His job is just part-time—three or four days a week, so it fits in well with his drinking."

"He's a good dad, isn't he?" said Danny.

"Yup. He's a damn fine dad."

22

THE NEXT DAY, AFTER A LUNCH OF POTATO SALAD AND HAM, Danny walked along with Russell to the little house at the end of Lyndale Drive. He liked that he and Janine lived on the same street, even though their houses were some distance apart.

She was in her backyard mowing the small patch of lawn. The push mower clattered quietly in the still afternoon.

When Danny approached, she stopped, and a smile lit up her face.

"You have green eyes," he said. "I never noticed before."

"Yes, I do."

"So green."

He sat on the stoop and watched her while she finished up the yard. A belt held up her cutoffs today. Maybe her dad had noticed how much of her you could see. There was a Yogi Bear decal sewn on one of the pockets now and what looked like part of a bracelet sewn on another. It sparkled in the sun.

"I like the way you sew extra stuff onto your clothes," Danny said.

"Thanks. We have a sewing machine that belonged to my mum. It was just kind of sitting there so I figured I'd learn how to use it. I'm just starting; it's fun. The beads and stuff I sew on by hand."

This was the first time Danny had heard any mention of a mum. He wanted to ask questions but decided to let it go for now. She probably needed some time to come to terms with having told him so much about her dad the day before.

After she put the mower away in the rickety old shed, they started walking towards the Red Top. He thought it might be nice to treat her to a root beer; he had money in his pocket. But everybody and their dog would be there. Literally. Dogs came. Besides, the Red Top was more for popular kids.

Russell ran on ahead, and they walked along, knocking into each other every so often. Danny couldn't seem to keep his limbs to himself. Dot had mentioned that morning that he was shooting up like a weed, and he knew it was true. He could feel it; his bones hurt from all the growing.

He wanted Janine to talk. She was still his friend; she had told him her biggest secret (as far as he knew—he supposed she could have a bigger one). But it was possible the friendship had new limits that he didn't know about yet. He still felt as though it had been shaken to its roots.

"Do you ever go to the Red Top?" he said.

"Nah, the Red Top's for losers. Let's turn here, so we don't have to see them laughing their idiot heads off."

He began to wonder if Janine was lacking in friends. It hadn't occurred to him before.

"I'm worried that I might be famous for hatin' Miss Hardass even if I haven't been goin' around talkin' about it. As well as for my slingshot skills."

He hadn't meant to say it yet, but there it was.

"Christ. You and your famousness," said Janine. "You really find a lot of things to worry about, don't you?"

"Well, they're legitimate worries."

She reached over and tousled his hair. "You know some big words for a kid."

Danny shook off her touch.

"Everybody hates Hardass," said Janine.

"Not as much as I do."

"Some do."

Danny couldn't believe that. And he didn't like that she had said it. No one's hate was as big as his, and he had thought Janine knew that. Tears threatened. He couldn't cry, especially after having his hair tousled.

Janine saw his tears; he felt her see them with a sideways look.

"Let me tell you another Hardass story," she said.

"Okay."

He glanced around to make sure no one was watching them, that none of the losers from the Red Top were following along behind. Nothing ever felt allowable about what they did, no matter what it was. It felt right, for the most part, but not allowable.

"It was in gym class again. A kid had an accident. Most of us were leaping around playing basketball, and all of a sudden Hardass blew her whistle. We all stopped in our tracks. She loves doing that. If you don't stop in your tracks when she blows her whistle, you have to do laps. God, I'd like to shove that whistle so far up her ass it comes out one of her eyes."

"Okay, so it's not about Cookie," Danny said, more to himself than Janine.

"No. So we're all standing there waiting for whatever dumb thing she's going to say, and she tells Morven Rankin to step forward, which she does. Then she tells her to turn around in a circle. By this time we've all pretty much seen what's going on."

"I know who Morven Rankin is," Danny said. "She's the unfortunate girl."

"Yeah. Morv's strange, but she's all right. And she sure doesn't need Hardass on her case. Anyway, there's a red patch on her white shorts between her legs. She had started her period."

"Oh."

Danny felt his ears turn red. He knew about periods. There had been a big to-do when Cookie'd had her first one, involving her not being prepared. All he could remember of his mother's involvement was irritation. It was Danny who went to Wade's to pick up the equipment. He wore his baseball cap and a pair of sunglasses and waited till there was no one in the store except Mr. Wade and Ross, the pharmacist. Ross served him.

Danny said, "Stuff for a period, please."

Ross said, "Pardon?"

"Stuff for a period. For a girl."

"Oh. Sure thing." Ross raised a finger. "Hang on, and I'll get you set up."

He gathered together a few items, put them in a bag, and charged it to Mrs. Blue's account, without asking how Danny wanted to pay. When he handed the bag over the counter he smiled and said, "You're a good man, Danny Blue."

Danny had brought cash and was disappointed that Ross recognized him through his disguise, but grateful that it went as smoothly as it did. It could have been so much worse: Ross could have had a harder time figuring out what he was talking about; kids from school could have come in and noticed what he was buying and tortured him forever; the store could have been out of the sinister supplies, meaning he'd have to go further afield. Also, he had worried that Ross would refuse to sell him the stuff, like he did when kids came in for cigarettes and doobs.

At least Cookie had been at home when it happened. It was a disaster, but a private one, except for Ross, and he was obviously accustomed to periods and probably worse.

Danny still didn't know all there was to know about them, and that was fine with him. It didn't seem like the kind of thing he had to concern himself with yet, if ever.

But here was Janine, merrily talking as though it was the most natural thing in the world. Maybe it was at her house, but certainly not at his.

He pictured going home, walking into the living room, and saying, *period.* He wondered if that would be enough to open his mum's eyes wide. If it wasn't, he could say, *menstrual period.* He'd have to do it when Dot wasn't there.

"What's so funny?" said Janine.

"Nothing."

"Anyway, Hardass berates Morven and calls her a filthy, ignorant girl and tells her to go to the change room and hose herself down. That's what she said. *Hose yourself down.* Like she was talking about a car or an elephant. Poor Morv finally got it and looked down at herself. And guess what happened then."

"What?"

"She fainted."

"What was Cookie doin' during all of this?" Danny said.

His pleasure in knowing that it wasn't his sister's predicament was like a golden apple resting in the palm of his hand. On this occasion she had been safe, separate from the nightmare unfolding for another girl. He felt bad for Morven, but from a distance.

Janine turned to look at him.

"I don't know," she said. "This story isn't about Cookie. What I'm trying to get across is that way more people than just you and me would be happy if something bad happened to Hardass. Can you imagine if Morven's brother had walked by the gym and witnessed that scene the way you saw the thing with Cookie? For all we know, he did and he just didn't show himself, and right now him and Morven are planning their own revenge."

Danny tried to digest the story. He had trouble picturing it happening to Morven. It was always Cookie, and the red was huge and running down her pale unsteady legs.

"That's a very unpleasant story," he said.

"Yeah, I know, but I had a point I wanted to make."

They'd arrived at the river. They sat down in the grass and watched the miniature kids on the other side, messing around near the water.

"Danny?"

"Yeah?"

"You need more than one friend."

"Is that so?"

He felt, as he had so often lately, that if not for certain body parts holding him in, he would have slid out all over the ground.

"Are you sayin' this because of all the stupid questions I ask?" he said.

"No."

"Why then?"

"Because it only makes sense."

"How?"

"Well, for one thing, what if the one friend up and dies?"

"Yeah, I guess."

He knew she was right. What if she hadn't come along after Paul had deserted him?

"You're not dyin', are you?"

"No, I'm not dying. It's just...it's good to spread yourself around a little."

He didn't want to spread himself around at all.

"I'll get back to havin' friends after the Miss Hardass thing is over."

Friends would get in the way now. How could she not see that?

"I have to get goin'." He stood up.

"Why?"

"Because."

"Is it because of what I said?"

"No."

"Why, then?"

"I told Dot I'd help her beat rugs."

She seemed to accept that.

A familiar lump had formed inside his chest, like a good-sized sweet crabapple—not a small sour one.

"I'll walk you," said Janine.

Boys were supposed to walk girls home, not the other way around. Her offer drove home the fact that she didn't think of him as a guy, not in the Rock Sand sense of the word. But she would; she had to. He could wait out Rock Sand.

"Do you wanna come back for supper?" he said when they approached his house.

He didn't want to lose her.

"We have full-fledged meals when my aunt's here."

"Are you sure you want me to?"

"Yeah."

"Won't everybody mind?"

"No way. My mum might not even see you, and Aunt Dot is a farm wife. She's used to makin' loads of food and havin' visitors. They've even got hired hands who she cooks for."

"Okay then."

So...he had a future.

23

DANNY TOSSED TWO MATS OVER THE RAILING OF THE STOOP to add credence to his rug-beating story.

"Just airing one or two things out," he said to Dot when he saw the questioning look on her face.

It was just mid-afternoon so Danny headed out again after telling Dot that he had invited Janine for supper. He found a secluded spot and sat staring out at the river. The day was cloudy, but the trees still cast their shadows on the water. It was, as always, travelling towards downtown. Here and there it looked as if it was going nowhere, but still, it moved. Those must be the spots where the current came into play—the current that everyone went on about—the one that caused one person a year to drown. Cookie was this year's person.

The banging on the back door had sent the toast clear out of Danny's hand onto the kitchen floor. Before either he or his mother could respond the door slammed open, and a soaking wet Frank Foote gasped, "Call an ambulance. It's Cookie. She was in the river."

They stood mute for what seemed a long time when Danny remembered it later. He worried that he hadn't acted fast enough. Neither of them had known that she wasn't in her bed. His mum pointed to the telephone in the hallway, and Frank lurched forward to make the call, drenching the floor with river water. A puppy was suddenly scrambling around the kitchen making squeaking sounds. Frank's puppy. Danny was out the door in his pajamas and bare feet, at the riverbank in seconds. He couldn't find her at first, not till Frank caught up and pointed a little further downstream. Then he saw her. She was on her front at the bottom of the bank, barely out of the water. Frank must have dragged her in and turned her head to the side, eyes to the river. Danny slid down and tried to look at her face. If he could just have pushed the swollen river aside. It kept getting in his way.

Barbara Blue stood at the top of the riverbank staring down, and Frank joined Danny at the bottom. He still had streams of water on his face—tears or river or both. He moved forward to help, and they turned her over.

Cookie's wide-open eyes and blue lips shook him, but Danny began mouth-to-mouth respiration. He had learned it at the Sherbrook Pool, where he had earned his intermediate badge last winter. Her lips felt like cold rubber, like cold inner tube.

"The ambulance is coming," Frank said.

Danny kept on.

Cookie was wearing her housecoat with deep, buttoned pockets. There were buttons up the front too. Danny was glad of that. If she had been wearing one with a tie it might have opened and come off, and she might have been naked, and Frank would have seen her, and the ambulance men would see her, and he would see her. *Cookie*. He kept on with the mouth to mouth.

Frank put a hand on his shoulder.

"I can hear the ambulance, Danny. Help is almost here."

He heard his mum say, "She has a hole in her heart," as though that had something to do with anything.

The ambulance men told Danny and Frank to stand back, and they worked over Cookie for a minute or two.

"I'm sorry, boys," said one and he headed up the bank to where Barbara Blue stood waiting.

Danny fell to his knees by his sister and pressed his face into the soaked terry cloth that covered her narrow chest. She smelled of the river. He wedged a hand under each side of her and hung on. A keening sound escaped from inside him, and Frank knelt down and put a hand on his back.

The ambulance man struggled back down the embankment with a stretcher.

Danny didn't want to let her go. If he let her go she would be gone. He wanted to stay with her at the river, at least until he died.

"Danny?" His mum's voice wafted down.

"I'll go," Frank said. "You'll be okay?"

"Mmph," he said.

Sometimes it occurred to Danny to go over to Frank's house and stand next to him, the boy who tried to save her. But he couldn't do it; not now, anyway, these days when so many of his thoughts ran towards destruction. He felt himself too great a contrast to Frank Foote, who did such a first-rate job of caring for his own doomed sister.

He thought about how blue Frank had been from the icy water of the Red and wondered if they had thanked him enough. He had even had the presence of mind to shut his puppy up in their house till the ambulance had taken Cookie away. No lights, no siren.

She had begun drawing nooses and daggers in the margins of her scribblers during the last months of her life. Other things too. Danny often didn't know what they were; she wasn't a very good drawer. But they all had to do with pain and death. Droplets of blood. Whose blood? Her own, Miss Hartley's, their mother's?

One time he came upon her as she was drawing a big squarish object with saw-toothed edges on two sides.

"What's that?" he said.

"A razor blade."

"Why are you drawing razor blades?"

"It's not razor blades. It's *a* razor blade. And I'm drawing it because in art class Mr. Loepky told us to draw a picture of the World Series."

Gillette advertised during the World Series games so it made sense in an odd sort of way. Drawing a razor blade was easier than drawing a ball player or bleachers full of fans, or even a bat or a ball. But it still didn't sit well with him. When she got out her watercolours and dipped her brush in red paint, he was sure she was going to add blood to the blade. He breathed a sigh of relief when she carefully printed *How're Ya Fixed For Blades?* at the bottom of the page.

It was Gillette's slogan. But did it have to be red?

He headed back up to the drive now, home to Dot's Sunday roast and to their dinner guest.

When Janine arrived her hair was nicely combed, and Danny caught a whiff of flowery shampoo when he greeted her at the gate.

He took her inside and introduced her to Aunt Dot, who greeted her and said, "Do your folks know you won't be home for supper, dear?"

"Yes, ma'am. It's just my dad, and he says to thank you very much."

"Well, you tell him that you're most welcome. We're happy to have you. Maybe next time your dad can come too."

Danny blushed. He hadn't thought to anticipate all the things Dot might say to embarrass him while Janine was there. Up to now, he had left all talk of *next times* to Janine.

"It smells great in here," she said.

"That's the roast," said Dot. "We're about ready to sit down. Danny, take Janine in to meet your mum, and I'll get everything on the table."

Danny hadn't bargained on this. He and Janine went into the hall and he poked his head around the corner to see what sort of shape his mum was in. Her eyes were closed, and she didn't look too bad, but he didn't want these two parts of his life to intermingle. He didn't want his mum's sick aura to touch Janine. He made murmuring sounds for Dot's benefit, motioned to Janine to do the same, and then guided her back through the kitchen to the dining room.

The table was set for three.

"You can just slip into Danny's mum's place there, Janine," said Dot. "She won't be joining us."

"Well, isn't that a surprise," said Danny. He was irritated with her for telling him to introduce Janine to his mum. He hadn't done it, but still.

Janine had two helpings of everything: roast beef, carrots and sweet onions that had been cooked around it, mashed potatoes and gravy, Yorkshire pudding, and apple brown betty for dessert. Aunt Dot gloried in watching her eat.

"Thanks, Aunt Dot," Janine said, as she pushed away from the table. "That was one of the best meals I've ever had."

Dot was flushed with pleasure. "You're so welcome, my dear. You must come again."

Janine insisted on clearing up, and Danny helped. Dot went into the front room to sit with her sister. The kids left the kitchen spick and span.

"God, that was good," said Janine before she left him at the lane.

He wanted her never to leave. He thought about walking her home but it seemed not quite suitable, seeing as she had walked him home earlier.

24

DURING THE PAST FEW DAYS THERE HAD BEEN NO MORE TALK of whisking Danny and his mother out to the farm, but he knew he'd have to remain on his toes as far as Dot was concerned.

She was in the kitchen preparing to go home. This involved attaching notes to casseroles and rearranging the fridge by moving the older stuff to the front.

"I've laid in some groceries, Danny. There are some things that are going to run out before I come back—milk and such—and I may not have covered everything you like. We really should sit down, you and I, and make a master list."

"We can manage, Auntie Dot. I'm good at shopping for groceries."

She tousled his hair. He wished people would stop doing that. He'd just combed it and added a little Wildroot Cream-Oil that he'd picked up at Wade's last time he was there.

"I know you are, dear." Dot wiped her hand on her apron.

"There's a carrier on my bike. It holds a lot."

They had eaten lunch, and Danny was itching to get out of the house.

"Your mum's set up on the couch again." Dot said it as if it was normal. "Edwin's going to be here in a few minutes to pick me up. Did you brush your teeth, honey?"

He sighed.

"I'm sorry, dear. I know you don't need that type of reminder." She sighed too and sat down at the kitchen table.

"Sit with me for a minute, Danny."

"I have to go," he said. "Things to do."

"Just for a minute."

He pulled out a chair and perched on the edge of it.

Dot made a steeple of her fingers.

"This girl, Janine, isn't she a little...I don't know...mature for you?"

Danny wondered for a second if she was referring to the two nicely contained mounds underneath Janine's T-shirt.

"No," he said.

He thought about things Janine had said that hinted at experiences beyond his and he saw how Dot might think she was right about this. But it didn't matter. He was just a couple of years and one or two experiences behind Janine. He would catch up to her, no sweat.

"Don't get me wrong, honey. She seems like a nice girl. It's just that she's...well...she must be at least Cookie's age, isn't she?"

"Yeah. She's pretty much exactly Cookie's age."

His aunt didn't say anything for a minute or two. Danny hoped she was thinking that he thought of Janine as an older sister, a sort of substitute for Cookie.

"I haven't seen Paul in a while," Dot said. "Or those other fellas, Stu and Stumpy, is it?"

"Stubby."

He wished he could talk things over with Cookie now. She'd know it was okay for him to be friends with Janine and might even have the words for him to say so Dot would think so too. She'd often been good at knowing what other people should do or say—just not herself.

Too bad he hadn't been friends with Janine before Cookie died. Too bad Cookie had never brought her home. They could have hung around, the three of them. He and Janine could have saved her together.

"Janine was Cookie's best friend," Danny said.

It wasn't untrue.

"Oh," said Dot. "I didn't know that. I guess it makes sense, then, that you'd want to spend time together."

"Yeah."

"To help each other with losing Cookie."

"Yeah."

He was soon out the door, marvelling at his own genius.

As he practised at the river he wondered how Janine was feeling in the aftermath of eating supper with him and Dot. Fine, he supposed.

Then his thoughts turned again to Cookie, to the aftermath of her death.

Because of the uncertainty surrounding it, the City Medical Officer of Health was called in. They looked into it: talked to Frank, to Danny, to Barbara Blue. They talked to the ambulance attendants, and studied the riverbank. Then they wrote up a report and ruled what happened to Cookie *death by misadventure.*

Frank explained to them that she was knocking against the river's edge when he saw her. He was out early with his new dog. It was the pup that spotted her first. She was caught between a rock and a large branch. He had to go right into the water to free her from the branch. Yes, he admitted—he was a strong swimmer, a strong treader of water. He was able to lift her up onto the shore. She was very light.

The autopsy report said that she had water in her lungs. That meant she drowned. If she hadn't had water in her lungs it would have meant that she died first and then fell in.

So Danny imagined her drowning—swallowing water, breathing water, till there was no place inside her that allowed for any more.

The report also said that there were marks on her body where she'd been cut, inches below her naval and on her breasts and just inside her hipbones. Cuts made with a knife, some of which had healed and left scars, some with scabs, some brand new. No one told Danny that part. He overheard Dot and Edwin discussing it using their most serious voices.

Uncle Edwin was the only person he could ask about the particulars.

"Why didn't the weight of Cookie sink her?" he said. "I know she didn't weigh much, but still."

"It would have, Daniel, along with the pull of the current. Long enough that she took in enough water to drown. But then the current would have pushed her up again, wedging her into her resting place between the tree limb and the rock. Currents are funny that way."

"Funny," said Danny.

"And then, as you know, her housecoat was caught on the limb."

"Frank uncaught it."

"Yes. It was lucky that she got caught that way, so that Frank and his pup found her."

"Yeah," said Danny. "Lucky."

His uncle explained about eddies, but Danny wasn't listening anymore. He pictured Cookie holding her breath till she couldn't and then breathing water instead of air. Then he pictured her not holding her breath at all, just welcoming the filthy river till it took her over. He hoped it didn't take too long.

Someone found the plate that had held the pineapple upside-down cake that Danny, Cookie, and their mother had eaten for dessert at Cookie's last supper. It had been licked clean.

She'd had two cans of beans and two cans of Klik in the deep pockets of her housecoat. No one talked about that. But that's how Danny knew she was dead on purpose. She had used them to weigh herself down.

He didn't know if other people thought she had meant to do it. Edwin made a big to-do about the slick flatness of the grass where they figured she had gone in, as though she had slipped unintentionally at the top of the low cliff, gone over the side, and kept on sliding.

Danny and Russell passed that way now, and he stopped to look.

There hadn't been a whisper of suicide, but he knew that's what it was. Also, deep in his heart, he knew that Miss Hartley wasn't the sole cause of Cookie's agonizing misery. Still, someone had to pay, and she was by far the best of all possible targets, she with her poisonous words and brutal acts of cruelty.

25

It took Danny a couple of days to realize that something potentially very useful was happening. It was shortly after Dot had gone home.

Construction began in the empty lot on the north side of the high school. He noticed it one evening on his way home from baseball at the flood bowl. He had signed up after Janine's speech about needing more than one friend.

The friend part was going nowhere, but he didn't expect or even want it to. He didn't hate baseball and he wasn't terrible at it. He never got picked last because there were three or four other guys who were worse than he was.

His position was usually centre field; sometimes he played shortstop between first and second. The good players played at the official shortstop position between second and third. When he occasionally caught a ball, his fellow teammates shouted things like, "Atta way to be, Danno," and he liked that.

It was getting tiresome, though. He had to force himself to go and he didn't always make it.

Paul and Stubby played, but so far neither of them had been on his team. Paul wasn't mean to Danny, but neither did he seek him out, and Danny didn't try. Trying didn't feel right. Maybe later, when it was all over.

In the good old days, Danny and Paul would have spent a large portion of their time at the construction site beside the school. This one was pretty boring compared to some. A couple of summers ago they had revelled in the chaos of two classrooms being built on the west side of Nordale. For the whole season it kept them occupied in the evenings, when the workmen had gone home. They fashioned forts and caves and a high-wire area, where they placed a two-by-four over a couple of sawhorses and performed amazing feats of balance and skill. Sometimes they pretended they were workmen.

"Hand me that level, will ya, Bert," Paul would say. "This window is lookin' a little lopsided. And I wanna shim up those joists."

"Sure thing, Marv. Just wait till I finish here with the winch. It's actin' up again."

The day after Danny had noticed this new site he went back while the men were at work and watched them dig, level, and prepare to lay cement. When one of them sat down on a crate for a smoke and a drink from his thermos, Danny sauntered over.

"What are you building?" he said.

"Just a parking lot for the teachers, buddy boy. Nothing very exciting."

Danny couldn't think of anything more to say, so he stepped away and left the man to his cigarette and coffee. There were some kids on the other side of the school grounds playing baseball. He wanted to join them and wondered why it had suddenly become so hard. Joining in used to come naturally, like drinking cool water to quench his thirst. He sat down in a sunny spot against the school, where he couldn't see either the parking lot or the game, and watched instead the pictures inside his head, mostly of Janine.

Two mornings later, he presented his mum with a bowl of Rice Krispies and made two pieces of toast for himself. He buttered them and looked for jam. What he found was an empty jar of E.D. Smith apricot. Why would someone put an empty jar of jam back in the cupboard, he wondered, and then realized it had probably been him.

He spread brown sugar on his toast and as he ate it he made a grocery list without asking his mum if she wanted anything. He took some bills from the drawer and folded them into his pocket.

On the ride home from the A&P Danny congratulated himself. It was the best job of shopping he'd done so far. There was cherry jam, bread, eggs, peanuts in the shell, milk—everything on his list plus a few items that he hadn't thought to buy before: Sugar Pops, two kinds of cheese that weren't Velveeta, and crackers that weren't soda crackers. They were called Sociables and they looked good on the box. He concentrated on the road to avoid trouble with the eggs. He whistled as he cycled.

When he got home the couch was silent.

It came to him as he put the groceries away. The new parking lot was directly adjacent to the north side of the school grounds. If he and Janine were to practise in that area, it would make all the sense in the world for one of them to accidentally hit Miss Hartley on her temple and watch her die instead of get into her car.

In his head when he described it to Janine he said, *the north side of the school*, hoping she would be impressed with his grasp of directions and forget that he had not known which way was east. He could also say, *on the way home from baseball*, so she would know that he was playing with others. And then he would quit but not tell her. It seemed dumber all the time to be putting himself through it just because a girl thought he should have more than one friend.

He had the sense of time running out. Winter was a long way off, but when he pictured it, he saw an impossible place, with snow-covered streets and thick mitts and heavy hooded parkas.

26

DANNY HAD PLANNED ON TWO NEW PIECES OF TOAST, WITH jam this time, but he couldn't wait.

As he rode over to Janine's, he thought about Cookie. In 1966 he would be older than she ever was, ever would be. He supposed that when he was ninety he would still think of her as his big sister because he had never experienced her as anything else.

Why had she been so messed up? There was a time when she ate like a regular kid and hated throwing up as much as he did.

He remembered her love of Cherry Blossoms. She had thought they were almost too good to be true, the same way he thought about yo-yos and kaleidoscopes. Danny thought they were a gyp. He thought they shouldn't cost as much as other chocolate bars; they seemed so small. She explained to him that they were as big as the others. She pointed out the weight on the box compared to the weight on a Jersey Milk. He still didn't buy it.

She was particular about chocolate bars. For instance, she liked Jersey Milks better than Dairy Milks. Danny hadn't been able to tell the difference. She made him sit down for a taste test, and he couldn't say why exactly, but he found he agreed. Jersey Milk was better.

"Told ya," she'd said.

That was a long time ago.

He almost missed Janine. She was on her bike.

"I have to go grocery shopping." She skidded to a stop. "Do you want to come with me?"

"Sure."

He didn't tell her that he had just been.

"Do you have money in case you want to get something?" she said.

"Yup. Go home, Russell. We're gonna be ridin' in traffic."

Russell made an about-face and trotted off back up the lane.

"Will she really go home?" said Janine.

"Yup. She'll probably head out again soon after she gets there, but for sure she'll go home first."

They pedalled over to Dominion against the warm dusty wind. Janine had a big carrier too.

"We've got a lot in common," said Danny.

"Like what?"

"We both have big carriers on our bikes. I know loads of kids with no carriers at all."

They parked and got a cart.

Janine whisked through the aisles, throwing things into it.

"Don't you have a list?" Danny said.

"No.

"Don't you forget stuff without a list?"

"No."

She stopped so abruptly that Danny banged into the back of her.

"Don't move," she said. "Don't look anywhere. Back up. Hardass is over there in the frozen foods. She's with another woman."

"Let me look." Danny moved to get past her.

"Stop. Use your head."

"What?"

"We don't want her to see us together, you idiot."

"Why?"

Janine ignored his question and approached the end of the aisle again.

"They're not actually sharing a cart, but they're definitely together," she said when she came back. "It must be her sister. Unbelievable."

"What's unbelievable?"

She ignored him again.

"Let me have a look," Danny said.

"You can in a minute."

"Why do you think it's her sister? Couldn't it just be a friend?"

"Shh! They look a lot alike. Christ, they look exactly alike." Janine took another peek. "The shape of them, their size. Plus, I doubt if Hardass has any friends."

"Let me see."

"Okay, quick. They're comparing items. One second at most."

Danny peered around the cans of pineapple stacked at the end of the aisle. "They look alike except for their hair."

"They sure do," said Janine, "right down to their flat asses."

"I can't see those," said Danny, straining again to look.

"Okay, pull back."

"They don't dress much alike," Danny said.

"So?"

"Maybe they're sisters, but not twins."

"Who said they were twins?"

"I don't know. Me?"

"Who cares? We can use this."

"How?"

"I don't know."

Janine took another look. "They gotta be twins. This is unreal."

"I wonder why they don't dress alike if they're twins."

Janine sighed. "Jesus, Danny. Twins don't dress alike after the age of six, when they go to school and get teased to death and realize their mums have been making fools of them all through the first years of their lives. You absolutely flabbergast me with the things you don't know."

He poked his head out again and stared in plain sight at the two women chuckling over the frozen foods. He didn't care if they saw him. It was the only thing he could think of doing to pay Janine back for her meanness.

"They're laughin'," he said.

"Bitches. That makes me sick. They shouldn't be allowed to laugh."

She pulled his T-shirt till it stretched out about a foot and a half.

"You're wreckin' my shirt." He stepped back out of sight. "I wonder if they live together."

"Probably not," said Janine. "They have separate shopping carts. Unless they live together, but keep their food separate. I can see them doing that—yelling at each other if, say, Hardass's tomatoes touch the sister's lettuce. Coming to blows. Maybe the sister'll end up killing Hardass, and we can sit back and relax."

"That'd be great," said Danny. "But then..." *Then, we wouldn't get to do it.* He stopped himself before he said it. "Maybe they live together but have two fridges," he said instead.

Janine chuckled.

She reminded him of Jake when she laughed. He remembered the splendour of her honest laughter, as father and daughter sat next to one another and shared a joke in their backyard.

"I think it's most likely that they live in separate houses," she said. "The sister might have a husband. Most women do."

"Miss Hardass doesn't," Danny said.

"Probably because every man she's ever met in her entire life hates her," said Janine. "You gotta get out of here. We don't want them to see us together. Meet me back at my house. It'll be okay if they see me on my own."

"I'm not clear on why they can't see us together if it's gonna be an accident," said Danny.

"Oh, yeah. Well…it just seems right is all."

27

"Quick. Get on your bike," Janine said as she steered hers into the backyard.

"Why?"

Danny was sitting on the grass, patting Pearl, who was on her side with her eyes closed.

Janine dumped her groceries on the stoop.

"Hurry up. They're still there. We have to follow them and find out where they live."

Danny stood up. "I should really go home and make lunch for my mum."

"Are you insane?" said Janine. "Come on." She was back on her bike and heading out of the yard.

"Why do we need to know where they live?" Danny had caught up, and they were careening side by side through the streets.

She didn't answer; he knew she heard him.

"I really should go home and make my mum some lunch," he said again.

"What will happen if you don't?"

It wasn't the first time Danny wondered that himself. She often didn't eat much of what he presented to her anyway. What would happen if he didn't take a tray to her three times a day? Would she get up and make something for herself? Would she starve? Would she die?

"She'd get skinnier and skinnier, and I'd probably get taken away from her. Not by the Children's Aid Society, but by Aunt Dot."

"I like Aunt Dot," said Janine.

"Me too. But I don't wanna go and live with her."

"I get it. This won't take long."

She sped ahead of him, and he pushed to catch up.

They wheeled into the parking lot as Miss Hartley and her sister were loading their groceries into the trunk of the dark blue Beetle.

"Hide," said Janine.

There wasn't a lot to hide behind, so Danny crossed Marion Street to Anderson's Animal Hospital and went inside. The cacophony was such that no one noticed him standing sentry at the window. He waited till the women were on their way down Marion before he emerged and shouted across at Janine. They headed after the Volkswagen.

It wasn't much of a trip.

"Hardass drives like an old lady," Janine said over her shoulder. "Slow down a little."

"You're tremendously bossy today," said Danny.

They followed the two women to a big old house on rue Valade in the old section of St. Boniface where people spoke French. Miss Hartley dropped her sister off and gunned the car as she drove away.

"I guess she only drives slow when her sister's in the car," said Danny.

He watched as Janine wrestled her bike behind a tree.

"We don't need to hide anymore," he said. "I'm not sure why we had to hide in the first place."

"If we do something to the sister, we don't want her to have seen us beforehand."

"Why would we do something to the sister?"

Janine didn't answer him so he asked again.

"I don't know, do I?" she said.

It was a corner house. The sister had two bulging paper bags full of groceries. She fought with the latch on the gate and then struggled up a staircase at the back of the house. She entered a doorway on the second floor.

"You'd think Miss Hardass could've helped her with her bags," said Danny.

"She's not that kind of person."

A plump brown wiener dog walked up to them and began to bark.

"*Tais-toi, maudisse*!" said Janine. "*Vas-t'en*! Go away!"

The dog stayed where it was and kept barking.

"Go and check the mailbox."

"Why?" said Danny.

"Just do it. And then we should get out of here. This dog isn't going to stop barking."

"What am I lookin' for?"

"Anything."

Danny found three mailboxes lined up next to the front door. They had nameplates attached. The first one said Roger Dubois, the second one, Mrs. Randolph Flood, and the third one, Miss Gretchen Hartley. *Miss Hardass?* Danny didn't know her first name. Could there be a third sister? The discovery that Miss Hartley lived in the house (if indeed it was her) felt like an over-the-top gift, if for no other reason than it gave him something fabulous to report to Janine.

Next to the door there were three doorbells, also with names attached to them. Miss Hartley was on the top floor. by the looks of it, Mrs. Randolph Flood in the middle, and Roger Dubois on the main floor.

He rang the bottom bell just because, and ran back to where Janine stood behind the tree.

"I've got some news," he said. "Let's go to the park."

"What?" said Janine. "What news?"

"Wait'll we get there."

He hopped on his bike. "Let's stop at the Spanish Court on the way and get something to eat, my treat, and then I'll tell you."

When they got to the monument in Coronation Park they concentrated on their Fudgsicles for a few minutes. Janine licked hers from the bottom up to keep the ice cream from running down her wrist. Danny's caught the sleeve of his long-sleeved shirt.

"Okay, what?" said Janine.

"What's Miss Hardass's first name? Do you know?"

"Gretchen."

"'Kay. She lives on the top floor, and her sister lives on the second. Her name is Mrs. Randolph Flood."

Janine was as excited as he was.

"Jeez, if she lives there too, it was lucky she didn't come back while we were still there."

"Yeah. She couldn't have gone far. She'll be needin' to get her frozen stuff in the fridge."

"Mrs., eh?"

"What?"

"Mrs. Randolph Flood, you said."

"Yeah. Why are we excited about this? What does knowin' where they live have to do with anything?"

"I don't know yet. Maybe nothing. Maybe something."

"Our plan is still gonna take place in the school parking lot, isn't it? You haven't changed your mind about that, have you?"

"Parking lot?"

Danny realized in all the excitement that he had forgotten what he had set out to tell her in the first place.

"That's good," said Janine when he told her of his discovery. "That's very good. But we have to wait till fall for that, when school's back in. We might want to do something minor before then, to shake them up a little. Not a lot, just a little. And it could involve knowing where they live."

"I'm not sure why the sister needs shakin' up," said Danny. "Maybe we should do the big thing before fall now we know where they live. What if Miss Hardass changes schools or something?"

"We'll monitor them," said Janine. "We'll dog their every move."

"What if they move to France?"

"Then we'll quit dogging their moves. Don't borrow trouble, Danny."

"What the hell does that mean?"

"It means don't worry about things that may never happen. In this case, things that more than 99.9 per cent for sure won't happen. I wonder if the sister has a husband."

"Well, she is a Mrs."

"I'm not sure if I want her to have a husband or not," said Janine. "It confuses the picture."

"What picture?"

"I don't know yet. You've got chocolate all around your mouth and all over your sleeve. Why are you wearing a long-sleeved shirt when it's a thousand above?"

Danny rubbed his arm across his face. He couldn't tell her that he wore long sleeves to cover up his weakling arms. He had never even considered his arms till he saw Rock Sand's muscles bulging out of his T-shirt. And Janine had admired them; she had touched a bicep.

"I'm thinkin' the husband is gone or dead," he said.

"Why?"

"If you have a husband, you're unlikely to live on the second floor of an old house. You're more likely to live in an entire house."

Janine smiled at him. It was the kind of smile she used when she tousled his hair and it made him feel as if he knew nothing. He stayed out of reach.

"It seems stupid that they live in the French part of town," he said.

"Why?"

"'Cause they're not French."

"So what? I'm French and I live in an English part of town."

"You're French?"

"Yeah. What did you think?"

"Nothing, I guess." Danny said, although he had been wondering where she'd learned her French swear words.

"Did you not think my name sounded kind of French?"

Danny realized that he didn't know her last name.

"Yeah. I guess." It was way too late to ask her now.

"Why do you think people make fun of me for the way I talk?"

"I didn't know they did. I like the way you talk."

He loved the way she talked, but he didn't want to say the word love in case she thought he loved her, which he did.

"My dad's name is really Jacques," Janine went on. "But he didn't like the way English people pronounced it, like Jock, so he changed it to Jake."

"Do you speak French?" Danny said.

"We spoke nothing but French for the first few years of my life. My dad and I still speak it sometimes around the house."

It hadn't occurred to Danny before that the way she talked was because she had a hint of a French accent.

"I wish I could speak French," he said.

"You take it in school, don't you?"

"School doesn't count."

"Yeah, they don't do a very good job of it. They teach grammar and stuff, but not how to speak. I got a hundred in French last term."

"Really?"

"Yup. It was the first hundred I ever got. I couldn't believe it. Let's get going."

"Do I still have chocolate on my face?"

"*Oui.*"

"I know what that means." Danny dragged his sleeve across his face again.

They rode down the back lane of Claremont towards Janine's house. Frank Foote was in his yard playing catch with another boy. His sister was sitting in her wheelchair on the patio watching them, or facing them, anyway. Frank waved at Danny and Janine, and they waved back.

"Frank doesn't make fun of me," said Janine.

"No," said Danny. "He wouldn't." He didn't know if Janine knew that Frank had been the one to find Cookie. He suspected she did. Probably everyone in Norwood knew everything about what had happened that day.

"You know what's really stupid?" she said. "Speaking of things that are stupid?"

"What?"

"The way Mrs. Flood calls herself Mrs. Randolph Flood as though her own first name is Randolph."

"Maybe it is." Danny smiled so she wouldn't think he was a moron who didn't know that women weren't named Randolph and who couldn't eat without getting food on his face like a toddler.

"We could maybe use that to torture her in some way," said Janine.

"How?"

"I don't know yet."

Danny was concerned about the way Janine's ideas of revenge had taken a turn and begun to focus on Mrs. Flood. As far as he knew there was no reason to torture Mrs. Randolph Flood.

"Come inside while I put this stuff away."

They were back at Janine's house where the groceries sat on the stoop where she had left them.

Danny followed her in and sat down at the kitchen table. A lot of the things she was putting away were the same types of things he bought when he went shopping.

"Oh, jeez, the ice cream has melted," said Janine.

"What did you expect?"

"Let's eat it right now. We can just pretend it's soft ice cream, but better than usual because it Neapolitan."

She opened up the carton, got a couple of spoons, and they set to.

"Cookie would have loved this," said Danny. "In the olden days, I mean. First Fudgsicles and now soft ice cream."

"Were you close to your sister?"

"Yeah, pretty close, I guess."

"What was up with her, Danny? Why did she puke all the time?"

"You know about that?"

"Yeah, I heard her in the washroom at school. More than once. I know other kids heard her sometimes too. I saw her at the river once but I'm pretty sure she didn't see me."

"So, does everybody know then?"

"Well, I never told anyone, but I can't say about the others. It probably got around. I heard a couple of them making gagging sounds as she walked by them one day. I told them to lay off, but it didn't help. No way were they going to listen to me."

"I don't really understand it," Danny said. "The way she was. I know she wanted to look like Audrey Hepburn. She was her idol. Ever since she saw *Breakfast at Tiffany's*."

"Jeez, I don't blame her. Audrey Hepburn is beautiful."

"I guess so. Cookie used to ask me if I thought she was fat. I'd say no, but I didn't know what more to say. I wish I'd known what more to say."

"It wasn't your fault, Danny."

"I'd hear her cryin' and I'd knock on her door, but she wouldn't let me in. Everything was a secret with her. I didn't get it, still don't."

"Some things are beyond getting," said Janine. She swirled the three flavours of ice cream together.

"My mum used to criticize her…tell her she took after the broad-beamed side of the family."

"That wasn't very nice of your mum."

Danny put down his spoon.

"Aunt Dot is worried that you're too mature for me to be hangin' around with," he said.

"Screw Aunt Dot."

"I thought you liked her."

"I do, but screw her anyway."

"She eased up a bit when I told her you were Cookie's friend."

"Good. That's good that you told her I was her friend. I hope Cookie knew that I was, or would have been, or something."

"I hope so too," said Danny. "I guess it looks weird from the outside lookin' in—you and me hangin' around together. People must think so."

"Who?"

"I don't know. People. Others."

"So what?"

"So nothing, I guess. I'm mostly just thinkin' about how it fits in with the whole Miss Hardass thing."

"What about Uncle Edwin?" Janine said. "What does he think?"

"I don't know. Probably nothing, unless Dot starts harpin' on at him about it."

He stood up. "I gotta go home and make my mum a very late lunch."

"Come back when you're done," said Janine. "We need to work on our tactics."

28

On the ride home Danny wondered what their tactics were going to be. He didn't want them to lose sight of the original plan and he thought that Janine went off on tangents too easily. She probably couldn't stay focussed because her mind kept drifting off to kissing Rock Sand.

It was possible that they stuck their tongues in each other's mouths. He wished she would save her tongue for him. Next time he saw her he would try to catch a glimpse of it, see how it moved inside her mouth.

When he got home he sprawled on the Muskoka chair and stared at the pool. Russell began hurling herself at the screen door, so Danny got up and let her out. Lena was inside. He had forgotten she was coming.

He wished he could talk to Cookie about the best way to avenge her death. Was Miss Hartley the right target? How about those girls who made gagging sounds as Cookie walked by? They deserved something. Where would she stand on the subject? Maybe nowhere. She'd probably be thinking about cake.

One day last winter Danny had come home from school a little earlier than usual. His mum was on one of her rare outings, to see a doctor about her muscle spasms.

When he walked into the house on that frozen February day a warm chocolaty aroma welcomed him. Cookie sat at the kitchen table with a partially baked cake in front of her. She looked to have been eating the crusty parts from the top and around the edges. He wanted to run, but he didn't.

"I couldn't wait for it to be done," she said.

Her face was a blotchy red with embarrassment, and tears ran down her gaunt cheeks. She put down her spoon. There was chocolate on her face and her clothes and her hands and her forearms. There was chocolate in her hair.

She ran out of the room, and Danny soon heard water thundering into the bathtub.

He threw away the rest of the cake. There was no point to it. This was the most bizarre thing he had ever walked in on. All he could think to do was clean up the mess.

When his mother walked in the door he was putting his winter moccasins back on, not sure where he was going. She was a little worse for the wear from her outing, so he didn't have any trouble bolting out the door with little in the way of an explanation.

It must have been the worst thing in the world being Cookie, Danny thought now. Of course there were worse things. He had seen pictures from the war, but that was war. This was regular life. Surely it hadn't had to be that way.

Russell was lying beside his chair, on her side with her eyes open. Danny stared at her till he was sure of the up and down of her breathing.

The things Cookie had done didn't make her feel good, or even okay. They did the opposite of those things. He knew that much because of her crying.

It was as though she had been starving, like those pictures of the people in concentration camps. So she filled herself up. But then she emptied herself out so she was starving again. Her methods for whatever it was she was trying to accomplish (satisfying her hunger? looking like Audrey Hepburn?) were at odds with each other. Surely she saw that. But it wasn't a matter of seeing, he supposed. He had started a letter to Audrey Hepburn once to enlist her help. But he hadn't finished it and wouldn't have known where to send it if he had.

He didn't want to think about it anymore. Sometimes it seemed as if there was way more stuff he didn't want to think about than stuff he did.

His thoughts turned to Janine and Miss Hartley and Mrs. Flood and Rock Sand and back to Janine, and a tiny ray of optimism poked through when he realized he could see her again as soon as he wanted to.

He didn't want to have to work around Lena, so he hopped on his bike and headed back over to Janine's.

"What did you make for lunch?" she said.

"Nothing," said Danny, and they both laughed.

29

"I've smelled booze on Hardass's breath," said Janine.

They were at the river.

"Really?"

Danny caught glimpses of her wet tongue as she talked. He wanted to ask her to give it to him.

"Yup. She and her sister probably drink their heads off."

They chewed grass ends in silence for a while.

"They probably get drunk and try to talk French to each other," said Danny. "And then go out and make fools of themselves tryin' to talk French to people in the neighbourhood."

Russell bounded across the field to where they sat, the back half of her body twisting from side to side the way it did.

"The paper boy must have finished his rounds." Danny welcomed his dog.

"We're going to have to get around to spying on them," said Janine.

"We don't wanna get too diverted," said Danny. "Our slingshot practice should still be the most important thing."

"The spying can be mixed in with our practice," said Janine. "It'll make both things more fun."

So they spied. And they practised.

Mrs. Flood did not go out to work each day.

"Maybe she's a teacher, like Hardass," said Janine.

They concluded that Roger Dubois, the tenant of the third apartment, was away on a holiday, as they never saw him. They never saw any man at the house on rue Valade, so they also concluded that Mrs. Flood no longer had a husband.

"She's a divorcée," said Danny.

"Or a widow," said Janine.

"Nah, a divorcée."

"She could be a spinster," said Janine, "like Hardass. And she just calls herself Mrs. Flood so people will think that once upon a time a man liked her."

"Nope. She's a divorcée." Danny liked the word. It conjured up pictures of spike heels and whiskey laughs and blouses with sweat marks underneath the arms.

During the last week of August they discovered that she worked at Queen Elizabeth School. Miss Hartley dropped her off before driving over to Nelson Mac. The teachers were getting ready for the school year.

"Why are we spendin' so much time on the divorcée Flood?" Danny said.

They were in Coronation Park, on their way home from the library, where Janine had dropped off seven books and picked up four more.

"I don't know. It's something to do. It's kind of interesting, isn't it?"

"Yeah, I guess."

"Rock went to Q.E. I wonder if he had her for anything," said Janine.

"Rock went to Q.E. I wonder if he had her for anything." Danny said it in a high mimicky voice.

"Shut up, Danny."

"Sorry."

"You could be friends with him if you weren't such a jerk."

"I'm not a jerk. And anyway, if I start havin' a seventeen-year-old guy friend, Aunt Dot will have me committed to an insane asylum."

"He just turned eighteen."

"Way worse."

"It's okay to have a best friend, Danny, but you need others too, so you don't count entirely on the one person."

"Yeah, you've already pretty much said that."

"Well, it's true."

"Who's your best friend?"

"I don't really have one, but you're the person who I tell the most stuff to. Like about my dad and that."

"I'm kinda new, aren't I, as friends go?"

"Yeah, but I think we're sort of kindred spirits, like Anne of Green Gables and Diana."

Danny hadn't read *Anne of Green Gables* but Cookie had. It was still on the bookshelf in her room.

"Why do you think that?"

"I just do, that's all."

"What's it to do with?"

"Well...I think I understand your wish to avenge Cookie's death. To hurt someone."

Hurt.

"And there's a certain amount of comfort in that."

"Comfort?"

"Yeah. I feel like this plan of ours kind of intertwines us."

Danny wanted badly to be intertwined with her but he wasn't sure about the comfort part. He wanted to be with her all the time, but he rarely felt comfortable. Maybe he didn't know what comfort was.

"What about Rock Sand?" he said. "Is he a kindred spirit?"

"Yeah, but it's different with him."

"How?"

"Well...I'm not sure how to explain it to you, but you'll get it in a year or two."

Blood rushed to Danny's head. "Don't say that."

"Say what?"

"What you just said."

She hadn't said *when you're a little older* like people usually did when they thought he was too dense to get something, but what she said meant the exact same thing.

He kicked the base of a well-established tree so hard that he hurt his foot.

"Careful there," she said, as though he were four years old.

"I have to go now." He limped across St. Mary's Road and down Claremont towards the river.

Janine didn't come after him; Danny looked back a couple of times.

He wondered if Rock Sand felt that Janine was a kindred spirit. He probably had no clue what it meant.

When he got to the river he took his slingshot out of his back pocket and shot a few stones, aiming at nothing. Just the act of settling the stone, pulling the sling, and watching it soar over the water soothed him.

Russell ran towards him from the direction of home and circled around.

Being friends with a girl was way too hard, especially an older one who thought she was queen of the world. He should be good at it, having hung around with Cookie all those years; she was a girl, after all. But Janine was nothing like Cookie. Maybe she was right. Maybe he didn't yet possess the wherewithal to process all the words and starry-eyed gazes of a fifteen-year-old girl. She was still fifteen—would be until December 9th. He had asked.

She had said they were intertwined. It was the best thing she'd said to him so far, but then it was annihilated with her talk of Rock Sand. And that was his own fault; he shouldn't have mentioned him.

"Oooh," he said. His body ached. "I wanna touch her, Russ. I wanna intertwine with her."

He walked slowly along, and Russell followed with considerably more enthusiasm.

A cool wind blew—an unlikely wind for August. Again, time felt as if it were running out, but it couldn't be. It was all around him—all the time in the world. He wanted to go back to Janine, but it was too late. She would have had enough of him for today.

He arrived home with a sore big toe. He was ashamed of himself. She had told him her innermost secrets, and he hadn't come close to telling her that that was his new most precious treasure.

For supper he put one of Dot's casseroles in the oven. When he dished it up, he saw that it was her ham and chicken concoction. As he ate at the kitchen table he was almost certain he heard his mother say, *Mmm.* When he retrieved her tray he found that she had eaten the entire portion on her plate. He washed the dishes, put the lid on the remains of the casserole, and put it in the fridge, wondering for a split second if it would still be there in the morning. Of course it would. Cookie was no longer there to eliminate any chance of leftovers.

He noticed some spillage and wiped it up. Lena didn't clean anything that wasn't out in the open for all to see. If Dot was going to keep on with spot checks, he was going to have to improve his efforts. He didn't want to end up living on a farm near Baldur because a small fridge spillage put her over the top.

30

One of the things Danny hated the most was when he dreamed of Cookie and made plans with her to do something, like play crokinole or take a bus farther than they ever had before, and then awoke and remembered she was dead, and the hollow pain filled him up all over again. He loved the dreams, but the waking part hurt so bad.

If only her death could remain a constant in his consciousness so the remembering didn't keep springing itself on him. How many times did she have to die?

He stood at the entrance to the front room. His mother surprised him by being upright, with an open magazine on her lap. She didn't look to be reading it, but even so.

"I can't stand thinking that Cookie wanted to die."

He startled her with his words.

She turned her head so that she was almost looking at him, but she didn't reply.

"We should have tried harder," he said.

"It wasn't easy." She turned a page without looking at it.

"So? What's easy got to do with anything?"

She reached for one of her pill bottles and began to slide into a horizontal position. The magazine fell to the floor.

Danny didn't go away, though he knew it was what she wanted.

"She had big troubles," he said. "We should have tried to help."

"We didn't know how big her troubles were."

"We're her brother and mum. We should have known."

Danny thought about the revelation after Cookie's death of the damage she had done to her body with something sharp—the cuts and scabs and scars.

"A person shouldn't be left all alone to manage her problems when she's only fifteen and on the road to death."

"What made you so smart all of a sudden?"

"I'm not so smart. I'm just saying."

"Are you going somewhere with this, Danny?"

"We should have known. That's where I'm going. And that's what I can't stand. How we just let her die. I can't stand that we did that."

Danny wanted to hurt his mother. He wanted to take his pocketknife and carve Cordelia into her face to remind her of how she had failed her daughter.

"Do you imagine that I don't spend all my time thinking about the things I should have done for that girl?"

Danny didn't know what to say to that. He left her and went outside to sit by the pool.

He realized that that was the first time he and his mum had talked about Cookie's death. If you could call it a talk. And he realized, also for the first time, that she too believed that her daughter had intentionally ended her life, that she knew that *death by misadventure* was all wrong.

Danny was tired of spying and tired of practising. There was nothing he wanted more than to knock on Paul's door and meet up with Stubby and Stu and go looking for adventure. Seeking adventure—that's what they had called it. They probably still did. They were probably seeking adventure right this minute. He wondered if, now that some time had gone by, Paul would have him back. Never mind his plan or his concentration.

He walked over to 117 Cedar Place and knocked on the door. Mrs. Carter answered. She was wearing Bermuda shorts that showed off her lovely legs.

"Oh, hello, Danny. I haven't seen you in a while."

Was there a coolness to her tone? He couldn't bear it if there was.

"Hi, Mrs. Carter. Is Paul in?"

"No, dear. He's out somewhere with Stubby and Stu. I don't know what they had in mind. Seeking adventure, I suppose."

She smiled at having stolen their phrase.

"Okay. Thanks, Mrs. Carter."

"I'll tell him you called around."

"'Kay."

"Don't be a stranger," she called after him.

She had called him *dear* and said *don't be a stranger*, so that must mean she didn't hate him or hope that he'd never hang around with Paul again. He hadn't heard that stranger phrase before, but figured it must mean don't stay away too long.

But who cared if Mrs. Carter didn't hate him? What was he going to do, seek adventure with her?

Maybe Stubby and Stu didn't hate him as much as Paul did. He thought about looking for his three former friends. But Paul was the boss.

He didn't go to baseball anymore. It served no purpose. Maybe once school started again he could fall in with new guys and stop fretting about the old ones. There'd be kids from all over starting high school at Nelson Mac.

Danny slouched home, his heart achy inside his chest.

Janine was right: you needed more than one friend.

31

DANNY WAITED TILL SCHOOL WAS BACK IN BEFORE HE VISITED Janine again. He was in grade nine now, at Nelson Mac, and he had seen her at a distance, always alone. He hadn't approached her in case she didn't want him to.

The last time he'd left her he'd been in a huff—not a friendship-destroying one—but a huff nonetheless.

He biked over after four with Russell along for support. She was sitting on the stoop with Pearl. He approached slowly, not wanting to startle her.

He wanted to say *I love you*, but he just said, "Hi."

"Hi, Danny."

"You look sad," he said, and she did too, as if something bad had happened. Maybe Rock didn't want to kiss her anymore.

"No, I'm good," she said. "Sit down."

He wondered if maybe her dad was on a bender. But then he heard sounds from inside and knew Jake was home safe.

The sun was warm on the stoop, but the warmth inside the breeze was gone, along with summer. Pearl was stretched out, but not as languorously as she had been in the summer months. Russell stationed herself in the middle of the yard.

"About our project," Danny said.

"Maybe we should wait till spring," said Janine.

"No way. I won't be as good in the spring after a winter of not practising."

"Yes, you will."

"Maybe not."

"Anyway, I thought we decided I was going to do it."

"No, we didn't. I can't believe you think we decided that."

"Oh. I thought we did."

"How's school?"

"Okay, I guess. How is it with you?"

"Not bad. The girls in my class have Miss Hardass for phys ed. It's weird seein' her around."

"All the girls in the whole school have Hardass for phys ed," said Janine. "It'd be weird to not see her around."

"There are different kinds of weird," said Danny.

He ran his hand gently down the length of Pearl.

"Things are looser at Nelson Mac than at Nordale," he went on. "Like we don't have to line up for anything. I like that about it. And if you're in the hall or something, somewhere where you're not supposed to be, nobody grills you. Plus, there's way more kids; that's good too. It's not so noticeable that people hate you."

"That'll change," said Janine, "people hating you, I mean."

She said it by way of comfort, he supposed.

"I notice you don't seem to have much in the way of friends," he said.

"Very observant."

"Well…I wouldn't mention it if…it's just…you told me, more than once, I might add, that I need to have more than one friend."

"Yeah, but you can."

"And you can't?"

"It's different with me."

"Why?"

"'Cause I'm poor, 'cause I wear the same clothes every day, 'cause my dad's an alky, and I don't have a mum, 'cause I'm not pretty, and I cut my own hair, all kinds of reasons."

"I think you're pretty. Your hair suits you, and your clothes are interesting because of the things you sew onto them."

"Thanks." She smiled, but she didn't mean it.

She was wearing a jean jacket with Goofy on the arm and sparkles that looked like diamonds on one of the pockets.

"Being poor means no one wants to hang around with you unless they're poor too," Janine said.

"I don't think that's true," said Danny. "I'm not poor, and I wanna hang around with you. Plus, loads of poor kids go to Nelson Mac. I think you're way off base with this idea."

"Do you?"

A margin of light lit her face when she said this, as though it was a new thought, a brand new good thought.

"Yes."

Pearl stretched and rolled onto her back. Danny rubbed her tummy, and she purred her crackly purr.

"My dad's not an alky," Danny said, "but he's nowhere. And my mum is nailed to a couch. I think that equals poor. Plus, I wear pretty much the same thing every day."

Janine rubbed Pearl's ears. All this attention seemed too much for her. She leapt up and ran around the corner of the house. Russell immediately took her place on the stoop.

"What happened to your mum?" Danny said.

Janine stood up. "Let's go," she said.

"Where are we goin'?"

"To the river. You can leave your bike here. Come on, Russ."

They made the short trek and found a spot on the grass near the edge of the top bank.

"Somebody killed her," said Janine. "My mum."

Danny's scalp tingled.

"It was a lady did it. A big shot vice-principal. She rammed into our tiny Studebaker with her gigantic Edsel and killed her. She died the instant we were hit." Tears filled her eyes.

How do you act when someone tells you something like this? *I'm sorry for your loss* was okay for Jake's dead brother, Daniel, but it wasn't good enough for this. Danny tried to remember other things that people had said to him after Cookie died. All he could remember was that the words made no sense. They had seemed unrelated to what had happened. They could have been placed in a small word pile and lit on fire, and no one would have missed them. *My condolences.* That was another one. *May I offer my condolences.* Add that one to the pile. He knew way better than to say it. At its best, it could be a joke.

"The big shot was drunk," said Janine, "and she didn't go to prison. She didn't even almost go to prison."

"She should have been hanged," said Danny.

Janine spurted out a laugh through her tears.

"Yeah, I thought so. Hanged at the very least."

"By the neck until dead. What was her name?"

"Miss Chapman."

"Miss Chapped Ass. Let's go get her."

"Believe me, I've thought about it. Me and my dad both. But we can't. It'd be too obvious."

"When did it happen?"

"Four years ago. But it still rips my guts apart. And I know my dad's guts are still ripped apart too. It's why he goes on benders. That's my theory, anyway."

They sat, Danny pulling up blades of grass and chewing on the white parts, Janine turning her face to the lowering sun, allowing her tears.

"Chapped Ass—thanks for that, Danny—didn't even say she was sorry. Not to us anyway."

Danny loved to hear her say his name. It didn't happen often enough.

"She probably said it to some cop," said Janine, "while she was busy giving him a blow job."

He hadn't heard anything like that from her before. Blowjob: he still hadn't figured out the blow part. It couldn't be right. He could imagine his dick inside a mouth for sure, being licked, sucked on, having all kinds of things happen to it there, but not being blown like some sort of live whistle. He stirred inside his jeans and tried to concentrate on the fallen tree below them where he used to come to build fires with the friends he no longer had.

"My mum had just gotten her licence," said Janine. "My dad was in the passenger seat, and I was in the back. We were playing I Spy. Dad and me. My mum was concentrating on her driving. I remember him saying, *I spy with my little eye something that is red.* And the next thing I remember is my mum's blood and then the stink coming off Chapped Ass who stood by the side of the road with a cop's arm around her. Ambulance workers saw to my mum, and somebody told me to stay with the killer and the cop.

"My dad was getting in the way. They had to keep telling him to stand back. Finally he did stand back and then he noticed that Chapped Ass stank of booze. Four cops had to restrain him—one for each limb. I knew my mum was dead. You couldn't look the way she did and not be dead."

Danny forced himself not to ask about the way she looked. He pictured Cookie inside her coffin, with so much goop on her face that she looked like a stranger. She hadn't worn much makeup before her death, just pink lipstick sometimes.

He had worried for a second that God wouldn't recognize her and then he remembered that God wasn't there and that even if he was, he was an asshole, so who cared anyway.

Russell walked up to them now with a large tree limb in her mouth. She could barely manage it. Danny threw it for her anyway, not very far, and she walked after it.

"Is this why you said you understood my wish to hurt someone?" Danny said.

"What? Oh. Yeah, I guess."

"Your mum and my sister both died on account of teachers."

"Chapped Ass isn't a teacher. She's a vice-principal."

"Same thing. You have to start out as a teacher to become a principal."

"Vice-principal," said Janine. "Plus Hardass didn't actually kill Cookie."

Danny turned his head and looked at her steady green eyes.

"Yes, she did."

He stared into her eyes longer than was comfortable. It gave him a chilly thrill, like the time he didn't say *You're welcome* to his mum when she thanked him.

"Okay," said Janine. "I give. Hardass is directly responsible for Cookie's death."

"Okay," said Danny. "Good then."

It was because he had looked at her for so long and so steadily that she came around to his way of thinking; he was sure of it. The power of the discovery felt huge. He hadn't known it was going to happen. He hoped he could pull it off again.

"Before my mum was killed we used to have suppers like the one Aunt Dot made," said Janine. "My dad still talks about them."

Danny thought then that it wasn't so far-fetched that they invite Jake over sometime to enjoy one of Dot's meals. He stood up and heaved Russell's tree limb again.

"Maybe we should forget about Mrs. Flood," Janine said. "This is getting to be too much."

"My sentiments exactly," said Danny.

He hadn't spent much time thinking about her at all, except for wondering why Janine wasted so much time on her.

32

THE SUN HAD DISAPPEARED AND IT STARTED TO RAIN GENTLY, a fine rain that was almost fog. The season was getting away on them.

"We gotta set a date," Danny said.

"There's no hurry."

"Yes, there is."

"No, there isn't. There's no reason it couldn't be done in winter."

"What, are you crazy? What about snow? What about mitts and hats? Why are you draggin' your feet?"

"I'm not. We could do it on a nice winter day."

"A nice winter day doesn't mean Miss Hardass won't be wearin' a hat or a hood."

"The cover would be better light-wise," said Janine.

"The cover would be pitch black," said Danny. "And no one practises with slingshots in the winter. You've lost interest."

"No, I haven't."

"Yes, you have."

They watched Russell gnaw on the limb. She finally seemed to realize it was more for gnawing than for chasing.

"Where's your dad, Danny?"

"Where'd that come from?" he said.

"I don't know. From because I told you about my mum, I guess."

When sound information about their dad had finally come their way several years ago it was from Aunt Dot, who was visiting at the time.

"Auntie Dot?" Danny had said.

"Yes, pet."

"Where's our dad?"

She had turned an unbecoming colour of red and stammered a little. "I think that's something for your mum to tell you about."

"But she won't. She just won't. She keeps saying he's dead, but we're pretty sure she's lying. If he were just dead, she wouldn't be so weird about it. Loads of people are dead. It's gotta be something worse than that."

Cookie was standing behind him for moral support. She was licking Jell-O powder out of its waxy paper. Lime.

Dot turned to her and tried to talk her out of her choice of snacks. Cookie left the room and tromped upstairs. She licked as she walked, not missing a beat.

Danny knew that even if Dot would tell them something, she'd need to consult with their mother first. He went upstairs to his own room. Cookie had closed her door; he left his open. He sat in his chair with his feet on the windowsill and looked out at the river.

Voices rose up from the living room. Quiet murmurs turned to hisses like never before. Aunt Dot called them both downstairs. They met in the hallway. Cookie's lips were green, and she had a slightly dazed look about her. When they passed the front room, Uncle Edwin was in the big chair, sheltered behind the *Free Press*.

They settled themselves at the kitchen table, and their mother leaned against a doorframe with her arms folded in front of her, inside the sleeves of a sloppy cardigan. She gave them her new version of what had become of their dad. It went as follows:

"I began having my health problems soon after you were born, Danny. Your dad couldn't manage it. He left us two years later."

"Our dad isn't dead."

"No."

"Why did you tell us that he was?"

"I don't know. I guess I didn't feel up to telling you what happened and I thought you were too young to understand it. You probably still are."

"What's to understand?"

She had no answer for that.

"Where is he?"

"I don't know."

She pushed herself away from the doorframe with one of her thin shoulders and turned to leave them.

"Is that it?"

She stopped but didn't turn around. "Yes, that's it." She made for her bedroom.

"What caused your health problems?" Danny called after her. "Was it because I was born? Did I give them to you?"

The door clicked shut behind her.

"No," said Dot, who had been busying herself at the counter transferring cookies from a cookie sheet to a plate. "Definitely not."

"Why does she hate us, Auntie Dot?" Cookie said.

"Oh, sweetheart, she doesn't hate you." Dot crouched down and put her arms around Cookie, who stiffened ever so slightly.

"She's just worried, that's all. About her health mainly. The doctors have given a name to what she has but that doesn't really help because they don't know how to treat it. All they can really do is give her something for the pain and to help her sleep. Life isn't very much fun for her lately."

"What name did they give it?" said Cookie.

"Fibrositis," said Dot. "It's a puzzling disease, honey, one they don't seem to know much about."

"Will she have it forever?" said Danny.

Dot placed the plate of chocolate chip cookies between them instead of answering that question, but tried to fill in some other gaping holes in the story.

Their mother's condition worsened, and their family doctor hadn't been able to diagnose it back then. He came to the conclusion that it was all in her head and sent her to a psychiatrist who prescribed drugs that didn't work.

"A tiredness got its clutches into her and wouldn't let her be, but it wasn't the kind of tiredness that helps you fall asleep," said Dot. "It was very hard on her."

"What kind of tiredness was it?" said Cookie.

Dot sighed. "Well, it's hard to describe. It probably doesn't make good sense to say it was the kind of tiredness that keeps you awake, but that's the best I can do."

She covered one of Danny's hands with her own.

"I lived here for a year," she said. "You probably don't remember."

"No," they said together.

"What about our dad?" Danny retrieved his hand.

"Well, he was here for two or so years after you were born, honey, but then, like your mum said, he went away.

"He provides for you," she went on. "That's where the money in the drawer comes from. He sends it to me, and I put it there. He sends me enough that I can pay all your bills. More than enough."

"Is he rich?" Cookie said around a mouthful of cookie.

Danny reached for one, seeing that if he didn't, he'd miss out entirely.

"He seems to be a wealthy man. He was an engineer before he left, so I guess he still is."

"He drives a train?" Danny perked up at this.

"No, honey, a different kind of engineer. He designs bridges and things like that. He's very smart. That's why you and your sister are so clever."

"What if he dies," said Cookie, "and the money in the drawer stops coming?"

"Don't worry about that." Dot smoothed Cookie's hair back from her forehead. "You'll always be provided for."

Edwin's newspaper crackled from the front room, and Dot adjusted her posture.

"Anyway, your mother got some better. They put her on a drug that eased her pain for a time. She began caring for you two, doing the things a mother should do. When I thought she was well enough, I went home to the farm."

"Where is he?" said Danny.

"He travels a lot for his work." She pushed the plate of cookies towards him.

"But his home. Where's his home?"

Dot hesitated and then said, "I don't know, honey."

That was how it was left; that was all they got. Danny felt as though he didn't know a heck of a lot more than he did before, except that for sure their dad was alive. He had tried to feel happy about that but couldn't. His dad wasn't a magic man. He travelled, but not with a circus. He drew pictures of bridges, maybe shared them with a few people. Not with him.

Danny gave Janine a condensed version of the story, and she wanted to celebrate the fact that his dad was alive, but he couldn't muster up any celebratory feelings.

33

LATE SATURDAY AFTERNOON, AFTER THE FIRST WEEK OF school, Danny went down to The Bay and sat on the mezzanine floor to watch the people come and go. He missed Paul. He missed Cookie and all the trouble she carried with her. He even missed himself, the way he used to be. Please let it go back to the way it was, he prayed to the God he left behind at Sunday school.

With no one there to talk to about the sights around him his glum feeling grew. He supposed the Paddlewheel wouldn't make him feel any better so he left The Bay and looked up and down Portage Avenue. He crossed the street to the Manhattan restaurant. Its sign had always tantalized him with its sparkly cocktail glass with the cherry inside.

When he walked in he needed a moment or two to adjust his eyes to the dimness. There were booths along one side and a long counter that ran practically the whole length of the restaurant. He took a seat at the counter about halfway down and accepted a menu from a weary-looking waitress.

He felt self-conscious. He'd often sat alone at the counter in Wade's and drunk milkshakes, and he and Paul had been all over the place on their bikes trying out different spots for Cokes, but this was his first time in a downtown restaurant on his own. And this place didn't have a whole-family kind of name, like Picardy's or The Chocolate Shop, where kids could easily come and go. This place was for grownups. He was surprised the waitress didn't kick him out. She seemed more interested in the newspaper on the counter in front of her. She took a pencil from above her ear and scribbled.

The room was thick with cigarette smoke, like the living room at home. He glanced over his shoulder to get a better idea of the place now that his eyes had fully adjusted. One other person sat at the counter—a man in a suit, who he had passed on his way in. Only a few of the booths were occupied.

Danny's eyes roamed slowly, and a jolt just about knocked him off his stool when they came to rest on a familiar form. In a booth near the back of the restaurant sat Miss Hartley. No, Mrs. Flood—her hair was blonde. It was the sister. Janine was convinced the blonde hair was from a bottle.

"Like Marlon Brando," Danny had said, and she said nothing in return. They had exhausted that conversation; he wouldn't touch on it again.

Both of her hands clutched a glass that was identical to the one outside on the neon sign. Then one hand let go and reached across the table. Her manner caused Danny to think she was reaching for a man.

"Are you ready to order, sweetie?"

It was the weary waitress, pencil back on top of her ear.

"May I have a Coke, please?"

"Nothing to eat?" Her voice was raspy, well used, not unpleasant. It reminded Danny of the sound the stockings made when the woman's legs rubbed together on Sydney I. Robinson day.

"Not just now, thanks," he said.

She left him the menu and poured him a Coke.

What was happening was something he'd want to report to Janine in detail, so he got up and headed towards the back of the restaurant where there was a sign saying *Restrooms.* He needed to see who she was reaching for. He looked straight ahead as he passed the booth, but on his way back from the restroom he glanced towards it.

Rock Sand and Mrs. Flood were deep in discussion; it was more than a casual chat. Danny panicked in case Rock saw and recognized him but he didn't have to worry. His eyes weren't interested in anything but Mrs. Flood. Both his hands surrounded one of hers, and he had a teasing smile on his face. A dirty smile.

Danny sat down and took a long drink of his Coke. Mrs. Flood didn't know him so he could have another look now he was out of

Rock's line of vision. There was a mirror behind the counter. He shifted two stools down where he had a better view of her face and their hands.

Rock turned her hand over and placed their palms together. Then he ran a finger down the centre of her palm, slowly, all the way to the end of her middle finger. Danny shivered. Then they weren't touching at all but Mrs. Flood left her hand where it was, palm up. She wanted more. Rock took her hand again, and it disappeared. Danny pictured it going to Rock's grubby mouth to receive a filthy kiss. Then she pulled away, and he heard Rock laugh. Maybe he had tried to suck a finger, and she wouldn't let him — not in public.

This wasn't a student-teacher relationship, not even a former student-teacher relationship. It was something wrong and sordid. It might be too big to share with Janine. Her concentration had scattered at the first sighting of Mrs. Flood. This new information would smash it to smithereens. Maybe she was psychic — she had somehow known that the sister was someone to hate.

"Nine-letter word: region shared by Argentina and Chile, fifth letter — *g*."

Danny was startled into realizing the waitress was looking at him while she spoke. She was doing a crossword puzzle. It was the type of thing Aunt Dot called out from time to time. When he processed what she said, he blurted out, "Patagonia."

"My God, you're right," she said after a moment or two and laughed a whiskey laugh.

He slurped down the rest of his drink and left a quarter on the counter: fifteen cents for the coke and a dime for the waitress. It was the first time in his life he'd left a tip. He was a private detective paying for information. He liked the feeling.

"So long, genius," the waitress called after him.

Out on the street again, he crossed over and and hopped on a St. Mary's bus. He smiled all the way down Portage Avenue and across the two bridges into Norwood. At the Spanish Court bungalows he got off, and feeling like a genius detective, wound his way home through the leafy streets.

He pictured the way Rock and Mrs. Flood were and was certain that they had done it with each other. The way the palms of their hands had touched. Rock's finger down the middle of hers.

There was no denying the pleasure he felt at those two creeps being together. It meant that Rock had eyes for someone other than Janine.

This was tricky. When Janine had said they should forget about Mrs. Flood he had felt so optimistic about getting back on track. He didn't want to tell her what he had seen.

On the other hand, he wanted her to know so she could forget about that louse, so she could well and truly hate him and allow her love to take another path.

But then there was the problem of her concentration and the possible total derailment of their plan. It needed way more thought.

If he didn't tell her, she'd know he was holding something back. He knew she would; she was psychic.

When he got home he got out a piece of paper and a pencil to make a list of the pros and cons.

He thought again about the palms of their hands and how they touched. He wondered if it would be possible to place his palm against Janine's, to somehow fit it in to something they were doing, without her knowing how much he wanted to, without her knowing he was a fool.

34

DANNY DIDN'T GET AROUND TO HIS LIST OF PROS AND CONS, but he did wait until the next day to go over to Janine's. She was sitting on her back stoop with Pearl. They were staring at each other.

He sat down next to her and told her what he had seen.

"You're jealous of Rock so you're making stuff up," she said.

"I knew you'd say that."

He gave more details in an effort to convince her.

"The divorcée Flood had a cocktail in front of her. It was pink, like the neon one out front."

"He really touched her hand?"

"Yup. And then he let it go, and then he touched it again, and she pulled it away."

He didn't mention their palms, couldn't mention the finger.

She was silent for a long time, and Danny worried about her thoughts.

Inside his head he heard Rock Sand's laugh when Mrs. Flood pulled away.

Finally Janine said, "I saw her with him before."

"What?"

I saw her with him before, outside Fromson's."

"What the hell are you talkin' about? You had seen her before we saw her with Miss Hardass?"

"Yeah."

"Why didn't you tell me? You acted like you'd never seen her before."

"No, I didn't. I acted like I'd never seen her with Hardass before."

"What's the diff? You should have told me. How could you not have told me that you saw someone that looked exactly like Miss Hardass but with different-coloured hair?"

"I don't think I completely got it then," said Janine. "I mean, they were a ways away from me at Fromson's, and her fancy shoes and everything. I didn't think..."

"But then at Dominion. Why didn't you tell me then? You must have gotten it then. You're not retarded. Or are you? Christ, I thought we told each other stuff."

"I don't know why I didn't tell you, okay? I don't have to tell you every screaming thought in my head, do I?"

"Wow, you were already jealous. You were jealous of the divorcée Flood then, just like you're jealous of her now. You didn't tell me about seein' her, or about seein' them together because..."

"Shut up."

He had said too much. All he could do now was try not to say anything bad about Rock Sand. Maybe they could still not have a fight.

"There was nothing to tell," she said. "There was no touching or meaningful looks or anything. I thought it was just a grocery store kind of encounter. You know how you talk to strangers in stores sometimes."

"Not really."

He felt her slump beside him and knew it was up to him to make her sit up straight again, but he couldn't think how. He couldn't think of a word to say that he wasn't positive that he'd want to take back.

"Okay, c'mon." Janine stood up.

"Where are we goin'?"

"To confront him. What else?"

"Do I have to be there for it?"

"Yup."

"What if he lies?"

"I'll know."

"You might not."

"I will."

"How will you go about askin' him?"

"I don't know yet."

"Don't mention me."

"I won't."

Danny both did and didn't want to be there. He wanted to see how it went, to see Rock lessen in Janine's eyes, but he didn't want to be accused of anything, like ratting him out, and then be beaten up as a result, by those unnaturally muscular arms. Popeye arms.

Or what if he denied it, and Janine believed his lies? What if she wasn't as great as she thought she was at knowing when people weren't telling the truth?

They had gotten as far as her front steps where they sat down again. Pearl was flat in the grass now, staring at a black-capped chickadee perched on a low branch in a cotoneaster. She looked insane in her concentration.

"Have you decided yet what you're gonna say?" Danny said.

"Not word for word. I'm going to ease into it."

"How?"

"I don't know yet. Jesus."

They found Rock in the back lane behind his house. His head was deep inside the engine compartment of his car. A strip of fish-white flesh stood out between the bottom of his T-shirt and his jeans. It looked as if it had never before seen the light of day.

"Hi, Rock," said Janine.

"Hi, Jan." He didn't look up.

Danny thought that was rude and decided not to say hello.

"Did you have Hardass as a teacher when you went to Nelson Mac?" Janine said.

"Who?"

"Miss Hartley. The phys ed teacher."

He turned his head to the side and looked at her.

"No. Of course not. She was the girls' teacher."

He turned back to the black insides of his car.

"Did you know she has a sister?" said Janine. "A twin maybe?"

Danny saw a stiffening of his back and hoped Janine saw it too.

"Her name's Mrs. Flood," she went on.

"The divorcée Flood," Danny said quietly.

"She teaches at Q.E. We thought you might know her."

Danny elbowed her in the ribs for saying *we*.

Rock stood upright and wiped his hands on a clean rag that looked as though it had been ironed.

"What is this?" he said. "What are you trying to say?"

"Nothing in particular," said Janine. "Well, do you?"

"Do I what?"

"Know her."

"I had her for history. What's it to you?"

"Nothing. We were just wondering."

Again with the *we*.

"Wondering what?"

"Do you still know her?" Janine barrelled forward with her questions.

Rock's eyes wavered and then went flat.

"Of course not. She's a teacher. Why would I still know a lame-ass history teacher?"

"You tell me."

"Get lost, you two. I'm busy."

He buried his head inside his car.

They walked away down the lane.

"He's lying," said Janine.

"Told you."

"Shut up."

"I don't think you did a very good job of easin' into it like you said you were gonna," said Danny.

"So what? We got what we came for."

"You should have started with the weather or what are you doin' or something like that. I would've."

"Well if you would've, why didn't you? Anyway, what's the diff? *Je m'en fiche.* We know he's a liar and a weasel."

Janine's eyes filled with tears. Danny hoped she wouldn't cry for that no-good hoodlum with grease all over his hands. He pictured those hands mauling her and he couldn't stand that she would cry for him.

"I'm sorry that you're disappointed," he said.

"No, you're not."

"Yes, I am. I don't want you to feel bad about anything. Even if…"

"Never mind. I know what you mean."

"He knows now that we know," Danny said.

"So what? That doesn't have to be a secret."

"Oh. I thought it did."

"It doesn't."

"I think it would be better if it was."

"Why?"

"I'm not sure."

"Well, it isn't a secret, and that's that."

They wound their way back to Janine's house and sat down on the front steps.

The sky was the bright blue of coming autumn, and cumulus clouds scudded across it in the cool wind.

"Let's go around to the stoop," Danny said.

"Why?"

"He can see us from his house if he comes around front."

"So?"

"Well he's not gonna beat *you* up, is he? You're a girl. I'm gonna be the one he kills."

"Shh, my dad's sleeping."

"I'm gonna be the fall guy in all this," Danny said.

"There isn't going to be a fall guy." The tears that threatened were gone. "Except maybe Mrs. Flood."

They went around to the back and sat on the stoop beside Pearl, who was stretched out in the cool sun. Danny rubbed her tummy and wondered if there was a black-capped chickadee inside it.

"He would have gone to Queen Elizabeth for grades seven and eight," Danny said, "before the addition was built on Nordale. That's probably why I'd never heard of him."

"I feel sick," said Janine. "Like I'm going to puke. I knew it. I knew there was a good reason for us to spy on her."

"Please don't puke."

"We can use this. We can use this big time." She looked over both shoulders.

"How?"

"I don't know yet."

She stood up. "Let's walk."

They headed off in the direction of the icehouse.

"It's probably not against the law what they're doing," Janine said, "but it might be against school laws and for sure against the former Mr. Flood's laws. Maybe Rock is what happened to their marriage."

"If Mr. Flood exists," said Danny. "He could be dead. She could be the widow Flood."

"It makes me sick to think of them actually doing it," said Janine.

"Maybe they're not."

Danny thought about their palms touching, and the finger thing, and he knew they were.

"They are," said Janine.

"Yeah, I guess."

"How could he want to do it with her? She's gotta be at least thirty-five."

Danny thought the question was, *why would she want to do it with him?* but he held his tongue.

"Maybe she lured him in with her red lipstick and high heels," he said.

"And she thought he could do things to her that Mr. Flood didn't do," said Janine.

"What kinds of things?"

"I don't know. Wild things."

"Maybe he thought the same," said Danny, "with her bein' old and all. That she could teach him stuff—things that Mr. Flood had done that he might not know about yet. It could work both ways."

"Shut up, Danny." She said it softly, and her eyes filled up again.

He stopped talking for a while, let her pull herself together.

"Even if they aren't doing it," Janine finally said, "we can pretend they are for our purposes."

"They are," said Danny. "They are doin' it."

She looked at him. "Do you know something more that you're not telling me?"

"No."

He thought about demonstrating, using Janine's palm as an aid, but it seemed way too complicated. She might think that he wanted to do it to her, which he did, but she couldn't know that yet.

Danny didn't know what their purposes were, but he did know one thing.

"Janine…" It was the first time he had called her by her name. It felt strange…exciting, but in a self-conscious way.

"What?" She didn't show any outward signs of noticing.

"Well, this whole new tack doesn't have anything to do with Miss Hardass. It's just something you're goin' off on because you're jealous. The thing that you don't know what it is, but that we're gonna do, can't take over from our original plan. It just can't."

"I'm not jealous," she said. "What do you know about jealous?"

Everything.

"It's just…I don't want all our planning to go down the tubes. Maybe we should forget about this new batch of information till we've accomplished the Miss Hardass angle."

"It's all connected."

"No, it's not."

Jealousy was blinding her, but he was teetering on the precipice of pissing her off. He couldn't go back to the nowhere land where he had lived without her.

"I need to think," said Janine.

"Okay. Thinking is often good."

He knew it was Rock Sand who owned her heart. But maybe now, once the dust settled, he would own less of it. A small corner of it would be free for him.

They turned onto Monck Avenue and passed a hedge made up of lilac bushes. Danny picked a leaf.

"A lilac leaf is a perfect example of what a leaf should look like and feel like," he said.

He ripped it in two and held it to his nose and inhaled.

"And smell like. I wonder why lilac leaves don't change colour in the fall."

"Beats me," said Janine.

The wind was blowing the first leaves off the trees. It irritated Danny. If the wind didn't blow so hard, the leaves could stay longer. If it didn't blow at all, maybe some of them could stay all winter. Wind pissed him off.

"Lilac leaves are almost the last to fall," he said. "I wonder if it has to do with them stayin' green."

"Do you mind?" said Janine. "I'm trying to think."

"Sorry."

They passed Morven Rankin and her brother, George. They were both wearing baseball gloves.

"Hi, George. Hi, Morven," said Danny.

"Hey there, Danny. Hi, Janine," George said.

Morven just stared. George nudged her with his elbow, but she kept on staring. Janine didn't even look up; they were as bad as each other.

"Why didn't you say hi?" said Danny. "That's the girl who you told me the menstrual story about."

"What? Oh." Janine turned around and waved. "Hi, Rankins."

George waved back.

They walked as far as the community club, where they sat by the tennis courts and watched grownups hit balls back and forth.

"How about the flamin'-shit-on-the-doorstep gag?" said Danny.

"Not good enough."

35

"I'VE COME UP WITH SOMETHING," SAID JANINE.

"What?"

They were sitting on the grass by the empty wading pool at the community club. Girls carrying their tap dancing shoes came and went.

"It's a variation on the fiery shit in a bag."

"Okay," Danny said. "Let's hear it."

"*Danny has a girlfriend*," two little girls sang as they walked by. "*Danny has a girlfriend*."

"My dad has these roofers' nails," said Janine. "They're excellent nails with good flat tops big enough they can stand up on their own."

"Yeah?"

"Okay, so we place some nails standing up, inside the shit, inside the bag. We pour a bit of gasoline on it. Then we ring her doorbell, set a match to the works, and run like hell."

"You're talkin' about the divorcée Flood, right?"

"Of course. Who else?"

"Well, I keep hopin' we're gonna be talkin' about Miss Hardass."

"Relax," said Janine, "We'll get to her."

"*You've got Janine's cooties*," sang another girl as she tagged her friend.

The friend tagged her back.

"No, you."

"You."

"No, you."

"Let's get out of here," said Janine.

They took off down Lawndale, away from the taunts of the eight-year-olds.

"Remember when I said that Cookie was kind to me?" Janine said.

"Yeah?"

"It was when kids said things like that about me, to me: that whole cooties thing. If she saw it happening she would always come over and kind of make it seem like we were playing together, as if she wanted to be with me. And the kids would back off. It was before she got weird, when she was still half-assed popular back at Nordale."

"I wonder why she had to go and get weird," said Danny.

"Probably all kinds of reasons," said Janine. "And don't forget Hardass. She was on Cookie's back right from the start, from the beginning of grade nine. Always on her about not being any good at anything. I don't know why she picked on Cookie—lots of kids are terrible at sports—but she never gave her a break. Once she..."

"Once she what?" said Danny.

"Nothing."

"Are you thinkin' about the locker room thing?" said Danny. "Cookie told me about that."

"Yeah, there was that. It was really horrible. God, I detest that bitch. Did Cookie tell you that she's always in the locker room with us? For no good reason. That's bizarre in itself, right? I mean, we have our underwear on, but still, it's creepy. A couple of the girls took their bras off once and walked up to ask her a question—pushing it, you know, tits all over the place, but pretending nothing was out of the ordinary. And she didn't say anything, didn't tell them to put their bras back on, just drank it all in. Is that perverted or what?"

"Which girls?"

Janine chuckled. "Oh, Danny, Danny."

He stepped out of reach so she couldn't tousle his hair. Her voice had tousling all through it.

When they got to the river they sat down close to the edge.

"Who's gonna do the placing of the nails?" said Danny.

"I'll do it. I'll wear rubber gloves."

"Oh. Rubber gloves. That's a good idea."

"Well, what did you think, I'm going to do it with my bare hands?"

"No, I guess not."

"This is going to be great. We'll do it after dark. We want her to be sure to see the flames. It'll scare the piss out of her."

"And we don't want anyone to see us. Maybe we should wear disguises."

"What sort of disguises?"

"I've still got a Lone Ranger mask and hat."

"I've got a pair of horn-rimmed glasses with a false nose attached."

"This is why it's not good that Rock knows that we know about them," Danny said. "He'll figure it's us and he'll rat us out."

"She won't tell him about it," said Janine. "She won't want him to know that anyone hates her that much. Plus, she won't want him to know that she had shit attached to her feet."

"Are you sure?"

"Mm-hmm. She'll think it'll make her less attractive in his eyes."

"Will it?"

"Probably. Who wants to suck on toes that have been covered in shit? Even if they've been washed a billion times."

"No one, I guess," Danny said. He wasn't sure he would want to suck on anyone's toes no matter what, but he didn't say so. Something else to think about.

"I hope she's wearing flimsy slippers or bare feet," said Janine. "That's another good thing about doing it late. She's more likely not to have shoes on."

They picked Friday, September 18th. Dot was home on the farm, and Jake was working the three-to-eleven shift at the bakery. The sun set at a little after 7:30. They didn't have to wait long after that for the cover of night, but to be on the safe side they decided on 10:00.

In the late afternoon they searched for dog shit in the grass by the river. They wanted it fresh. Janine had brought an old ladle, rubber gloves, and two plastic bags. They walked slowly, Russell trotting along ahead, till they found what they needed. Russell didn't even try to contain her excitement.

Back at Janine's house she transferred it to a flimsy paper bag, positioned the nails, and put it back into plastic for the journey to rue Valade. She put the ladle and gloves in a bag of their own and tossed them in the garbage out back of the shed.

Danny went home to make supper. It was almost 7:00 but he knew his mum wouldn't care. He wasn't hungry. He heated up some Chuckwagon Dinner for his mum and noticed for the first time how horrible it was. Thin stew, an embarrassment of stew. How could he have eaten it before without questioning it? He threw it out. Not even his mum deserved Chuckwagon Dinner. He heated up some tomato soup and placed a pile of soda crackers beside it on her tray. She put out her cigarette.

"Thanks, Danny," she said.

"You're welcome, Mum."

He felt okay about the dog shit; it was a good prank. But the nails made him uneasy. He didn't like imagining how it would feel if he was the one doing the stomping. And what if they got caught? This wasn't his fight. What a waste of getting caught if it wasn't even something he wanted to do.

But then, Miss Hartley wasn't Janine's fight, and she was gung-ho about that. At least she used to be. Maybe she just needed any fight, it didn't matter whose.

They mustn't forget that Miss Hartley lived upstairs. They had to keep an eye on her apartment as well as Mrs. Flood's for any sign of interference.

He put several kitchen matches in his pocket and said goodbye to Russell at the back door. There was no room for a dog in the plan.

Janine was ready with the bag and a small jar of gasoline. They had a little time to kill so they played a few hands of rummy. At 9:30 they hopped on their bikes and cycled slowly over to rue Valade, stopping across from Saint Boniface Hospital to don their disguises. At 9:45 it was as dark as it was going to get.

"I hope that stupid wiener dog isn't around," Janine said, as they parked their bikes on rue Dollard by the fir tree across from the house.

Danny felt as though he hadn't been much help so far.

"Do you want me to be the guy to do it?" he said.

"We'll both do it. I'll position the shit and pour the gas, and then you drop the match and ring the bell, simultaneously if possible. Christ, I forgot matches."

"I've got lots."

"Really?"

"Yup," said Danny, a hero for a moment or two.

"Okay, let's just stand here and get our bearings."

"We better not stand for long. There's no one around right now. We oughta take advantage of that."

"The lights are on in her apartment," said Janine. "That's good."

Danny looked up and saw the stream of light running the length of the second floor.

"And none are on in Miss Hardass's," said Danny. "That's also good."

"Be sure to ring the right bell," said Janine. "The middle one."

He was tempted to ring the wrong bell to pay her back for thinking she needed to remind him to ring the right one.

"Will we wait to see what happens?" he said.

"Can't. We have to be gone."

"What's the point then, if we don't get to see how it goes?"

"We'll hear how it goes. That's good enough for me."

The golden light up in the rooms looked as if it should be welcoming someone home, not housing the screams of a divorcée.

"What if someone else answers the door?" Danny said.

"We have to take that chance."

"What if no one answers, and we burn the whole street down?"

"Danny, for Christ's sake."

"What if..."

"Shut up."

They stood under the branches of the blue spruce. A car drove by towards Taché. Two teenagers walked past on the other side of the street. They were holding hands, and the girl's head rested against the boy's shoulder.

"Okay," said Janine. "We'll wait till those two lovebirds are out of sight and then, if there's no other action, we'll make our move."

There was no other action.

"Okay, on the count of three. One, two, three."

It went off without a hitch. The flames shot up higher than Danny had anticipated. Janine's arm shot out and pushed him back. They ran to their bikes and were in a back lane a block away before they heard the howls of pain.

They kept on riding, Janine with a devilish smile on her face, Danny with a sick feeling in the pit of his stomach. His only thought was that he was glad he hadn't eaten any supper. If he had he would have spewed it all over himself.

36

JANINE SPIED IN THE COMING DAYS. DANNY DIDN'T HAVE IT IN him to join her. She reported that Mrs. Flood was using one crutch. It delighted her. Danny didn't want to see another roof nail as long as he lived.

It puzzled him that the imagined sensation of stomping on nails didn't bother Janine. He admired her for it one minute, and the next wondered if it was such a good thing. Maybe she didn't let herself imagine it.

His plan for Miss Hartley didn't allow for physical suffering, but he admitted to himself that he hadn't thought about it before now.

On Wednesday afternoon of the following week Danny found a perfect stone in the back lane behind Birchdale Betty's house. It was smooth, round, and the perfect size for his task. He carried it around in his pocket to help him with his continually threatened focus.

Dot returned on Friday. On Saturday afternoon Danny was upstairs when he heard hisses rising up from the living room. He crept into the hallway and sat at the top of the stairs.

"Barbara, we've been over this so many times over the years. I find it unconscionable that you haven't told him."

"Well, I haven't."

"You've said you would countless times. You convinced me that you meant it."

"I did mean it, Dot. It has just never seemed like the right time."

"Believe me, Barbara, I don't like harping on at you. But I can't believe that *the right time* hasn't presented itself in so many years."

"It's hard to believe you don't like harping at me."

"That's not fair, Barb. It's because I love you and Danny and want what's best for you both. You should tell him, so he understands there was more to it than his being born, and you getting sick. He might be dwelling on it, for all we know. And he doesn't have Cookie anymore, his ally in all things father-related."

"Jesus, Dot. Could you at least sit down so I don't have to strain my neck?"

Danny heard Dot's voice come up from a slightly different location.

"When we told him all those years ago that Art was alive, I was under the impression that he thought it was somehow his fault that his dad left. That may still be the case."

"That's ridiculous."

"No. It isn't."

"You tell him then."

"It's not my place to tell him."

"You could have fooled me."

"We can tell him together."

Danny snuck down the stairs and out the back door.

Art? Was his dad's name Art? He could scarcely believe he had never known, never asked.

He wanted whatever they were arguing about to disappear. It sounded bad; it sounded like an avalanche. He didn't want to smother under an avalanche. That would be worse than drowning.

Maybe his dad was in jail; maybe he was a murderer; maybe he fought on the side of the Germans and was a torturer; maybe he was the newly dead Adolf Eichmann and had been hiding behind the name Art Blue. He fingered the stone in his pocket as he trudged along the riverbank with Russell galloping ahead.

His mum had said it was ridiculous that he thought Art leaving was his fault. That was good news, anyway.

When he got home, Aunt Dot was the first to speak.

"Danny, could you come into the front room, please? Your mother has something she'd like to talk to you about."

His mum was in a chair with a blanket over her knees. An invalid still, but an upright one. He wondered if what she had been doing since Cookie's death qualified as a nervous breakdown.

"What's my dad's name?" he said.

"Arthur," said his mum.

"That's my name. That's my middle name."

"Yes."

"Arthur what?"

"Arthur Scirrow."

"Is his last name Blue?"

"Yes."

"Sit down, honey," Dot said.

"I don't think I want to sit down." He leaned against the archway between the front room and the hall. "This is something bad, isn't it? Something big and bad."

"It's something that happened, dear, at the time you were born."

Dot looked at her sister. "Barbara?"

Barbara lit a cigarette and blew the smoke out straight in front of her. Maybe she thought that was talking.

"It's hard for her," Dot said. "She doesn't want to tell you, but I more or less insisted on it, so I guess it falls to me."

"You don't have to tell me," Danny said. "I'm fine with not knowing whatever it is."

"When you were born," said Dot, paying him no mind, "there was another baby too. Another baby boy."

Danny slid down the archway and sat on the floor.

"Your mum and dad called him James."

Danny stared at the hardwood. The lines inside the wood were sinuous and lovely. He had never noticed them before. He waited for the rest of it.

"The baby died," said Dot. "A few days after he was born."

"Six days." It was his mother's voice now.

"I'm a twin," said Danny.

"Yes."

"Where is he?"

"St. Vital Cemetery."

"Near Cookie?"

"No."

"Why not?"

She uttered a squeak of annoyance.

"I don't know, honey," said Dot. "It doesn't really matter, does it?"

"I don't know. I don't know what matters."

"It was about space," said his mum. "There wasn't enough space beside James."

"Who came first? Him or me?"

"What?"

"Who was born first, me or…or James?"

"You."

"Why did he die?"

He stared at the lines in the wood. No one answered.

"Why did he die?"

"He…" Dot stopped.

"He was dropped." His mum's voice quavered. "And his tiny head hit the floor."

Danny heard a ringing in his ears that he'd never heard before. He stood up.

"My dad dropped him."

"Yes, honey," said Dot. "He didn't mean to, but he dropped him. It was an accident."

He walked out of the room and out the back door. The first order of business was to get away from the ringing.

Dot called after him, but he ran. If he ran far enough and fast enough it would stop, and he would be able to think clearly about the two pieces of information he had been given. One at a time. He wished he just had one for now. The first one: he had a twin brother. A dead one, but that seemed secondary at the moment.

He stopped running. He wished he hadn't asked why James had died.

"James," he said.

He shouldn't have asked. His mum would have been happy never to tell him. Dot probably would have made her, eventually, but he would have been safe from the information today.

When Janine's house came into view the ringing stopped, but he didn't want to see her or anyone else. He went home for his bike. As he rode to St. Vital Cemetery, he took in nothing of his surroundings.

And then he roamed. Roamed and roamed.

Finally there it was: a small slab of stone. *James Scirrow Blue. June 24 1950–June 29 1950.*

Danny didn't want him to be so far away from Cookie; he wanted them side by side.

His brother lay in the shade of an oak; Danny lay down beside him. He looked up at the deep blue sky through the changing leaves and felt the solid earth beneath him.

He wondered if he were to find his dad and tell him that it was okay, that as far as he was concerned it was okay, if his dad would have him.

When he stood up and looked around he realized that he was standing pretty much where the Cadillac man had stood when they had looked at each other over the graves. That had been on his birthday. His and James's birthday. He tried to picture the man but couldn't.

Danny walked over to speak to Cookie. Just a few words, there was too much in his head. He wanted to tell her that Janine liked her and would have been her friend. Maybe she already knew. Who knows what kinds of things girls tell each other? Especially messed-up, unsettled girls. Then he retrieved his bike from the parking lot and rode home.

The sun was low in the sky by now, the sunset a fiery background for the world across the river.

His mum was alone in the living room.

"What kind of car does my dad drive?"

His mother coughed out the last drag of a cigarette.

"I don't know."

Dot's kitchen clattering grew quiet, and she scooted into the living room, drying her hands on a tea towel.

"Does he know that Cookie died?" said Danny.

"Yes," his mum said. "He knows."

He stared at her. "Why do we have his last name if you hate him so much?"

"I don't hate him, Danny."

"He didn't mean to drop the baby."

"I know that."

"Can't you please forgive him and let him come back?"

"It's not that simple."

"Could you please explain it to me then, so I get it better and stop wanting him to come home?"

"No, not today, I can't."

"Some day?"

"I don't know."

"Maybe?"

"Maybe."

37

In the early morning just before he woke up Danny dreamed about Cookie. They were at The Bay, looking for a Christmas present for their mum. They checked their coats on the mezzanine floor so they wouldn't be weighed down. The idea was to start at the top, on the sixth floor and sail their way down to the basement where they would end up for chocolate malts, or *Bay basements,* as they called them.

They found earrings for their mum. Sparkly ones that clipped on.

He woke up before the chocolate malt part. Just as well, he thought. Cookie might have behaved badly if they'd gotten to the chocolate malts.

So James was his second thought when he woke up, not his first. He imagined being inside of his mother, not alone. He pictured the first six days of his life. Not alone. He missed James more than he could have imagined missing anyone and he knew through to his marrow that that would never change. He had missed him before he had ever heard of him.

Cookie would have been barely two years old, but maybe deep inside her head, she'd had a hazy recollection of another baby boy. Just not enough of a memory to talk about out loud. Danny wanted to turn back the clock and take Cookie to a hypnotist who would take her back in time. And then she would tell him everything, every minute detail, of those first six days.

He dreamed of a day when he could ask it of his mother.

The statement she uttered on Sydney I. Robinson day: *my dear lost boy.* It took on a whole new meaning. The realization was no comfort, but at least the words made sense now. And it didn't seem strange to him that she loved his dead brother more than him.

A quiet wave of buoyancy passed through Danny when he smelled bacon cooking and heard it sizzling in the pan. *James.*

He got dressed and went downstairs.

The three of them settled themselves around the kitchen table.

Danny looked at his mother the way he had looked at Janine when he convinced her that Miss Hartley was directly responsible for Cookie's death (even though he had always known it wasn't true). He looked straight into her grey eyes.

She met his gaze.

"Did he look like me?"

"Yes," she said. "Very much like you."

"Were we identical or fraternal twins?" He had learned about that in science.

"I don't know for sure. It was too soon to tell. But I think identical."

"Did we weigh the same?"

"You weighed a wee bit more."

No one touched a bite.

"Did he cry?"

"Yes, you both cried."

"Who cried more?"

"Danny…" said Dot.

"No, Dot. It's okay. You cried more, Danny. I remember thinking afterwards you must have known."

"Known?"

"Yes. Known you were going to lose him. That's crazy, I know." She finally cast her eyes down.

"No, it's not crazy."

Tears welled up in her eyes, and he felt a pull towards her, but he couldn't move.

Dot stood up and put an arm around her sister and handed her a Kleenex from her apron pocket.

He went upstairs after breakfast and sat in his chair. He realized he would be unable to tell Janine the story of James. He didn't want her to see his dad in a bad light.

38

DANNY TALKED JANINE INTO GETTING THE JOB DONE BEFORE Thanksgiving, and then she talked him into letting her do it. He had lost track of any reason why she shouldn't.

Pumpkins were on sale at Dominion. He figured the rinds would be perfect for some last-minute practice and to use as targets the night of the "accident." They could place chunks on top of the posts that edged the new parking lot. A big pumpkin was too unwieldy for his bike, so he bought three smallish ones and fit them into his carrier.

Dot was at the house when he got home. As usual, he hadn't known she was coming.

"Pumpkins." There was pleasure in her voice. "Are you going to carve some jack-o'-lanterns, honey?"

"Yup."

"Save the pulp and I'll whip up a pie or two."

"'Kay."

"I'm just here till tomorrow morning. The rapeseed is coming off the fields and I have to get home."

She slid some scalloped potatoes into the oven.

"Uh, Paul has invited me over for supper," Danny said. "I already said okay."

"That's fine, dear. I'm not making anything fancy."

Danny took the pumpkins, a sharp knife, and a bowl out to a spot behind the shed to get away from the eagle eye of his aunt. He cut up the pumpkins and separated the pulp from the rind. He put the pulp in the bowl and took it in the house.

"Thanks, dear. How's the carving going?"

"Slow."

"Would you like a hand?"

"No, thanks."

He went back outside, where he divided the target-sized chunks of rind into two plastic bags and hid one inside the shed for the next day.

After cleaning up the mess, he willed Aunt Dot to be out of question range and ran inside for his jacket and slingshot. He put Russell in the house, shouted a good-bye to his aunt, and headed back to the school with the bag of rinds banging against his thigh and some excellent stones in his pockets.

It was just after 5:30 and edges were beginning to blur in the fading light. The sky was a pastel blue behind the transparent clouds, one or two shades paler than the '57 Cadillac that haunted his daydreams.

Janine was already there.

"Pumpkin rinds," she said.

"Yup."

"Good idea. All I brought is a few cans. Now we won't have to waste time on retrieval."

"That's what I was thinkin'," said Danny.

It was what they were calling the dress rehearsal. The eve of the grand performance: everything in place but the real thing.

He set up the rinds on the fence posts that had been built on two sides of the parking lot. They were flat on top, just like the ones in his yard.

Janine shot at them. He set up more rinds, and she shot at those, missing some just in case someone was watching

"Uh oh," she said. "There's Russell."

Sure enough, there was Russell running full speed towards them.

"My aunt Dot's here," said Danny. "She must have let her out."

"Is she going to be here tomorrow?"

"No, thank Christ. She's leavin' in the morning."

They shot at the remaining rinds and left them where they lay, as evidence of the reality of their practice area. Few people had been by to witness their charade, which disappointed them both.

When Danny and Russell got home, Dot was in the kitchen rolling out the crust for pies.

"Hello, Danny. You're home early. It's good you and Paul have taken up again. I went outside to have a look at your jack-o'-lanterns, but I couldn't find them."

"I ruined them. I threw them away."

"All of them?"

"Yup."

39

THE NEXT MORNING DOT KNOCKED ON DANNY'S BEDROOM door.

"Shit." He whispered it to Russell, who lay beside him on the bed.

"May I come in, Danny?"

"Sure."

"Your mum's still sleeping. She finally managed to nod off after being awake most of the night."

She perched on the edge of his bed.

"I see a change in her," she said.

"You do?"

"Yes, honey, I do. I think she's coming round some. She's trying to take fewer pills, and I think it's making a difference. She seems a little more…alert, I guess is the word."

Danny hadn't noticed, but he hadn't been paying the slightest attention. And now he was in the middle of realizing that today was the day, so he had to struggle to listen to his aunt.

"I just wanted to mention it so you could maybe try to be…I don't know, receptive to her if she makes an effort."

He heard the sound of her voice, but the individual words were lost on him.

"It's most likely she'll continue to have trouble sleeping, what with cutting back on the pills, but we can hope that'll improve."

Danny's mind was on the school grounds with Janine and the setting sun.

"I wanted you to know, I've put the idea of you coming out to the farm on hold. I've spoken to Lena, and she's going to do a little more cooking. I know you want to stay here, Danny, with your friends and activities and such, so we'll continue on as we are and hope that your mum continues to make progress."

Good. She was saying something good.

She stood up and smoothed her skirt.

Danny threw back the covers and swung his legs over the side of the bed. His pajamas had trains on them and stopped halfway up his calves.

Dot smiled. "Looks like you need some new pajamas. This is quite a growth kick you're on."

She leaned over and kissed him on top of his head. As she left the room she described pumpkin pies and casseroles and what was where. She kept talking all the way down the stairs.

It was a windless Tuesday. The girls' basketball team had a game after school so Miss Hartley would be there till 6:30 or so. After classes, as arranged, they both went home to feed their parents.

Danny made Kraft Dinner and wondered if it was the last thing he would ever make. The whole day had been like that, right from when he set his two feet on the floor to get out of bed. He had no intention of dying, but he felt a finality in every move he made. It wasn't unpleasant.

For a second he caught the aroma of a chocolate cake baking and he felt a familiar movement inside his chest. Then both were gone.

The powdered cheese from the Kraft Dinner seemed distasteful to him for the first time. *Yuck*. More like powdered orange chemicals. Agent Orange. The stuff the Americans used to poison Vietnam and everybody who lived there. He'd heard about it on television back before Cookie died.

When he presented the pile of muck to his mother, she said, "Thanks, Danny. One of these days soon, I'm going to get up off this chesterfield and cook you your favourite supper."

That was a shock. He didn't want shocks on this of all days. It was enough that Dot had come and gone.

"You're welcome," he said.

He didn't know what his favourite supper was. Did he have one? Would she have an answer to that if he asked? He didn't want to put either of them through it.

Back in the kitchen, he couldn't get his food to go down so he threw the orange mess into the garbage.

Russell watched him do it.

"Sorry," Danny said.

His mother ate every bite of hers.

Russell didn't like being left at home, but Danny closed both back doors firmly against her eager little face. Then he stopped at the shed to pick up the remaining pumpkin rinds.

He worried that they had left it too late. Even one week ago things would have been clearer, cleaner. But Janine had argued for the change in light. She could handle it. She could do this.

"Have you got the stone?" She stood with her hands in her back pockets, leaning against the school at the western entrance.

"'Course."

He'd carried it in his pocket since the day he found it.

Miss Hartley's Volkswagen and Mr. Potter's Hudson were the only cars left in the teachers' new parking lot. The bus that had brought the visiting team and their fans was parked in front of the school.

"I thought her car was blue," said Danny.

"Nope. Green. More of a bluey green, really."

"I could have sworn it was blue."

"Blue. Green. What's the diff?"

Janine was shooting stones at anything.

"The diff is one's blue and one's green," said Danny. "Maybe she got it painted."

Janine emptied her pockets of stones and moved them into a tidy pile with her foot.

"So, teach me," she said.

There were more people around than on the previous evening. Mostly kids coming and going through the school doors. Game day.

"It feels weird," said Danny. "You're better than me."

"We've been through this. And don't talk so loud if you're going to say things that aren't fake."

"Okay." Danny cleared his throat. "The main thing is concentration. It's a bit like bows and arrows in that way."

"Do you shoot bows and arrows?"

"No."

"Then how do you know?"

"I don't. But it figures."

He crouched down and studied her stones.

"The size of the projectile is important too." He hefted one in his hand. "You look to have done a good job choosing yours."

"What should I aim at?"

"I'll place these pumpkin rinds on top of the fence posts, and we'll start with those."

"Okay, good. I'll shout out which one I'm aiming at, like when you call out the balls and pockets when you're playing pool."

"Do you play pool?"

"A little. I've gone with my dad to the Coronation pool hall."

"Is this real talk or fake?" Danny said quietly.

"Real."

"Okay. Down to business." He put one rind on each of ten posts.

"Second from the left," said Janine and missed the shot.

"Nice try," said Danny. "Was that real or fake?"

"Fake, you moron."

"Shh."

"Okay, from now on everything's fake. Okay?"

"Okay."

"Third from the right." She missed again.

They discussed each shot and celebrated loudly when she hit one and then another.

Their play-acting wasn't for nothing. Other kids were playing baseball at the south end of the field, out of listening range, but not out of sight. And Mr. Roberts at the corner house on Balsam Place was messing around in his front yard. The Coniston bus stopped at the corner of Highfield and Pinedale, and two men and one woman got off. The men trudged home across the school grounds. The woman took the sidewalk.

They talked louder when people went by.

"Good shot."

"Watch this. Oops."

"Not bad, not bad."

The flow of people began to lessen, and the light began to fade.

"Let's not do it today." Danny looked at his watch. "It's gettin' too dark."

"There she is," said Janine.

It was 6:35, and Miss Hartley exited the building.

Janine reached out her hand, eyes on the teacher, and Danny took the chosen stone from his pocket and placed it on her palm. She settled it in the pocket of her slingshot and waited for her moment.

Miss Hartley walked towards her car, teetering on high heels, something Danny had never seen before. She was more inclined towards low heels and running shoes. She rummaged in her handbag. Stopped, started, stopped.

Water sounds floated over from Birchdale Betty's yard.

She started again, and Danny worried that Janine had missed her chance. Miss Hartley had found her keys and paused for two seconds at the driver's door.

Janine took her shot, and the teacher went down like a wounded marionette, fell to rest in a crumpled pile.

They looked at each other and turned towards the back lane between Pinedale and Balsam. Mr. Roberts was gone. At first they walked quickly, their sneakers crunching on the gravel.

"Who's there?" Birchdale Betty called over from her yard. Her hearing was legendary. She was watering her fir trees—something she did every fall before winter set in.

Their footsteps quickened to a run, down Highfield to the river.

"We should have stayed." Danny gasped for breath. "We were gonna stay."

"Running seemed the only thing to do."

"I know, but we have to go back."

"It's too late."

"What if somebody saw us?"

"I don't think anyone did."

"Birchdale Betty yelled."

"She doesn't count," said Janine.

Danny's heart would not slow down. "I don't know. This might be the only time in history when people pay attention to what she says." Blood pounded in his head. "It might not be too late to go back."

They stood inside the deepening dark until breath came more easily.

"We should have gone over the afterwards part more." Danny sat down in the tall grass. "So we knew exactly what we were gonna do."

"It's okay," said Janine.

"What do you mean it's okay? How can it possibly be okay?"

"I missed the shot." She sat down beside him.

"What?"

"I didn't make the shot. My wrist twitched."

"But…she went down. She fell down beside her car."

"I know that."

"At the exact same time that…"

"I didn't hit her."

"This is impossible."

"I would think so too if I didn't know otherwise."

"Maybe you just think you didn't hit her. Your mind could be playin' tricks on you."

"I hit her car," said Janine. "I heard the plink."

"What happened to her, then?"

"I don't know."

Danny imagined the shape of her now, getting lost in the shadows of the autumn night.

Then the sound of an ambulance wailed in the distance, came closer, was right on top of them. They both stood up.

"Maybe she died of fright when she heard the plink," said Danny. "Let's go back."

"No. If we were going to check on her we should have done it at the time. That would have been the normal thing to do, not checking on her seven hundred hours later, after we've thought about it, and everybody else in the world is already there."

"We could watch from a distance."

"No."

"What'll we do then?"

"We'll wait till tomorrow to see what happened."

"Easy for you." Danny didn't know why that was so, but it seemed to be the case.

"Danny. Look at me."

She held him by the shoulders, and her eyes drilled holes into his.

"We didn't do it. We didn't pull it off. There's nothing for us to get into trouble for."

Danny stared back without flinching.

"If you say so."

"I do. I say so."

They walked down the riverbank as far as they could towards St. Mary's Road and then climbed up onto Lyndale Drive.

"You never miss," said Danny.

"I missed tonight," said Janine.

They went to Bober's for some penny candy.

Danny stood in front of the gum machine and stared at the round balls inside the plastic bubble. Only two blacks visible in the sea of white, blue, red, green, orange, yellow, pink. Lots of pink. Whose idea was this? Every kid wants black. The familiar rage tore through him. There should be a gum machine that had all blacks. He wondered if there was such a thing anywhere in the world.

He bought a package of Black Cat gum—the kind in sticks.

Janine stole a licorice pipe and a few caramels.

"I can't believe you stole, tonight of all nights," Danny said when they were back on the street.

"I've never paid for candy at Bober's," said Janine. "I'm not about to start now."

"Jesus Christ," said Danny. "I have to go home."

"Why?" she said. "It can't even be eight o'clock."

"I've had enough for one day."

She let him go without further argument, and he headed home down Coniston. He didn't have the wherewithal even to open his pack of gum; the act of chewing seemed far too strenuous.

Russell greeted him at the door in a full-out frenzy.

His mother called out. "Is that you, Danny?"

"No. It's Danny Kaye," he said.

"Come and see me a minute."

She was sitting up.

"Let me look at you."

Had the whole world changed tonight?

"You look shaken. Is something wrong?"

"No."

She had lipstick on.

He plodded up the stairs to his room. This was no time for his mum to start paying attention to him. He hoped her sudden burst of energy would burn itself out overnight.

After a half hour or so he tiptoed back downstairs and phoned Janine. There was no answer. She was probably across the street giving Rock Sand a blow job.

"Danny?" said his mum.

He snuck back up the stairs to his room and closed the door.

40

DANNY DIDN'T GO TO SLEEP THAT NIGHT. HE DIDN'T EVEN get out of his clothes. At 3:00 a.m. he slipped out the back door and pressed through the night air over to Janine's. It was warm for October. Her house was in total darkness. He thought about throwing stones at her bedroom window, but realized he didn't know which room in the tiny bungalow was hers. He went over to the school grounds, to the spot where they had put on their charade.

So, the word of two kids against the word of a mad woman. Maybe it wouldn't come to that. Birchdale Betty may not have seen them, and Janine was awful sure that she'd missed her shot. But in that case, what happened? It all seemed impossible. Nothing could line itself up inside his head.

He went home and lay down on his bed till after the sun came up.

Thoughts, mostly unwanted, came and went. If Miss Hartley was dead, Mrs. Flood had lost a sister: a twin. It staggered him that he hadn't thought about that before. They had laughed together; he had seen them.

When he went downstairs, his mother was in the kitchen stirring oatmeal porridge on top of the stove.

She smiled at him. The tiniest smile imaginable.

"Good morning, Danny."

She must have said that to him before; it was a regular-type thing for people to say. But he couldn't remember it if she had. And she wasn't regular, hadn't been for years. He struggled one more time to remember who she had been before her illness led her so often to the couch, and Cookie's death glued her to it. He didn't want to prefer the couch person, but in many ways she was easier.

His mouth opened but no words came out. He forced himself to eat a bowl of porridge. He couldn't let her down on her first try. She stood and looked out the kitchen window while he ate. Neither of them spoke. And then she went back to the living room.

Danny rinsed his bowl. The oatmeal sat like gumbo in his gut. He walked out into the crisp fall morning. The brightness of the sun pained his eyes; it held little warmth. Leaves drifted down, and squirrels ran about preparing for winter. He wished it were one year ago, and that he could change the world he lived in.

He followed the familiar route to school. Nothing seemed different on the street. Kids passed him; he passed other kids. One or two of them said hi. No boys, just girls.

Maybe Miss Hartley would be there. Maybe it hadn't happened. What had happened? He thought about Janine and wondered how she felt this morning. Cool, calm, and collected, he guessed, but she was convinced that she had missed. He wondered how she would be feeling if she didn't think she'd missed, if she would be anxious the way he was. He suspected not.

Miss Hartley wasn't there. The girls in Danny's class were excited because they would have a substitute for phys ed. That was all that the excitement seemed to be about. He listened carefully all day to anything anyone had to say. Nothing caught his attention.

He didn't see Janine so he walked over to her house after school.

All the crabapple trees along the lane were empty of fruit; they had been picked clean weeks ago. The apples that hadn't been picked lay rotting on the ground. Danny regretted not having eaten more of them when they had been at their peak of deliciousness.

Janine was raking, out back where the willow tree was. He remembered his plan to fashion a new slingshot with its wood. It hadn't happened. That plan was from a lifetime ago.

"Why are you rakin'?" he said. "Most of the leaves are still on the tree."

She looked up and smiled. "I like raking."

"Would you like some help? I could help."

"No, it's okay. We haven't exactly got the biggest yard in the universe. I'm about done for now."

"Miss Hardass wasn't at school."

"Yeah, I know. We had a sub for phys ed. Well, it isn't a surprise, is it? Something happened to her."

"What? What happened to her?"

"I don't know." Janine rested the rake against the side of the house.

"She couldn't be dead or there would have been a bigger to-do at the school," Danny said. "There was just girls bein' happy because she was away."

"It's too bad. It would've been great if she'd died without us having anything to do with it."

She was so sure.

"No, it wouldn't have," said Danny. "Not with us bein' there and runnin' away instead of helpin'."

And leaving her with a twin sister who would miss her forever.

"You worry too much, Danny. Give yourself a break." Janine squinted into the lowering sun. "What do you want to do?"

"I don't know."

"Let's eat."

They went in the house and Janine opened the fridge and every cupboard in the kitchen that had food in it. They ate bread and butter and peanut butter and jam, and cookies, and marshmallows, and what was left of a bought pumpkin pie.

"Aunt Dot made real pumpkin pies when she was here," said Danny.

"Really? Why are we eating this one? We should be at your house."

On his way home Danny realized that he hadn't thought about Miss Hartley for practically the whole space of his visit with Janine. She didn't seem to have any worries at all about the situation. She had tried to kill someone, hadn't succeeded, and now, to her, it was as though nothing had happened. Danny supposed she had bigger worries, according to her, anyway, about her dad and Children's Aid and all, but just the same. He wished he could be like her. Or maybe not.

She missed the shot, but did that make her not guilty? And what about him? Was he not guilty?

A trace of a good feeling came and went.

There would be no punishment; he had not done it. He was guilty for having set out to do it, but no one need know, except Janine.

He supposed the trace of good feeling was fleeting because it was only skin-deep—it had to do only with the outwardness of what hadn't happened. It didn't run deep like the guilt.

When Danny got home he heated up a can of cream of celery soup (with milk) for his mum and then went up to his room. He noticed the *Little Lulu* comics where he had left them on the floor. He had lost interest in reading them. Who cared what Janine used to read a thousand years ago? He took them to Cookie's room and put them back where he had found them in the closet beside a pile of old stuffed animals. The sight of her pink rabbit nudged the familiar hollow ache in his chest. When he picked it up he saw the corner of a Hilroy scribbler poking out from under the other animals. He pulled it out. There was nothing written on the cover—not Cookie's name, not a subject. He opened it. Written at the top of the first page in her awkward left-handed writing were the words: *Thursday, September 26, 1963*

Danny realized he was looking at a diary. He turned a page, and then another. Most of the scribbler was empty. There were only three entries: one from last fall, one from April of this year—less than a month before she died, and one from...May 1—the day before Frank found her in the river. The last day of her life.

41

DANNY TOOK THE SCRIBBLER AND THE RABBIT BACK TO HIS own room and began to read.

Thursday, September 26, 1963

My mum says I have an unfortunate body type and that I take after my dad's side of the family. It would be better if I took after her, she says. I wonder if he loved her. Did she ever love him and his unfortunate body? He's barely a memory for me. I want to find him and make him come home. He could love me and look after me again like I believe he did once. If only I looked like Audrey Hepburn. Then he'd come home. That's a joke, but I mean it.

I want to go downtown, to the third floor at Eaton's, where I can choose something fantastic. Maybe chicken à la king and a jellyroll. I'll tell them I'm picking it up for my mother who's too sick to make supper. The last part is true. She's too sick to do anything but criticize me. The woman behind the counter will smile and think I'm a good daughter. I know I'm not. I steal money from the drawer. And I'm wasteful.

At the river I'll find a perfect place where I can do it all at once.

Someone caught me the other day in the washroom at school. Janine. She heard me and asked if I was all right, if I needed help. I like her. She's different from the other girls.

I said I was fine and no, I didn't need help. Something disagreed with me, I said.

She went away and left me alone.

If only I could go far away from school, from phys ed class, from my mum. And never, ever come back. I'd miss Danny—he's the only one I'd miss.

Sometimes I play hooky; I write my own notes with a different story every time: Cookie has the twenty-four-hour flu, she has food poisoning, she has a sore neck. I make up stuff that can clear itself up in one or two days and I sign my mum's name. Her signature is easy to copy. My marks are okay, but I have trouble concentrating because I have to think about all the stuff I want. And how I'm going to go about it. It takes up pretty much all my thoughts. It consumes me.

Yesterday I went into a house. I didn't decide to; I just did. It was as though it happened to me; I didn't make it happen. I cringe with thoughts of how it would have gone if I'd been caught. All the different scenarios. I'd have had to run and never stop. There's no way I could have faced it.

I don't want to do it again, but I don't know that I won't.

People in Norwood don't lock their doors. Some do, but most don't. Dads go to work; mums do too, but not very many; kids go to school, and they leave their doors open to the whole wide world.

I went to the other side of St. Mary's Road. Not that it would make any difference if I was caught over there, but somehow it felt safer to be far from home.

It was disappointing: fruits and vegetables, meat thawing on the counter. I did find leftover bubble and squeak in the fridge and made a considerable dent in that. And there was a cheese that was almost too good to be true: MacLaren's Imperial Cheese. It comes in a red cardboard container and is the best thing ever. Well…maybe not the best. There's always cake.

The only things I took with me were the Imperial cheese and a little paring knife from a wooden knife holder on the counter. Minimal damage. The risk was huge, but nothing bad happened.

At first it wasn't clear to me why I took the knife, but it is now.

Today I pressed its point into the smooth skin on the inside of my right forearm. I hesitated, and then with just a little more pressure, broke through, and a drop of blood appeared. No pain to speak of, nothing that even qualifies. I wondered why I'd never done it before. I poised the knife to cut again, but stopped. It would be difficult to explain such a wound.

Oh, Cookie. It felt like a terrible violation, to read her innermost thoughts this way, but Danny couldn't stop. How could he stop?

Friday, April 17, 1964

I went into another house today. It was really something. But now I feel sicker than I've ever felt before. And lonesome too.

It was east of St. Mary's, like the other time. The high school kids were already in class.

Sweets were on my mind. Cake. My dream cake is chocolate with chocolate icing, and cherry pie filling between the layers. My knife was on my mind too. It takes up a lot of space lately.

I found myself on Hillcrest Street. Hillcrest has no curbs. I like that about it; it seems homey somehow. I watched the young kids from the house go off to school. They'd be heading to King George or Queen Elizabeth. The schools on that side of St. Mary's Road are named after kings and queens or else they have religious names, like Holy Cross or Precious Blood. There are lots of Catholics over there.

When I strolled into the back lane I saw both parents get into a turquoise Chevy and drive away. I think it was a '58. Danny would know. The mother wore spike heels, like the ones my mum wore before things got so bad for her, when she used to wear her taffeta dress. It's been forever since she wore that dress. I don't even know if she still has it. It was beautiful, and she looked beautiful in it. A long, long time ago. I figure this mum must have a sit-down job. Still, her feet must ache by the end of the day.

My mum's feet have a horrible look to them—kind of scaly and bumpy. Mine are okay—smooth, with no extra bumps.

When the car turned the corner onto Caton Street, I sauntered into the yard without looking around: that would be a dead giveaway. A Dairy Milk bar rested on a ledge by the back door. Someone had probably set it there as a reminder to take it with them. I left it; I didn't want anything to be too obvious. Whoever left the chocolate bar would notice for sure if it was gone. If nothing else presented itself, I could grab it on my way out. They could blame it on the mailman.

I entered through the back door. The aroma surrounded me, lifted me, carried me up the three steps to the kitchen. I shut my eyes for a second against the sting of sunlight streaming in through the windows. The room was all aglitter, everything aglitter.

The chocolate cake was on the counter, cooling in its pan. The mother must have gotten up early to bake it, maybe for a birthday party later in the day. A bowl of chocolate icing, covered with Saran Wrap, sat beside it. The cake was still too warm to ice. It would just be one layer, unless the mum had a fancy idea about slicing it up and somehow fitting it back together. Some mums did things like that. Not mine.

Bending my face to the cake, I inhaled. I began to tremble and had to sit down.

The whole family was probably thinking about it right now. Their day would be geared towards it and the surrounding festivities. I knew I couldn't mess with it.

I made myself get up from the chrome and plastic chair and looked inside the fridge. There was a plate of fancy sandwiches, also wrapped. Fancy sandwiches. If someone asked me to name the two food items that I love most in all the world, I would say chocolate cake with chocolate icing, followed closely by fancy sandwiches.

I took them out and set them down on the table. I unwrapped them, thinking perhaps I could wiggle one or two loose from the pile without disrupting it. They would be for the same party as the cake.

A stout black cat startled me with its presence in the doorway. It stared up at me and then leapt up onto the counter and gently poked its nose into the cake. It wasn't interested, but it didn't move away. There was a tiny crumb on the tip of its nose. It sat down and resumed staring at me. Maybe it was trying to guard the cake, keep it safe from me. The idea was in my head that it had a chance.

I ate two of the sandwiches. One of them had a cream cheese and maraschino cherry filling, and the other one was egg salad with green olives. I ate two more. What else could I do? It was bigger than me. One was grated sandwich meat, probably Klik, mixed up with green relish and mayonnaise. A lovely idea. The other was chicken salad, with chopped celery and a sweeter dressing, likely Miracle Whip.

On I went.

The cat watched, kept me company.

I left two of each kind of sandwich, bunched them together to make a meagre pile, and put the plate back in the fridge.

Then I rummaged through the kitchen drawers for a spatula. The cake was cool enough to ice. With the spatula and a knife I iced it in its pan. The cat joined in by batting at the utensils. I didn't mind. When I was done I covered it with the clear wrap from the icing. I washed the bowl, spatula, and knife and left them in the dish rack to dry. Then I said goodbye to the cat and went out the back door, the way I had come, with the cake hidden inside my book binder.

The Dairy Milk bar in its brown and purple wrapper floated on the ledge in a pool of white sunlight. I left it behind. It would give whoever had placed it there a few extra seconds of calm.

What I did is too big not to cause a major kerfuffle, within the house at least, maybe further afield. I ruined someone's party, probably that of the little girl who had skipped happily down the street with her brother.

As I left the yard I knew my only hope for a future was if I had entered and exited the house unseen. No one approached me. I pray I'm in the clear.

That, for sure, was my last time. I have been lucky.

I made my way carefully to one of my spots by the river, carrying my binder like a platter. Then, once I freed the cake (it was a mess), I used the binder as a cushion, as the ground was damp. I devoured my ill-gotten treasure in peace. The river didn't care. The cake didn't taste any different on the way up. It hadn't been inside me long enough.

My binder is totalled. I left it at the river.

I'm a criminal, a thief.

At first I figured I could mail the cake pan back to the people whose day I had ruined. I could wash it and wrap it in brown paper and take it to the post office on Taché. But then I couldn't remember if it was 85 Hillcrest or 82, or maybe it was neither of those.

So I didn't mail it. I hid it at the river, not with my binder, but further along, so it would be harder to connect the two items if anyone ever finds them.

Now I hate myself more than anything—more than Miss Hartley, more than my mum's feet. I want to sleep for a year and wake up as Audrey Hepburn.

When I got home I came up to my room and retrieved my knife from its spot under my mattress.

Then I took off my clothes.

It's important that I cut in places that no one but me can see, even when I'm in my underwear. Can you imagine if Miss Hartley noticed? I can't change in the bathroom anymore, not since she called me a cockroach. Some of the girls don't mind even if you see their bare chests. I'd die if anyone saw mine. It's horrible—I hate my nipples. They stick out and make me sick. My breasts are one of the places that I cut. And inside my panties above...you know.

That's where I pressed the point of the blade, where I left off last time. I'm making a *J* for *John* and right now I'm working on the arc of the *J*. John is John Lennon; he's my favourite Beatle. I don't need to make a word, but I do need to cut myself. Making a word gives it a form of sorts, a kind of... legitimacy.

I cut just deep enough so the blood appeared and sat, didn't run over. The particularness of my effort pleased me, the precise extent of it. I waited till it dried and then put on my housecoat. It will form a scab, and then I'll peel it off. If it fades I can do it again. I want it to last a lifetime.

There is something fantastic about cutting myself that goes all the way to the core of me. Something switches over in my head. Expands. As if I know something no one else does. I long for it to take me over and save me from the other thing—the thing that I hate. *Please God.*

Danny called me for supper: macaroni and cheese. I made it myself last night before I went to bed so I wouldn't have to do anything much about supper today. I didn't know then that I wasn't going to school. Danny helped me last night by grating the cheese and he helped me again today by warming it up in the oven.

When I put just a wee bit on my plate I saw my mum and Danny exchange a glance. Sometimes I think they know what I do. Danny anyway. For sure they know about my secret eating (*where does the food go?*) but maybe not the rest of it. I don't think my mum notices much of anything. She's always in a dopey state because of all her pills. I think she sometimes even takes sleeping pills during the day. She's never going to get better, I know it. She sighed as she ate (her portion was even smaller than mine), as though it was the most trying thing she'd ever done.

Danny concentrated on his own meal, as if everything he needed was right there in front of him, on his Melmac plate.

I don't remember what it's like to sit down for supper and eat what's in front of me while thinking normal thoughts. Taking regular helpings, knowing what a regular helping is, having a little more if it's something I like. Looking forward to dessert. Leaving the table satisfied, neither still hungry nor stuffed to the gills. And then getting on with whatever comes next: homework, going outside, watching

Donna Reed. It seems like a million years ago. Maybe a glass of Jiffy at bedtime if Mum isn't around to drive us out of the kitchen.

What did that feel like? From here it looks like heaven. How could I have taken it for granted? Is there anyone else in the world like me? While I watched the Beatles on *Ed Sullivan* I wanted to concentrate on John (I love his voice the best), but all I could think about was going to the bathroom when it was over so I could get rid of the pork chop and mashed potatoes that I'd cooked for supper. When I hear "Please Please Me" it reminds me of pork chops and applesauce and how they taste coming up if they've been down there too long. It reminds the other girls at school that they want to kiss Paul McCartney more than they want anything, even chocolate cake. I hear them talk; I want to be them. I want to be anyone but me.

The house is quiet tonight. Quieter than usual, but not in a peaceful sense. I want to scream out into it and change my world. If you could see this house's quiet, it would be the colour of dust and strewn with shards of glass. The glass would be difficult to see and impossible to avoid.

Danny remembered that macaroni-and-cheese day. He hated knowing that she felt his judgment on her. And he hated caring so much if someone had seen her that day, in that other house where she didn't belong.

He read on, through the last entry.

Friday, May 1, 1964

We had pineapple upside-down cake for dessert. Mum made it. As I ate, I wondered about the next piece: would I have it now or later or never? I was hoping for never. Why can't I stop? Other people do. Danny and Mum do. One piece satisfies them. I wanted more right then, but was afraid to make the move. I didn't want to see them exchange that look.

A bad thing happened today. Early on, Danny and I talked about how odd it was that whenever our mum gets up the strength to make anything, it's always a dessert. Why not a main course? Something that's good for us. We decided that Danny would ask her about it, being careful with his words so as not to hurt her feelings. I couldn't imagine how he would pull it off.

When I used the bathroom after supper I ran water in the tub while I threw up so they wouldn't hear me. I wish we had more than one bathroom. I let the water out again without taking a bath. It seemed too hard. When I started upstairs I heard them talking in the kitchen so I sat down on the bottom landing and listened. I think I heard most of the conversation, mixed in as it was with the clattering of dishes. Mum sounded fairly cheerful at first (she was having a good day), the way me and Danny long for her to sound. It happens from time to time.

Danny said, *Why, when you decide to cook, is it always a dessert?*

I cringed at his choice of words. They weren't tactful enough.

You know, with Cookie and everything, he went on, *with her... with our problem with her.*

I felt as though someone had hit me in the stomach with a giant sledgehammer. *Our problem with her*. That's what he said. I hadn't known that I was a problem for other people. For Danny.

Then my mum said, *I'm sorry, Danny. I'm so sorry I don't do a better job of cooking for you kids. I guess, when I have the strength, I want to cook something fun.*

Danny made a snorting sound at that, as though the word *fun* couldn't possibly apply to anything that happens in our house.

And then Mum said something like, *And as for the problem with Cookie, I'm sure she'll outgrow it. I don't think what I choose to bake has much to do with it. It's normal to have dessert.*

Then Danny said, *But Cookie isn't normal. What she's doing to herself isn't normal.*

And Mum: *Teenagers often go through unusual phases. As I say, I think she'll grow out of it.*

She started blabbing about when she was young, and I stopped listening. Then I heard the snap of a tea towel, and Danny was through the kitchen door in an instant.

I didn't move fast enough, and he saw me.

He came towards me and said my name but I put up my hands against him coming any closer, and he stopped.

I grabbed onto the banister and ran upstairs. It hadn't occurred to me that I would be part of the question. It was supposed to be about our mum's cooking, not about me. We were supposed to be in it together. I closed my bedroom door behind me.

He didn't follow me at first. He would know there was nothing he could say to make it better. I missed him as I wondered if he would try. I wanted to talk to him about what had just happened, but I wanted it to be someone else that I would be talking about. Not him.

When the floorboards creaked I knew it was Danny outside my room.

He said my name a couple of times, but I covered my ears with my hands; I didn't want to hear any more words. My stomach felt empty and my mouth felt dry. I shivered under my quilt and couldn't remember the last time I was warm.

A little while later I took off my clothes and retrieved my knife from under the mattress. I caught a glimpse of myself in the mirror. I hate my mirror. When I look at my bare self all I see is fat, even though people tell me I've gotten too thin. If I'm so thin, what is this blubber that I can grab a hold of at my waist? I want to cut it off.

My hand was a little shaky so I cut deeper this time. I felt like I went inside the pain—right inside it; it held me close like it loved me—and this time I watched the blood run. I didn't stanch it, but pressed around the cut. I bled on my sheets, but I don't care. It was the best part of my day.

At midnight I got out of bed and started downstairs. I had been lying awake thinking about the cake. It will be a glaring omission tomorrow if I eat it; Danny and Mum will want some, but neither of them will be surprised if it's gone. There has been so much gone food.

I was on the top landing when I remembered what Danny had said earlier. I sat down where I stood. His words came back: *...our problem with her; ...Cookie isn't normal.*

Once I walked into a conversation between my mum and Aunt Dot, and Mum said, *You don't know what it's like for me.* She stopped talking when she saw me. I thought then that she was talking about her disease. Now on the stairs I realized that she might have been talking about me.

It's possible that Danny would say something like that to Paul when they're out seeking adventure. *You don't know what it's like for me.* Like Mum said to Dot.

It was hard to digest this new realization. I truly hadn't known that it was like anything for anyone else; I just thought it was like something for me. It makes me feel sick to think that anything about me is like something for anyone else.

My thoughts returned to the cake. If I eat it, there will be silence tomorrow. Not at first. At first Mum will say something like, *I was looking forward to a piece of that cake for my lunch today. My throat has been feeling so good lately. You've gone and eaten the whole thing.*

Sorry, Mum. I'll make another one.

Never mind.

She'll look at me with distaste, the way Miss Hartley does, the way I do myself when I look in a mirror.

And then there will be silence.

I thought about coming back to my room and using my knife again to help me stay away from the fridge. I could cut my nipples. That might hurt enough.

Instead I went to the cellar and chose two cans of pork and beans and two cans of Klik from the pantry and put them in the deep pockets of my housecoat. I'm back in my room now and I'm struggling. *The cake*. I'll go now to the river.

And that was all.

It was his fault. He had sent her over the edge. Never mind Miss Hartley and her vicious cruelty, never mind his mum and her criticisms of Cookie. He was worse than both of them because he was supposed to be her ally and he had torn that bond apart with his words. She had loved him more than anyone, and in return he had hurt her more than she could bear.

Danny returned the scribbler to where he had found it. He was sure he would never want to read it again. But he would wait till he was thinking clearly before deciding what to do with it, what Cookie would want him to do with it. Destroy it, in all likelihood, but he would wait till he knew for sure. It was the least he could do for her.

Back in his own room he closed the door behind him. A moment later Russell scratched at the door, and Danny got up to let him in. Then he lay down on his bed and wept.

42

WHEN DANNY WOKE UP IN THE MORNING HE WAS STILL IN his clothes. He changed quietly and went downstairs. His mum's bedroom door was closed. He looked in the living room and saw that the bedding was gone from the couch. Quickly, he brushed his teeth, splashed water on his face, and slipped out the back door.

It had become more important than ever to find out what had happened to Miss Hartley. He didn't know who to ask. Surely if she was dead, the school would be buzzing with the news. At lunchtime he stood inside the cloud of smoke outside the teachers' lounge and tried to hear what they were talking about. The words melded into one another and formed a limp murmur with no edges or personality. His ears weren't equipped for the job.

By the end of the day he had picked someone to ask. Morven Rankin was unpopular, more so even than he had become, but it didn't seem to have any effect on her; she didn't seem to care. One of the reasons she was unpopular was that she stared at people way too long. Her brother George tried to train her to do otherwise—Danny had heard him—but she didn't pay any attention to him, or if she did, she chose not to do as he said.

It probably hadn't even occurred to Morven to hate him or snub him. She didn't follow the rule of Paul as so many did. Plus, Danny didn't make fun of her. He didn't chant nasty rhymes at her or pass around her cooties, as he had seen the horrible girls doing back at Nordale, as they had done with Janine. Morven was all right, as Janine had said. And she had something in common with Cookie: Miss Hartley had humiliated her in front of the class, with the blood-between-her-legs incident.

The worst that could happen was that she wouldn't know what he was talking about. There had been talk forever that she was a couple of bricks short of a load, as Uncle Edwin would say.

A moment presented itself after classes ended for the day. He caught her alone just outside the school doors. She was facing away.

"Morven," Danny said.

She was slow to turn around. "Yes."

"I was wonderin'...do you know how long Miss Hartley is gonna be away?"

"Why?" said Morven.

He hadn't counted on that.

"Just curious," he said and stared at her, in the way he had learned to do. Maybe it would make her think they had something in common, since staring was what she was famous for.

"I don't know," said Morven. "Somebody said that the substitute said she's bereaved."

Bereaved. He had heard the word a lot at the time of Cookie's death. He and his mum had apparently been bereaved. So, if what Morven said was true, Miss Hartley's absence had nothing to do with her being dead. You had to be alive to be bereaved. He was dizzy with relief.

Russell ran across the school grounds to meet Danny, who introduced her to Morven. She held out her hand, and Russell licked it thoroughly on both sides and between the fingers.

"Thanks," said Morven.

Danny walked over to Janine's house with Russell stepping smartly at his side. He knocked on the screen door and Janine let them both in. She was making macaroni and cheese. Danny sat down—Russell alert beside his chair.

A cigarette burned in an ashtray on the kitchen table.

"Is your dad home?" Danny said.

"No."

"Is he on a bender?"

"No."

"Are you smokin'?"

"Yes."

She grated cheese on top of the macaroni, way more than anyone in his house had ever grated at one time. More than Cookie had, on the last macaroni she had ever made.

He wanted to tell Janine about Cookie's diary. But he was afraid to. What if she thought it was funny that Cookie broke into people's houses? What if she laughed? And he couldn't tell her that it was all his fault that Cookie died. He could barely tell that to himself.

"Would you like to hear the latest development," he said instead, "or have you totally lost interest?"

He took a drag on the cigarette and blew out the smoke without inhaling.

Janine slid the casserole dish in the oven and sat down across from him.

"Of course I want to hear, Danny. *Crisse*, I just wanted to finish what I was doing."

He told her what Morven had said. "I wonder who died," he added.

"Who cares?"

"Me."

"Why?"

"What if it was the divorcée Flood?"

"That'd be great," said Janine.

"What Morven said doesn't explain what happened on Tuesday when Miss Hardass collapsed beside her car."

"Maybe she collapsed from grief." Janine stood up and ran hot water over the cheese grater. "Maybe she got a phone call at the school just before she left, and that was the beginning of her bereavement."

Danny took another drag. "But there was an ambulance, a close-by ambulance. It must have been for her. You don't get ambulanced anywhere for bereavement."

"We don't know that it was for her," said Janine. "Plus, maybe if it was for her it was because whoever found her didn't know that her collapse was because of bereavement, and they called just to be on the safe side."

"Could be," said Danny.

"Guess what?" said Janine.

"What?"

"I was talking to my dad about slingshots and stuff. Don't worry," she said, responding to the look on Danny's face. "Not in connection to what we did or anything. I didn't tell him anything about that. Honest."

She let that sink in.

"Anyway, he told me that it would be nigh unto impossible to kill someone with a slingshot and a stone."

"What?"

"Nigh unto impossible. That's what he said."

Danny felt as though his whole self had been transferred out of his body to a mysterious destination. And what replaced it was nothing. He watched a girl clean up a kitchen counter. He felt a dog's head beneath one of his hands. A colourful cat sat in a doorway. A clock struck six in another room.

"That clock's way off." The girl rinsed a rag and sat down. "It's been off ever since I've known it."

"Can I have a whole cigarette?" The empty boy spoke.

"Sure, help yourself." She pushed an open pack of filterless Exports towards him.

Danny came back to himself as he lit up his smoke.

"You're going to have to inhale if you don't want to look like a simp," Janine said.

"We spent a lot of time workin' up to an impossible feat," he said.

"Yup."

"I don't know what to think."

He stared at Russell next to his chair and then at Pearl, who had stationed herself in the hall. "Little do Pearl and Russell know. They probably think all our thoughts and actions these past weeks have been about planning their next meals or whether or not we're gonna throw sticks for them."

"Or balls of yarn in Pearl's case," said Janine. "Do you want to stay for macaroni?"

"I don't think so, no."

Danny and Russell got up and walked out the back door. He dropped his cigarette into the damp grass.

On quivery legs at first, he began the walk down the lane. He felt like a gopher poking its head out from the earth after a prairie winter, adjusting its eyes to the light, taking a slow look around at the world it left a couple of seasons ago. It felt as if he had lived a whole life in the past few months, separate from his usual one. He could disconnect from it now, and set it aside, as his own being had done to itself just a few minutes ago. He wouldn't throw it away; it was too important to discard, but he could put it on a shelf, maybe in the shed along with his stones, and let it sit. Later, he could revisit it. Or not.

He could concentrate on Cookie herself now, not on what he was going to do about her. There was nothing to do but miss her and apologize to her, forever.

43

The next day Morven walked over to Danny in the schoolyard before the bell rang.

"Miss Hartley's sister died," she said.

"What?"

"Miss Hartley's sister died."

For a second Danny believed in another sister—one that wasn't a twin—who was much older than Miss Hartley and Mrs. Flood.

"Her twin," said Morven.

She started to walk away when Danny was unable to summon up any words. His head was very crowded.

"Wait. Morven." He ran to catch up. "Do you know what she died from?"

"A heart attack."

"Whoa." He touched the sleeve of her jacket when she started walking again, and she pulled it away.

"Sorry," said Danny. "Wasn't she too young to die from a heart attack?"

"Oh," said Morven. "I don't know about that part."

"Where did she die?"

"In the St. Boniface Hospital. That's what they say."

Thoughts shifted inside Danny's head, searching for a sequence that made sense.

"She had episodes forever," said Morven, back into it.

"Episodes?"

"Yeah, episodes to do with her heart. They say serious episodes."

Morven's answers were slow coming, but Danny didn't want them to come any faster.

"Thanks, Morven," he said.

"Welcome."

They both began to walk towards the school.

"Mr. Potter found her," she said.

He stopped, so she did too. The bell rang, and they both ignored it.

"Mr. Potter found her?"

"Yes. He found her on the ground in the parking lot and called for an ambulance. Birchdale Betty helped. He went inside her house to use her phone. It was closer than walking all the way to the other end of the school to where the office is. Plus, she offered. She was out there. Mr. Potter has been inside Birchdale Betty's house."

She seemed amazed by this last piece of information, and rightly so. No one, to anyone's knowledge, had ever been inside Birchdale Betty's house, and it was a matter of speculation by everyone in the neighbourhood, adults and kids alike. Was it insanely decorated, like her yard? Did she have old ladies tied up in the cellar? Did she keep her husband on a leash? Were there pickled toes in her pantry?

"You'd better get goin', Morven," said Danny. "You don't wanna be late on my account."

She headed towards the school, and Danny went home for his bike. He didn't hurry. He didn't care if he ever made it back to school.

Cars honked as he rode through traffic on his way over to rue Valade. He parked his bike by the spruce tree.

What he saw didn't come as a surprise; he had developed a theory on the ride over. Side by side, in the small parking area behind the house, were two Volkswagen Beetles: one blue, one green. Mrs. Flood had bought herself a car. It was the high-heeled twin sister who had crumpled to the ground in the parking lot. The deepening dusk had darkened the colour of her hair. Where had Miss Hartley been? It didn't matter.

Danny pedalled back to the school and knocked on the door of room 11-26. A familiar girl answered his knock. He had expected a stranger, someone from the other side of St. Mary's Road, one of the girls that should befriend Janine despite her poorness and self-cut hair. Before he said a word this girl turned to the class and said, "Janine. Your little boyfriend's here."

Amid tittering, Janine made her way to the door. She slammed it shut behind her.

"*Calice*, Danny, what are you doing? Trying to ruin my life?"

He told her what Morven had said, and what he had seen. As he told it, he noticed that she was wearing pale pink lipstick, almost white, and she had made an effort to curl her hair. He had never seen either of those things before. Also, there was something about her eyebrows. They were lesser somehow.

She was quiet as he spoke, and his words slowed as he took in her new look. He didn't like it. It went a ways towards taking her away from him.

The teacher opened the door. It was a man teacher.

Another thing Danny hadn't expected.

"Is this important?" he said, speaking to Janine.

"Yes."

She said it at the same time as Danny did, but for a different reason, he knew. She wanted everyone to think something serious, perhaps family related, had happened, and that was the reason a kid had come to call.

Two Volkswagens—one blue, one green; two teachers—one dead, one alive and not even injured—weren't important to anyone but a no-account kid who'd lost his sheen now that summer was gone, and lipstick and hair curlers had usurped him.

"Do you need to go home, Janine?" the teacher said.

"Yes, please."

"All right. Well, come inside and get your things, and we'll go down to the office and speak to Mr. Shearer."

"I don't want to go back inside," she said.

To Danny's amazement tears welled up in her eyes.

The teacher bought it and put a hand on her shoulder.

"Okay," he said. "You wait here. I'll be right back."

He went into the classroom, and Janine grabbed Danny's arm. "Let's go."

They ran out the side entrance of the school and slowed down when they got to Lawndale.

"My bike's at the school," said Danny.

"Go back and get it. I'll wait here."

He went back for his bike, willing the man teacher not to catch him and grill him and forever associate him with Janine.

"What should we do?" she said, when he joined her again.

For a second all the new things he would have wanted to tell her squeezed against each other inside his crowded head: that it was his fault that Cookie died—the person who loved her the most had hurt her the most—more than Miss Hartley, more than their mum, more than any laughing girls; that he had a twin brother named James who also died. But he couldn't tell her these things because he couldn't risk hearing that she didn't understand how much it all mattered.

He also wanted to tell her that he felt sad for Miss Hartley, evil witch though she was, because her twin sister was dead. But he kept quiet about that too, because he was afraid she would laugh at him with her new pink lipstick and hairdo. He was pretty sure she hadn't laughed at him yet, but that didn't mean she wouldn't now.

Danny stared into her cool green eyes, and she stared back with that unwavering gaze of hers.

"I told you Miss Hartley's car was blue," he said.

"Who cares?"

"Me."

He took off on his bike, left her where she stood.

"The high heels should have been a dead giveaway," he called over his shoulder. "Miss Hartley never wears high heels."

44

DANNY TURNED EAST AT THE FIRST CORNER TO PUT SOMETHING between them other than the empty space of Lawndale Avenue. The cold northeast wind pushed against him and took his breath away. It lifted road grit and threw it at his face till it stung. So he turned around and headed home. The wind felt better at his back.

When he got there he didn't want to go in the house; he didn't want to get warm. The Muskoka lawn chair still sat by the now empty pool. He sank into it and put aside thoughts of Janine.

He wanted to think about not having done it, wanted to recapture the modest elation that had roused in him. A private elation, it had turned out, but one he wanted to savour. But there wasn't going to be any elation, modest or otherwise. He had killed his own sister as surely as if he had taken a gun to her head.

Some of the words Cookie had written came back to him. *We were supposed to be in it together.* Oh, Cookie, we were in it together. Please know that, wherever you are. He couldn't bear to believe she was nowhere.

It felt now like everything bad in the whole world was his fault.

Mrs. Flood had died. Maybe the plink of the stone hitting the car had brought on the heart attack, but by the sounds of it, her days were numbered anyway, if Morven was to be believed: she'd had *episodes forever, serious episodes*. It might be his fault, but not completely.

But that no longer mattered. Being responsible for Cookie's death cancelled out everything.

Killing was far too horrendously gigantic of a thing to do. Along with destroying a person, you erased a lifetime of thoughts—all the memories and wisdom that lived inside that person. It mattered hugely in the grand scheme of things. That sort of destruction should never be done deliberately. No one should die because a killer had been born.

When he went in the house, the air felt cool. His mother was sitting at the kitchen table with a closed photo album in front of her. Danny had never seen it before. The window was open wide. A stream of cool air with an undercurrent of dust poured through.

"It smells good in here," said Danny.

"I thought I'd open a few windows and air the place out."

He walked through the house room by room and saw that all the windows were open except the one in his bedroom. She hadn't entered his room. He did so himself and lifted up that window too. The screens needed to be switched for the storm windows. He went back downstairs.

"Thanks for not going in my room."

"You look cold, Danny. Maybe we should close things up for now."

"No. That's okay. This is good." He sat down across from her at the table.

She was wearing plaid slacks, a white blouse, and a beige cardigan—clothes he remembered from before.

"What's wrong?" she said.

"Nothing."

It didn't look as if she'd be opening the photo album any time soon, so Danny stood up, grabbed his jacket from the back hall, and went back outside. It was hard to know how to behave now that his mum was up and around every so often. The weight of new expectations pressed down on him. She didn't seem to be wondering why he wasn't at school, so he decided to take the rest of the day off.

The sun had come out, and the wind had died down. Russell was resting in a sunbeam but stood up when Danny rounded the corner of the house.

They crossed Lyndale and walked into the long grass that lay sideways now from all the tramping down and from the cold. It had lost the greenness of summer.

Russell ran ahead, racing back from time to time to herd him.

Danny stopped at the spot where Frank had pulled Cookie out of the river. It didn't look any different from the rest of the riverbank, with its abrupt edge leading down to scrub and broken trees, to the branch that caught her. Except inside Danny's head, and he supposed inside Frank's. The ambulance workers probably hadn't been back this way, and he didn't know much about the inside of his mum's head, but for him, this particular section of the riverbank would always be Cookie. He walked the several yards upstream to where she had gone in, the grassier spot where the cake plate was found, licked clean.

He recalled someone in the death-by-misadventure camp mentioning that it was odd she had eaten the cake first, before the Klik and beans. As oddness went, Danny figured that was fairly low on the list. He supposed he was the only one on earth who knew that, if given the chance, Cookie had preferred to eat her dessert first. Her reasoning had been that anything could happen between the main course and dessert. The world could end, she could die, there could be an explosion that took out the whole kitchen. She didn't want to chance missing out on the best part of the meal. Their mother and Aunt Dot hadn't allowed it, of course, but if she and Danny were left to their own devices she, the long-ago Cookie, would talk him into doing it with her. He didn't object; he could see her point.

Danny's knowledge of that quirk of Cookie's would die when he did. It was in no one else's consciousness. That thought felt like an additional loss.

No one but he and his mother had seemed to suspect that Cookie'd had no intention of eating the canned goods. They were there inside her buttoned pockets to weigh her down. Danny knew his mother thought so too, from what she'd said that one and only day they'd talked about Cookie. *We couldn't have known.*

Something caught his eye. It glinted in a ray of the slanted sun. He slipped and slid down the riverbank on the damp dun grass. He pushed the scrub aside—young dogwoods with their dazzling red leaves.

There it was, the can opener: the one that Aunt Dot couldn't find on the day after Cookie's funeral. It was theirs, all right; there was the familiar blue plastic protecting the end of each handle. He picked it up, a rusty useless tool.

"Russell."

She hurtled down towards him.

"It was an accident."

Russell was soaking wet.

"The cans weren't in her pockets to weigh her down. She was gonna eat the Klik and the beans, Russ. She wasn't here to die, she was just gonna keep on eating."

Russell shook herself out and plowed up to the top of the bank. Danny followed, clutching the can opener in his fist.

"She slipped, Russ. She fell. It wasn't on purpose."

He knew there was a chance she'd interrupted her eating plans midstride and changed course down the path to death. But in his mind the better chance was that she had not, and that was the one he chose to believe.

It was, indeed, death by misadventure. He could live with that.

When he got home his mum was still at the kitchen table, but now the photo album was open. She was looking at pictures of Cookie.

It hadn't occurred to Danny before to wonder about the lack of family pictures. In other people's houses, Paul's for instance, they were all over the place: on top of the television, on the walls, on the dining room buffet.

He looked over his mum's shoulder and saw his sister as a baby, as a one-year-old, at two.

She turned a page and there were two snapshots of brand-new babies placed carefully side by side: Daniel Arthur and James Scirrow. Danny couldn't see any difference between them. He turned back a page and saw Cookie as a newborn. She didn't look much different from the boy babies.

"I guess we all get born looking pretty much the same," he said.

"Hmh."

Danny didn't know if it was a laugh or a cry. A tear landed on the page. He looked at her face and saw a trace of a smile, so he supposed her sound had been a little of each.

She brushed away the tear.

He set the can opener down on the table.

"I found it," he said. "Cookie had it."

She didn't remember that it had been lost and hadn't noticed that there was a new one in the drawer.

"I guess there's a lot I haven't noticed," she said. "I'm so sorry, Danny."

He wasn't sure what to do with the apology, so he told her his new theory about Cookie's death and left her to sit with it.

45

Little by little, details of the night of Mrs. Flood's death were revealed and became part of a new stream of lore to meander through the streets of Norwood.

The police were involved immediately because of the young age of the victim: she was just thirty-three. Too young to die.

Danny and Janine were not part of the investigation. That's how far out of anyone's consciousness they were regarding the dead woman. Birchdale Betty told the police that she had heard someone running away that night, but she couldn't get any more specific. The cops asked around to no avail.

When they spoke to Miss Hartley she explained about her sister's heart and other health problems, but they waited till they received the autopsy report before they closed the investigation. The final word was: *heart failure stemming from a congenital heart defect; complications from diabetes.*

Danny didn't even know about the police involvement till after it was over.

So it seemed no one in the universe except Danny and Janine knew about the stone that hit the car.

It was a little more difficult for Danny to find out what Mrs. Flood was doing in the school parking lot. No one seemed to be wondering about that but him. So he enlisted Morven again, and again she came through. She spoke to one of the girls on the basketball team and found out that Mrs. Flood was standing in as coach. Miss Hartley had left the school at 4:00 for a dental appointment that she had already postponed twice. It wasn't an important game, as games go, so she'd asked her sister to cover for her.

Danny thought it odd that a history teacher would fill in as a basketball coach and said as much to Morven. It didn't matter; it just seemed odd. So Morven sought out the girl again and discovered that Mrs. Flood had once been a physical education teacher before her health took a turn for the worse. That was when she switched to history. Apparently she *knew her stuff* when it came to basketball. That's the way Morven put it.

She seemed so happy to be doing Danny's bidding (he hadn't even specifically asked for this last piece of information) that he wished he had further assignments for her.

He wondered if Mrs. Flood had known she was going to die soon, and that that was at least part of the reason she had carried on with an eighteen-year-old greaser. Maybe she felt she had no reason to be cautious anymore, no reason not to act on every whim.

And he wondered what Miss Hartley thought of the affair—if it grossed her out, if she tried to talk her sister out of it. Maybe she hadn't even known.

When Danny got home from school on the Wednesday after Thanksgiving, a little over a week after Mrs. Flood's death, his mother was standing in the living room staring at the couch. It was cloth-upholstered and it used to be decent enough with its quiet earth tones, but she had ruined it with her constant dead weight and with spillage and with tearing at errant threads till they came loose and started a process of unravelling. He saw spots that were almost bare.

"It's a mess," she said.

"Yup." There was no getting around it.

When he got home from school on Thursday all the removable cushions were in the front yard. Inside he found his mother trying to drag the couch out from the wall.

"We're getting rid of it," she said. "There's a new one coming from Eaton's. I ordered it from the catalogue."

"Won't the Eaton's guys move it?"

"I can't wait that long."

"Here, let me give you a hand then."

He had his doubts about managing it, but then the doorbell rang, and two men from Eaton's announced themselves.

"I think out the front way would be best," said Barbara. "Fewer twists and turns."

They struggled in the doorway, cheerfully chipping paint here and there.

"Right to the curb, please." There was a lilt in her voice. "Fix the cushions on it, will you, Danny? I've phoned the Goodwill. It's a good solid couch for someone."

The men settled the new one, drank a glass of water apiece, and drove away.

"Do we have a tarpaulin?" Barbara glanced at the sky. "It looks like rain."

All Danny saw was blue sky, except for a narrow line of cloud in the southwest, across the river.

"Those clouds are coming this way," said his mum.

How did she know that? Couldn't they just as easily have moved off in the other direction? Plus there was no wind. She had always been good at weather.

As he went to fetch a tarp from the shed, his mother called after him, "Oh, Danny, I meant to tell you, a man was here from Children's Aid."

His stomach disappeared. "What did he want?"

"He wanted to know if someone named Janine Sénécal was staying here."

"Who?"

"Janine Sénécal."

He still hadn't gotten around to figuring out her last name after realizing it was too late to ask her without sounding like an idiot.

"What did you tell him?"

"I told him I didn't know anyone by that name."

It was true.

She left it at that. There were some good things about his mother.

He didn't want to think about Janine so he hopped on his bike and pedalled over to Wade's for a chocolate milkshake. As he poured the last bit from the silver container into his glass his eyes drifted over to a display of cards at the end of the counter. He picked one that said *With Sympathy* on the front and paid for it along with his milkshake.

When he got home he sat down for supper with his mum. She had made Scotch broth soup and toast, and he couldn't disappoint her by telling her he was full.

Afterwards he went up to his room and sat with the card a while before writing *Please accept my condolences* on the inside with his name underneath. He slipped it into its envelope, rode over to rue Valade, and put it in Miss Hartley's mailbox, not caring if she saw him. If she felt anything like the way he had felt in the weeks after Cookie's death she was sitting in a chair staring out a window at nothing.

He went to the parking area by the back lane and looked at the green Beetle up close. Sure enough, where the roof curved to meet the driver's door there was a tiny chip of paint missing.

46

ON A SUNNY DAY IN MID-NOVEMBER, AFTER THE FIRST snowfall that stayed, Danny walked down the lane to Janine's house. He squinted against the blinding white of the snow, and Russell frolicked as if she were still a pup. She never remembered from one winter to the next how great it was.

He heard the scrape of a shovel. Before he even saw the boy he knew that they were gone. He hadn't seen her at school, and neither of them had sought the other out.

The youngster was pushing snow off the stoop where the two of them used to sit. Danny had never seen it in winter before. A woman opened the back door.

"Good job, Billy."

Danny started to move on and then changed his mind.

"Can I help you?" said the woman.

"No," he said. "It's all right. I knew the people who used to live here. I thought they might still be around."

"Nope," said the boy.

"They're not long gone," said the woman. "We've been here less than a month."

"Do you know where they went?"

"No, sorry, dear. I just know they left in a hurry."

"Okay, thanks."

A cat appeared from around the side of the house.

"Pearl?" Danny said.

"Do you know her?" said the woman.

"Yes, I do."

"Her name is Pearl?"

"Yes."

"The rental agent said they couldn't take her, so we offered to let her stay on. She's no trouble. In fact, she's a good mouser."

"'Kay, good," he said.

Pearl came towards him, and he crouched down and held out his hand. She looked at him steadily as he scratched under her chin. He imagined that she was saying, *Where are they, Danny, where did they go?*

47

DANNY AND BARBARA WOUND THROUGH THE QUIET SUNDAY streets in the old DeSoto. It was her idea. They were going to see Cookie's grave.

The headstone no longer seemed important. He'd let his mother have her way. It was the only thing he could think of to give her: the opposite of going against her.

They parked and walked the short distance through freshly fallen snow. Barbara used a cane. It took him a moment or two to register what he was looking at. It was a different stone, one of a lighter hue. And on it were the words: *Cookie Ruby Blue*. All the other information was the same, but *Cordelia* was gone.

She put her hand on his shoulder.

"I'm sorry, Danny."

There it was again.

"You don't have to keep saying you're sorry."

"Don't I?"

"No. Once was lots."

"But there are so many things…"

Yes, there are. "It's okay," he said.

"Danny?"

"Yes?"

"About your dad?"

"Yes?"

"There are some things...that I can't explain. It's not that I don't want to. I just can't. If I ever I find that I can..."

The words he wanted from her weren't present in her world. Maybe they never would be. There was nothing he could do about that.

"I'm pretty sure I saw him," Danny said. "My dad, I mean."

He told her about the powder-blue Cadillac and how the man had stood by James's grave on his birthday, on their birthday. And he told her that he knew he'd been there the day they buried Cookie.

"I want to meet him, Mum."

"We'll see," she said.

"May we please move James over so he lies beside Cookie?" Danny said.

"Yes," said Barbara. "We'll see about that too."

48

THE WINTER OF '64–'65 WAS CLOUDIER THAN usual—darker—but maybe Danny just saw it that way. The light seemed to fall in a different way on the hockey rink, on the toboggan hill—more aslant somehow.

Paul drifted back into his life. When Danny looked back he couldn't remember the details of how that happened. He did remember that neither of them spoke at all of the past spring, summer, or fall.

He thought about looking for Janine, but never as more than an idea. There was barely a starting point. He was certain the Children's Aid Society had everything to do with their vanishing, but he thought he knew Jake and Janine well enough to know that if they were running, they wouldn't be found. And even if he did find her, what would he have to tell her, to ask of her?

Besides, his dreams of her were at the little house on Lyndale and on the streets of Norwood where they had walked and planned and fought. And at the river. That was where he wanted to see her, not somewhere else.

EPILOGUE

THE SCENT OF LILAC AND LILY-OF-THE-VALLEY FILLS THE AIR on a warm Saturday in spring of 2006. After his daily visit to his father at the Riverview Health Centre Daniel walks downtown from his home in the Norwood Flats. Outside Into the Music on McDermot Avenue he leans down to pat a Jack Russell terrier. It doesn't look to have any other breeds in it, unlike his long-ago Russell, the best dog he ever had. This dog licks his hand. Daniel lets it.

"She'll lick your hand all day if you let her." It's a woman's voice.

When he looks into her face he sees someone about his own age. Her lines are cut deep.

"Danny?"

"Yes."

"You don't know me."

And then he does. It's the voice. There is still the tiniest trace of a French accent combined now with something new, from a new place, perhaps. And then, when he tries harder, he sees her inside the weathered skin.

"Janine."

"You got tall," she says.

They don't embrace. There's a remnant left from all those years ago that precludes hugging.

"Let's get a drink," she says.

They sit outside at the King's Head so there is a place for her dog.

Daniel goes inside for the drinks: a pint for her, a half for him. The pub is almost empty. It's not quite lunchtime. At the outside tables a few young people are scattered, beautiful in their youth, in spite of their piercings and black hair and ubiquitous tattoos.

"What's her name?" Daniel says when they're settled. "Your dog, I mean."

"Jack." The dog looks up at her, and she smiles.

Her smile is the same as it was, with its downward edges. It reminds him that he never got to kiss her.

"It was either Jack or Russell," she says, "so we opted for Jack."

That is about as close as they get to the summer of '64.

It's there, like a presence at the table, but they don't talk about any of it.

"We?" he says.

"Me and my dad. When I came up to visit him a few years ago we decided to get him a dog to keep him company."

"Is he…?"

"No. He died on Monday. I've been here for a month or so. Lung cancer finally got him, but he smoked for over sixty years before it did."

She chuckles. "He never even tried to give it up."

Daniel pictures Jake in his undershirt, the filterless cigarette permanently attached to his lip, squinting at them from behind the screen door.

"What about you?" she says.

"My mum died a long time ago," says Daniel. "But not before she got me in touch with my dad. He's still alive. I see him almost every day."

"That's good," said Janine. "How about Aunt Dot?"

Another tap on the shoulder of 1964.

"She's long gone." Daniel smiled. "Good old Aunt Dot."

There are more catch-up words, nutshell words. Janine lived most of her life in Austin, Texas. She married a musician down there, then another, and then yet another. The last marriage took. Stephen is her husband's name, and he still plays gigs around the Austin area.

"I sewed mainly," she says. "Waited tables and sewed. I still sew for certain people, special clothes you know, mostly for bands, musicians."

"*Seamstress for the band*," says Daniel, and they smile, both knowing the lyric from the old song.

"Kids?" he says.

"No, no kids."

A little gust of wind blows through and lifts her white hair off her forehead. She is one of those people with the right skin tone for white hair. She looks just fine.

"The time never seemed right," she says. Lights a cigarette and coughs. "What about you?"

Daniel is married to a woman named Marsha, and they have three kids: two girls, Jean and Lara, and a boy, James, all grown. Lara is expecting a baby, his first grandchild. He has had a long career as an engineer, a builder of bridges. He's still working. Marsha taught home economics at Nelson Mac for many years after the kids were in school, but is retired now. She grows her own vegetables; she's a fine cook.

"Maybe a little too fine," he says and grins, in reference to the way he has filled out over the years.

"You look good," says Janine.

He doesn't tell her that people call him Daniel now because he wants to hear her say his old name again.

Please say it.

Does she know that Rock Sand died in a car crash before he was out of his teens, or that Birchdale Betty went to jail for extorting large sums of money from elderly widows?

He wants to ask her where they went that fall, she and her dad, and why. He decides it would be prying.

She looks into his eyes and says nothing.

As lives go, they knew each other for a very short time. Wrong as it had been—what they planned, what they did and didn't do—Daniel had believed that for a few moments in time they'd been on the same wavelength, on the same live wire. It had been something, really something. For him.

He feels a movement underneath the table and looks down to see Jack settling her chin next to his sandalled foot.

When Janine goes inside for more beer, Daniel speaks to the dog.

"I loved her once, Jack," he says. "My, how I loved her. But she let me down, man. She truly let me down."

About the Author

Alison Preston was born and raised in Winnipeg. After trying on a number of other Canadian cities, she returned to her hometown, where she currently resides. All of her books are set in the Norwood Flats area of Winnipeg, including *The Rain Barrel Baby, The Geranium Girls, Cherry Bites*, *Sunny Dreams,* and *The Girl in the Wall.*

A graduate of the University of Winnipeg, and a letter carrier for twenty-eight years, Alison won the Margaret Laurence Award for Fiction for *The Girl in the Wall* and has been twice nominated for the John Hirsch Award for Most Promising Manitoba Writer, following the publications of *The Rain Barrel Baby* (Signature Editions) and her first novel, *A Blue and Golden Year* (Turnstone Press). She was also shortlisted for the Carol Shields Winnipeg Book Award and the McNally Robinson Book of the Year Award for *Cherry Bites* and the Mary Scorer Award for Best Book by a Manitoba Publisher for *Sunny Dreams.*

Visit Alison's website at: www.alisonpreston.com

Eco-Audit
Printing this book using Rolland 55 Enviro White instead of virgin fibres paper saved the following resources:

Trees	Solid Waste	Water	Air Emissions
5	227 kg	18,499 L	744 kg